COSCOM
ENTERTAINMENT

BIGFOOT

VOLUME ONE

TERROR TALES

EDITED BY

ERIC S. BROWN AND A.P. FUCHS

COSCOM ENTERTAINMENT
WINNIPEG

ISBN 978-1-926712-75-8

Published by COSCOM ENTERTAINMENT
www.coscomentertainment.com
Text set in Garamond; Printed and Bound in the USA

COVER ART BY GARY MCCLUSKEY
EDITING CONSULTANT: KEITH GOUVEIA

TABLE OF CONTENTS

INTRODUCTION

BY

ERIC S. BROWN

ZOMBIES AND VAMPIRES are everywhere. They have become staples of modern horror in all its forms. They dominate the genre and the best sellers lists to the point that sometimes I think most of us forget there are other monsters, other creatures waiting in the darkness and the woods that are just as fearsome, if not more so. As a lifelong horror fan, I can relate to how easy it is to find your favorite type of subgenre and lose yourself in it so deeply you ignore everything else. To do so, however, denies you all the other frights that the genre has to offer and leaves you locked in a kind of tunnel vision that may one day grow old and stale.

After nearly a decade of writing almost entirely about zombies, I woke up from my narrow take on horror and realized there was so much more to write about. The roar of a monster I truly feared as a child called to me and I penned what might be definitive book of my career to date: *Bigfoot War*. In the 1970s, and even now in the direct-to-DVD horror market, Bigfoot was and is a monster to be reckoned with. He's a monster with such untapped potential in the literary world. *Bigfoot War* was my own personal attempt as an author to inject the mythos of the Sasquatch with a bit of apocalyptic steroids and let loose their fury on a scale I had never seen done before but always longed for as a fan.

The anthology you hold in your hands is a continuation of that effort to bring Bigfoot back to his rightful place in the monster food chain and have him be truly scary and not just some beef jerky spokes-beast in the mainstream. Within these pages you will find a whole new generation of up-and-coming horror authors as well as some seasoned pros seeking to do the same. Some of these tales are truly terrifying, some are gore fests that would make Fulci proud, but one thing they all have in common is they are fun to read.

If the horror genre is going to survive in our modern world, we must all get back to basics with stories such as these and focus above all on giving the reader an entertaining story that is not only enjoyable, but leaves them wanting more.

Hope you enjoy it.

SMALL TOWN, BIG TROUBLE

BY

DAVID BERNSTEIN

HANK DROVE DOWN Mott Street, an area of Seattle, Washington, where one could travel to elicit the services of a woman of the night. He hated the city with its over crowdedness, noise, and putrid odors, but it was part of his duty, his oath. Still, the task always made his stomach turn, no matter how many times he performed it.

He loved his small town of Fairhaven and the people in it, especially his immediate family: a wife and three children. They were his world and there wasn't anything he wouldn't do to protect them.

And that's why he was in Seattle picking up a prostitute.

"Hello, darling," he said, after rolling down the window of his Chevy Malibu.

The scantily-dressed vixen strolled over to the car, leaned into it.

It wasn't that he hated or even despised these poor souls of the night. No. But they were the easiest people to acquire without incident. And when they went missing, very few were looked for. Most were runaways or drug addicts, coming from broken homes. They were the ghosts of small town innocence, now lost and forgotten.

"You a police officer?" Hank asked, softly.

"Do you smell bacon?" the woman responded.

"Please, just answer the question."

"No, I'm not a cop." The woman lifted her top up, exposing her large breasts. "Good enough?" she asked.

Hank nodded, closing his eyes as he did so. He was so tired of the routine. He felt bad for the women in general, especially the ones he took. People lived hard lives, but prostitutes, if they lasted long enough, became like flavorless gum—chewed up and discarded.

"Hop in," he told her, trying to sound upbeat and not wanting to scare her off.

"Don't you want to know my rates?"

"No. I want it all and I'll pay whatever you ask."

The woman's eyes lit up. With a huge, gleaming grin, she opened the car door and got in.

Hank drove to a remote warehouse area down by the river, the same place he took all the prostitutes. Glancing around, the surrounding area seemed clear. He shut off the car's engine.

"Where you want to get it on, sugar?" she asked.

"Right here." He produced a handgun from the side of his chair. He pointed it at her and pulled the trigger. The weapon hardly made a sound.

The woman's eyes went wide with panic as she turned, fumbling for the door handle, but the tranquilizer in the dart that was lodged in her neck worked quickly. Her eyes began to droop, her movements slowing until she fell unconscious.

Hank popped the trunk, got out of the car and walked over to the passenger's side. He scooped her up, carried her to the trunk and gently laid her down.

◆　◆　◆

Crystal awoke some time later. Her head throbbed and her throat was dry, as if she'd been snacking on sand-coated crackers. What the hell happened? The last thing she remembered was . . . a gun. Someone had shot her.

Opening her eyes, she saw she was in a small clearing. A dense woodland area stood before her, illuminated only by the glow of the full moon. She tried moving—her mind confused, unfocused—but couldn't. Looking down at herself, she noticed she was tied in place to something. Some kind of wooden post. She yelled for help; her cries died in the black void beyond the trees.

"Do you have any family?" a male voice asked.

Crystal's heart leaped with a mixture of joy and fright. "Who's there?" she asked, straining against the ropes.

"There isn't a lot of time, so please answer my question."

"Who are you? Show yourself." When nothing happened, she asked, "What do you want with me?"

"Only the answer to my question."

"Yes, yes. I have family. A mother. A father. And a baby brother that care about me." The realization of her predicament was hitting her harder; tears welled in her eyes. She wanted to remain strong, not allowing the freak any satisfaction, but she couldn't help it. She was terrified.

"Give me their mailing address."

She froze. Was this guy going to send her parents a ransom letter? "Why?"

"So I can send them your money."

"Money? What money? I don't have any money."

"You had a hundred dollars in your purse. Add the two hundred I am going to give you. That will make three hundred dollars."

Crystal was speechless. What was this guy's game? She'd been scared out of her mind, thinking maybe he was going to kill her or torture her, or both. But he planned on *paying* her, wanting to send the money to her parents.

"You're not going to kill me?" she asked, a hint of hope in her voice.

"No. I'm not going to kill you."

Relief, like popping a Xanax, flooded her system. Had she just heard right? Was this guy just screwing with her, trying to teach her a lesson? Get her parents involved?

"Then why'd you tie me up like I'm some Joan of Arc? Is this how you get off? Because if that's the case, you didn't need to drug me." A hot kernel of anger grew in the pit of her stomach. "I would've done it free of charge."

"Give me your parents' address, please."

There was unease in the man's voice. He was almost pleading with her. "Look, you've had your fun. Now let me go."

"I can't do that."

"What's your deal, huh? You're not going to kill me so . . ." A loud animalistic roar erupted from the forest, silencing her mid-sentence. She said, "What the hell was that?"

"Please," the man said, "give me the address. This is your last chance to help your family before—"

"Screw you!" she yelled. "And to hell with my family! My dad was a loser and Mom was a junkie."

Another roar, nearer this time, came from the forest.

Crystal screeched. "Is that a bear?" She began sobbing, her chest aching as her heart thumped like the piston of an overworked diesel engine. "You've got to untie me. Please, Mister."

"I'm deeply sorry, but I can't. I have to be going now."

"No! Wait."

"Your money will be put to good use."

"Don't leave me."

A thunderous crashing sound of broken tree limbs and kicked-up forest debris filled her ears. Something big was heading in her direction.

Looking around, she saw no food in sight. Wasn't that what attracted animals? Especially bears?

The commotion grew louder as the thing neared. Maybe if she played dead—because that's what people were supposed to do when confronted by a bear—the animal would leave her alone.

Closing her eyes, Crystal let her body go limp, the ropes holding her upright. The crashing sounds abruptly ended as the creature stepped into the clearing. A putrid odor, like wet dog and rotten fish, filled her nostrils. She tried to remain still, had wanted to so badly, but the odor was too much. She coughed, barely breathing through her mouth to avoid the stench, and felt bile wanting to rise up into her throat. She kept her eyes closed, not wishing to see the animal.

A low, bass-filled growl came forth, followed by a dead-fish-like aroma.

She opened her eyes. Immediately it felt like someone slapped her in the chest.

She couldn't scream if she wanted to.

Crouching before her was a hairy, man-like beast. It's red, beady eyes—set deep within its skull—were filled with a malevolence she had never seen before. She was frozen with fear and caught in the thing's stare, like the victim of a vampire. Finally, she opened her mouth and managed a small scream. Then a louder one, until finally her shrill shriek echoed around her. The creature stood up, standing over six feet tall, and bellowed a roar. Its mouth was lined with jagged teeth that looked like they could chew steel, but it was the six-inch canines that caused her bladder to let loose. Saliva spewed from its mouth. She continued to scream.

In the blink of an eye, the beast swung its hairy arm and her point-of-view switched from looking at the thing's waist to the world suddenly flipping onto its side, staring at the beast's hairy feet.

Blood rained down from somewhere above her. A slurping sound.

A realization . . .

. . . then nothing.

◆　◆　◆

Hank sat in his truck, listening as the woman's screams went silent. Shaking his head, he closed his eyes and prayed.

For generations, his and three other families had been feeding the beast. As long as it received one human sacrifice a month, the town would be spared. It was a grueling, hard-to-swallow duty, but a necessary one nonetheless.

Using his cell phone, he called his best friend Joel. "It's done," he said, then quickly hung up. He dialed the third member of the "Bigfoot Family," as it was called. "It's done," he told Pete before hanging up. There was no need to say anything else to either man.

The legend dated back over a hundred and fifty years. It was said a disgruntled medicine man, that had lost his land to the bank, placed a curse on the town. Once a month, a human sacrifice was to be made in the forest to a blood-thirsty beast. Some believed the creature was the medicine man himself, that he had made a deal with a demon to be transformed into the Sesquac, a half-man-half-beast with a taste for human flesh.

Shortly after the man's proclamation that the town would fall, he disappeared into the Cascade Mountains never to be heard from again. No one took his threats seriously and the town went on as normal . . . until the bodies started piling up.

Night after night town's people were slaughtered, their bodies stripped of flesh, leaving nothing but gristle and bone. Hunting parties were dispatched to the surrounding forest, finding nothing but oversized humanoid footprints. Word spread fast of the medicine man's curse and a town meeting was called. After heated deliberation, the Bigfoot Families were established. It was the charge and responsibility of these three families to make sure the beast was appeased and the town kept safe.

It was originally thought to be a temporary position for the three families, maybe lasting a generation or two. The beast would eventually grow old and die. One hundred and fifty years later and the creature still roamed, the Bigfoot families having had to pass on the responsibility to new generations.

Hank waited an hour inside his pickup, giving the beast time to enjoy its meal before it returned to wherever it went. He trekked back to the killing ground to clean up the remains of the severed head and bury the bones.

◆　◆　◆

Three weeks later, a week before another sacrifice was to be made, Joel called Hank on his cell phone.

"What's up, buddy?" Hank asked, sitting in his worn recliner with a bottle of Labatt Blue in his hand.

"I can't do this anymore," Joel said, his voice cracking something awful, like a kid hitting puberty.

"Do what?"

"Go on with the family business. My son's almost of age to know the truth and be brought into our little group. I can't . . . I won't pass this on to him, Hank. I won't."

"Calm down," Hank said, sitting up in his chair and setting his beer down. He reached for his pack of smokes, pulled one out.

"Hank?"

"Hang on a sec." Placing the cigarette between his lips, he lit the smoke and took a long pull, inhaling the sweet tobacco deep into his lungs. He held his breath for a moment, then exhaled, satisfied.

"Hank, I'm serious."

"I know," Hank responded quietly. "I think I'm done, too."

"What? Really?" There was both a hint of relief and surprise in Joel's voice.

Hank took another deep draw from his cigarette, exhaling as he spoke. "Yeah. I've been thinking about it for a while now. "I'm glad you called."

"Oh, Hank. You have no idea how relieved I am to hear it. But what are we going to do? Tell Pete?"

"No, absolutely not," Hank said, firm. Pete Jorgan was a cowboy, a hot dog who had no qualms about the family business. He would never go along with them and would most likely cause a ruckus with the townspeople. And who knew what the town would do to his and Joel's family? No, this would have to stay between himself and Joel.

"We can't tell anyone," Hank said. "Not a soul, not even your wife. You understand what happens if this gets out?"

"Yeah, but what are we supposed to do? Leave town and let Pete recruit two more families to replace ours?"

"No. I want out, but not at the cost of the town folk. If we just up and left and anything happened to Pete, the town would be at the mercy of that beast."

"So what then?"

Hank took another drag off his smoke, then said, "We kill it."

"What? Are you nuts?"

"It's our only option. Well, *my* only option. I won't run and leave the town to suffer."

"Okay, okay," Joel said, his voice sounding a little calmer. "You're right. But it's been tried before and only to fail. Lives were lost. My great granddaddy lost his wife and eldest son to that creature."

"Things are better now," Hank said reassuringly. "Technology is better. Weapons are better. I've been working on a plan, have been for some time, should the need arise to kill it. It's risky, of course, but we have to take it." He paused, taking a last drag on his smoke before extinguishing it into his near-empty beer bottle. He waited for Joel's reply and when none came, he asked, "Are you with me?"

"Yes, Hank. I'm with you."

◆ ◆ ◆

The bait was set: another woman of the night from Seattle. She was tied to the post and still unconscious from the sedative.

With an unobstructed view of the clearing, Hank peered through the night vision scope mounted on his .30-06 bolt action rifle. The moon was out full again, illuminating the area adequately enough to see, but the night vision scope proved better.

Joel lay to his left also with a straight view of the clearing and armed with a .30-06 rifle and night vision scope. On their stomachs, leaves and forest debris covered them like seasoned army rangers waiting in the bush.

Hank had imagined the beast was no different than any other predatory animal of the forest, having keen senses beyond what any human possessed.

After speaking on the phone about killing the beast, Hank went over to Joel's house and had taken a set of clothes. Along with the set of his own he'd be wearing on the sacrifice night, he took Joel's shirt, pants, shoes and hat, and immersed them in the local pond for a few hours, marinating the fabric with pond scum before heading back to Joel's place. There, he allowed the clothes to dry in the dog house. He wanted no trace of human odor with them when they went into the forest.

The girl awoke and began yelling for help. The woods soon filled with the beast's roars before appearing at the clearing's edge. The woman fainted upon seeing the Bigfoot, silencing the air and making Hank's and Joel's job all the more difficult. Hank had been relying on the woman's pleas for help to cover up any noise they made.

He looked on, a nervous sweat trickling down the sides of his face, making him itch. He would have to bear it for now. Any movement, any noise, and the creature might bolt or attack. He wanted to turn to Joel, signal him not to move or make a sound. But he remained still, not wanting to alert the beast.

Inside the clearing, the creature looked around then began walking forward. Hank grinned as the monster's large head entered his scope's view. Letting out a controlled breath, he squeezed the trigger.

The weapon's crack echoed in his ears. Hank watched as the creature seemed to vanish, falling out of view. Joel didn't even have a chance to fire.

Hank was on his feet in seconds, sprinting toward the downed beast. He heard Joel close behind. Running up to the Bigfoot creature, Hank wanted to sink more bullets into its hide, but saw it wasn't going to be necessary. The thing lay still, a small hole where its right eye had been. The back of its head a mangled, blood-smeared, pulp; the exit wound appeared as if a bomb had gone off inside the monster's cranium. Blood, like strawberry syrup, pooled around the body as its left arm twitched.

Hank couldn't believe how easily the creature went down. The thing's skull looked thicker than a grizzly's. He'd had one heck of a lucky shot, having the bullet enter the softest part of the creature's body—a direct and easy line to the brain.

"You killed it!" Joel proclaimed, joyously. He jumped up and down like a cheerleader celebrating the winning touchdown.

Hank quickly grew uncomfortable, but it was finally over.

"Incredible!" Joel hollered, slapping him on the back. "One shot, one kill."

"We better get this lady back to the city," he said after a little time had gone by. "And then come back and clean this mess up."

"You going to tell, Pete?" Joel asked. "The town council?"

"Yes."

"We'll be heroes!" Joel said, before pausing. His face scrunched up in confusion. "You smell that?"

With an unlit cigarette in his mouth, Hank sniffed the air and nodded. A cold chill ran down his spine.

"Smells like this thing, only stronger," Joel said.

"No," Hank answered, his tone cold. "Smells like a bunch of the things."

From the woods came another beast, its movement almost soundless. It stood eight feet tall, making the one on the ground suddenly look like an adolescent. Then another beast came from the forest, followed by another and another.

"Hank?" Joel managed to squeak out.

Looking at Joel, he saw the front of the man's pants had darkened.

Hank raised his lighter to his mouth and lit the cigarette. The beasts hadn't even flinched at the sight of flame. He'd hoped it might scare them off, but it didn't. Closing his eyes, he took a long pull from the smoke, wishing he'd gotten his family out of town.

FRAME 353

BY

FRANCESCO COLLIA

ALL BRECK GREEN knew was that the shot was going to be brilliant. He could see the action unfold as an overlay on the storyboard he had been mentally assembling for years. The park's landscape had changed in the four decades since the original had been staged, but there was nothing so major that he couldn't Photoshop up in post. He'd tweak the color, tack on a branch or two and he'd have it. It was the actor that he needed to catch live, that authentic movement that still couldn't be replicated by a program, at least not one in his budget. Roger Patterson, the original's auteur, was a huckster and a hack, but he knew the same truth, knew the only thing that mattered was momentary believability. *The shot.* Breck watched his own version in the LCD screen and wondered how much inflation there had been in the Bigfoot costume market since 1967.

The shot. It was what he was hoping would alleviate some of the guilt that came with all of Dev's money. He knew the guilt was all his, that Dev would continue to write checks as long as he asked, but he needed something to show himself he had been asking for a purpose. The rest of the film was going to be lucky to be halfway coherent. He had written the script around this shot, the recreation of the fascination that locked on to him the first time he saw the infamous Patterson-Gimlin footage on one of those supernatural TV schlockfests when he was eight.

Now he waited. Here it was. Weeks of rehearsal, in-depth study and drills to get it just right, to get every step and arm swing just the way it was supposed to be. To nail that magical 352nd frame of the original film. The head turn. That was it, the money shot, the haunting glance of acknowledgement, of knowing, that told the viewer, especially one young enough to still keep a nightlight in reserve, that the world was not the place you thought it was.

Breck had grown up, of course, and grown out of his gullibility, but had never escaped that look, the power of which he had been seeking as an artist ever since. And now here it was, the moment of truth. He held his breath as the big lug got it. One take.

Exhale, he thought, *let it run*, and "Cut. Bring it in," Breck yelled, his hands jittering as his success sunk in. He held the camera not wanting to check, not wanting to know just yet if his initial excitement was unfounded, skewed by the rush. He looked up as Dev's jeep pulled up beside his car. Maybe he'd let his producer and best friend do the honors. Maybe he'd have to.

His star came lumbering up from behind. "How did I do?" He was a big kid, Crosley Barnes, a JUCO power forward Dev found through an online ad. Kid said he wanted to break into the movies if he couldn't make a go in the NBA.

"Who's your favorite actor?" asked Breck.

Crosley pulled the mask up to rest on his forehead. "That guy from *Avatar*."

"You were as good as that guy," said Breck. At least that wasn't a lie.

Dev came up with the same giddy smile he had since they'd started production on the project. Everyone, it seemed, was just waiting to go Hollywood. "Did I miss it?"

"I didn't," said Breck.

"Seriously? You got it? How does it look?"

Breck handed him the camera. "You tell me."

"Damn," said Crosley.

Breck followed the big guy's eyes and said the same thing. On her way from the jeep was one of those stunning girls you just didn't see out in the wild. One of those girls you only saw in the movies.

"Right," said Dev. "Guys, this is Taylor."

She tossed her long brown hair over one shoulder and extended a hand. Breck shook it and, if he had to, could have told you the exact distance in centimeters between the buttons running down her tight white shirt.

"I've never played a zookeeper before," said Taylor.

"Cryptozoologist," said Dev, who, despite his geek leanings, was acting the coolest of the three guys. Crosley still hadn't gotten past his own stare.

Taylor blushed, which only made matters worse. "I knew I was going to mess that up."

Dev had taken a step back and fired up the camera. Breck did his best to compose himself. "What have you played before?" he asked in a bit of a mumble. "In movies. What movies have you been in before?"

Taylor moved closer. "Only a few. Waiting for my break, you know. So far I've been a nurse—that was my last project. I've been a school teacher *and* a school girl. I got to keep the outfit from that one."

"Damn," Crosley repeated.

"You can go ahead and keep the outfit from this one, too," said Breck.

Taylor giggled and touched his shoulder. "These are my own clothes, silly."

Breck removed his cap and ran a finger along the drenched inner band.

"Dude," said Dev. "You see this?"

"No," said Breck.

"You didn't see this yet?"

"Still no."

"You should see this."

It was what Breck had feared. He had met Dev in college and knew right away that he was a good guy, a loyal guy. He also knew it would only be a matter of time before he took advantage of that. Not maliciously, but simply inevitably. Dev was kind and lonely and his family had money. It was almost entrapment.

"How bad is it?" asked Breck. The money was one thing, but what ate at him more was the thought of disappointing the one person who had believed in him. He had been selling Dev on this shot for as long as he knew him and he knew if he had failed now, after all the prep and practice, he was never going to get it right.

"Crosley, did you see anything out there?" asked Dev.

"What do you mean?"

"He means this," said Breck, handing the camera to the basketball player.

"What is that?" asked Crosley. The frame had been paused. Off to his right as he walked out of frame was a large brown spot that became a figure when he hit play. It moved toward him and then vanished back into the brush.

Dev and Breck looked at each other and they both tried to laugh it off. "C'mon now," said Dev. "We both can't be idiots at the same time."

"Well, whose turn is it?"

"It's my shadow," said Crosley.

"That's not how shadows work," said Breck.

"It's a bear, then."

"Maybe," said Dev. "Possibly. It's something. We should go check it out."

"Check out to see if it's a bear?" asked Taylor. "Uh, no."

"It's probably just a hiker who saw *this* thing lumbering through the woods," said Dev.

Crosley grinned at the thought of nailing his role.

"Then why did you say bear? No one starts with bear," said Taylor.

"Listen," said Breck, "I'm going to film it so you have to come. You're the scientist. This could be a breakthrough."

"It's going to be in the movie? Why wasn't it in the script?"

"It's improv. Guerilla filmmaking," said Breck. "No offense, big guy."

"Huh?" said Crosley.

"Forget it, Magilla. Let's go."

Dev motioned for Breck to hang back as Taylor followed Crosley to the new location.

"What's up?" asked Breck.

"Should we have what's-his-name come along?"

"Who?"

Dev gestured to Breck's car. "Lucious Redwolf."

Breck laughed. That was the name he had given him.

Dev left and returned with a middle-aged man in a fringed vest and moccasins. He was their Indian guide, the character lifted from Patterson and Gimlin's planned pseudo-documentary about tracking Sasquatch. The idea framed Breck's script, though he ditched the cowboys and miner for Taylor's breasts.

"Hey, Miguel," said Breck. "You doing okay?"

"Yeah, man. Is it my scene?"

"Change of plans. We're going to shoot a little something over there while we still have the light."

"All good. I already got paid."

His pay was a per diem bag of grass, not exactly scale, but he wasn't exactly union. He wasn't even a Native American and the filmmakers had joked Dev should've played the part since he was at least a real Indian. His parents were from Delhi. He was from San Bernadino.

"So what are we filming?" asked Crosley. It was a good question considering they were all standing around a particularly unremarkable patch of scrubland.

"This is where we saw . . . what *we* saw, right?" Everyone nodded in more-or-less certainty. "So now we film us searching for . . . what we saw." He paused and then pulled down Crosley's mask. "We film *you* searching for it."

"Very meta," said Dev.

"And this fits in the story?" asked Taylor.

"This *is* the story," said Breck. "It's *all* the story. Don't you see?"

"Oh, sure. Of course," said Taylor. "What do I do?"

"Nothing yet. But you will. Let's just get this down. I got ideas spinning all over the place. Ready?"

Crosley shrugged. "Just, what, go in there?" He pointed at the thicket.

"All the way. I want you to disappear into it."

"What if I find that hiker and you can't see me."

"Give us a shout and we'll swoop in. It'll be like a horror nature doc. No, this is good, this is going to be good. Okay, *Action*."

Crosley fell into character and hacked his way through the bushes and bramble.

Then he was gone.

"And cut," said Breck. He smiled, pleased with his directorial acumen.

"So now what?" asked Taylor.

"We wait for him to come back."

"I could do some waiting," said Miguel, sitting down against a tree.

"You know, we didn't tell him to come back," said Dev. "You just told him to shout if he found someone."

"Well, I guess he didn't find anyone." Breck waited while no one laughed. "What? You think he's not smart enough to come back on his own?"

"I think there's a way around over here," said Dev.

Breck thought it through. "I'm with you."

Taylor took off her shirt on the way and tied it around her waist. Her white tank top was tight and thin and Breck wanted to stop and kick himself for not having his camera on. He didn't think now was the right time to ask her to do it again, but he'd make sure to write an appropriate scene later.

After following the path into a curved patch of grass snuggled between the trees, Dev said, "I'm pretty sure this is where he would have come out."

"Then where is he?" asked Taylor.

Breck wished she would just stick to her lines.

"There's his mask," said Miguel. "Probably took it off to see where he was going."

"And to breathe," said Taylor. "Dave, you didn't tell me it was going to be so hot out here."

"Sorry," said Dev. "I thought you would have noticed the weather at some point earlier in the day."

Dev approached the mask, which Breck at first assumed was propped up on a stump, but as Dev got closer he saw it had been fitted onto a rock.

Odd, Breck thought and then retched as the rock came into detail. The costume's hair was dark and thick but not enough of either to conceal the unmistakable pool of fresh blood at its base. Blood and skin and gristle. Dev turned and threw up.

The others came running. Taylor screamed. Miguel's knees buckled and he almost fell. Breck started filming.

"You said there weren't any bears," said Taylor.

"I never said that," said Dev. "What we saw wasn't a bear."

"Then what did this?"

"I don't know. Maybe it was a bear. I don't know."

"Where's the rest of him?" asked Miguel, backing up the way they had come.

They stopped and scanned the area, though no one moved except Miguel who continued his retreat. "We should stay together," said Dev.

"Agreed," said Miguel. "Let's stay together back in the cars."

Just as Dev was about to assent, Miguel's legs flew up to the side and for a moment he was levitating horizontally, and then just as swiftly, his body jerked into the brush.

Day was coming to a close and the shadows were franticly at play in the remaining light. Breck couldn't make out what had happened. It had been too sudden, too unordinary to process on instinct.

Taylor moved toward him, her arm finding his waist. She didn't speak either and her face indicated she might not have been able to if she tried. Only Breck was in motion, panning the clearing in which they stood, desperately trying to capture on film the nearly tangible terror. When he got around to his companions, he lowered the camera and joined their huddled twosome. It was sinking in.

"Is this real?" asked Taylor, her grip on Dev tightening.

Dev was about to answer when he turned to his friend. Breck shook his head. "I didn't write *this*."

"So, what is it, then?" asked Dev.

"Is it a bear?" asked Taylor. "It could be a bear, right?"

"It could be," said Breck.

"But you don't think it is?"

"I don't know what it is."

"But what do you think it is?"

Breck didn't respond. What he thought was too ridiculous to voice.

"Could it be a *skoocoom?*" asked Taylor. They were all still looking at the spot where Miguel had last stood.

"Come again?"

"One of those cannibal ape men," she said. "The Indian guide . . . Miguel explains it in the script." She sighed and repeated his name softly.

"Um, well," said Breck. He was frightened by how *not ridiculous* the words actually sounded.

"Those are like Bigfoot, right?" she asked. "Bigfeet? They're all the same?"

"All the same myth," said Dev, with an authority deflated by the reality of their situation.

There was about a ten-yard radius around them in the glade, the only opening in the path Miguel had taken. All alternate avenues of escape meant an increasingly blind stumble through the undergrowth. The sun was just about gone.

"Does anyone have a gun or a knife?" asked Taylor.

"Why would we have a gun?" asked Breck.

"Because we're in the woods, maybe? Because you were so sure there are bears around here? What would you have done if we did see a bear?"

"I don't know," said Breck. "Make myself look bigger, right?"

"I thought it was play dead," said Dev.

"Have either of you ever even been in the woods before?"

"It's possible the answer's no," said Dev.

"Yeah, maybe not."

"So no knife either? Not that I think that would do anything."

"What about a flashlight?" asked Dev. He looked down to where her hands no longer were.

"I have this," said Breck, flipping on his camera's external light. It was bright.

"How much battery is left?"

Breck paused. He already knew. "Not enough. Twenty minutes?"

"How is that not enough?" asked Taylor.

"We don't know how long we're going to be here," said Dev.

"Here?"

"Here. Trapped here."

"That's your plan?"

"That's not a plan," said Dev. "That's our only choice. I'm not running that way not knowing what the hell grabbed Miguel and if it's still there, and I'm sure not running that way further to the middle of nowhere."

Taylor took a phone out of her pocket.

"Ok, that makes sense, too," said Dev.

Her thumb sat on the keypad. "Who do I even call?"

"The park rangers?" said Breck.

She lifted her thumb, then put it back down. "Do they have a special number or something?"

"Just call 911," said Dev.

"Do you even know where we are?"

"I know how to get here. Listen, they'll figure it out. Just call."

She did. And got nothing. "No bars."

Dev and Breck tried their phones. Nothing. "We need to walk around a bit."

The other two looked at him.

"A bit."

There was a rustle from the bushes by the opening. They were back together, cowering, waiting for something to follow the sound. The noise moved. It was all around them now, not a continuous movement, but dispersed and indiscriminate. They shivered as one when it got closer, turned as one to anticipate its pattern.

It stopped. They waited some more, waited for it to start again, for it to stay stopped. Time passed and evening had set in, light from an already-wan moon lost in the clouds.

Breck's eyes drifted to Crosley's remains. "That kid got decapitated."

Taylor squeezed his hand. It was the only practical response.

"We need to do something," said Breck. "We have to try to find a signal. Or make a run for it."

"Are you kidding?" asked Dev.

"Our cars aren't that far."

"Even if we get past where Miguel was are you so sure we can outrun it?"

"Outrun what? We don't even know what it is."

"And that's giving you confidence?" asked Dev. "Plus, it's pretty dark if you haven't noticed. I mean, I can barely see you."

The rustling started again before Breck could respond. It made its way around the clearing as before, but now there was something else. Something worse. A groan. A low, strained groan. Breck turned on the camera light and shined it at the opening.

"Oh no," said Taylor.

Miguel. He was on his knees. One hand pressed against his stomach, the other reaching, straining for them. He was bloody, cut and battered. He groaned again, his lips quivering to form syllables that the anguish in his eyes failed to distinguish as pleas or warnings.

Taylor broke toward him. Dev reacted too slowly and had to lunge to stop her, tackling her legs.

She kicked at him and screamed. "What are you doing?"

"It's a trap."

She kicked again, freeing her legs, but she stayed on the ground.

"Where has he been?" asked Dev. He was forcing calmness into his voice. "It wants us to go over there."

Taylor took his hand and slid back toward him. "Why doesn't it just come out here and get us?" There was no bitterness in her question.

"It's playing with us," said Breck, squatting beside them. "This is not a bear."

Miguel's hand slipped from his midsection and he cried out as his stomach spilled open. Taylor shrieked. They all did. Miguel made a final grab for them and collapsed face first onto the grass, body twitching.

Dev ordered Breck to turn off the light and they sat in the darkness together, but each alone with the ghost of evisceration. And Miguel's moans. Those they would continue to hear after his last breath, echoing well into the night.

Taylor had put her shirt back on as a chill set in. She held herself tight and tucked into Dev. Breck's light jacket wasn't doing much by way of warmth, though he still refrained from any chivalrous gesture. His eyes were locked on Miguel, or rather, just past his finally silent body.

"If it's just playing with us then there's no sense in waiting," he said just as Taylor was beginning to nod off. "We're all dead here. If we make a run for it maybe one of us makes it."

"I'm not going," said Dev.

"We all have to go or it's pointless."

Taylor sat up and rubbed her eyes. "So we wait for what? Morning?"

"It's not a vampire," said Breck.

"No, it's something else that doesn't exist."

No one spoke for several minutes, the conversation not over but on hold. Their chances of survival might have been incrementally better one way or another, but neither Breck nor Dev were fighters, literally or in any figurative heroic sense. That understanding placed their bet for them.

"First light we run," said Dev.

The decision opened a small window of release. In this bubble, the lull of nature, of camping, of its solitude and serenity, gave them all a respite. Breathing steadied. Nerves loosened. Taylor's eyes closed.

Breck inhaled deeply. "What's that smell?"

"There are a couple of corpses around us," said Dev with a pinch of humor.

"No, it's more like—"

Dev wailed. There was a sudden rush from where he sat and then his voice fell away. The air deadened with quiet, the moment frozen.

A dull, sickly thud resonated from across the clearing.

Breck dropped his camera. He fumbled it back into his hands and turned on the light. Taylor awoke. Another scream as his beam landed on Dev's body balled on its side. She clutched Breck's arm, almost knocking the camera from his hand. The light momentarily shot into the woods. Something moved. It was watching.

Silence descended again, filling the cracks of their remaining sanity. Dev shifted, lifted his head. Breck and Taylor gasped.

"I think my leg's broken," said Dev.

"Which one?" asked Breck. Then, quickly, "I don't know why I asked that."

"What happened?" asked Taylor.

"It . . . just tossed me."

"What was it?"

"I can only . . . testify . . . too big and hairy."

They went to him, braced him on their shoulders, and scurried him back. The camera's light was still on and Breck repositioned it to illuminate Dev's leg. His right shin was at an unorthodox angle and there was little doubt that beneath his jeans bone jutted through skin.

"You're going to have to take them off," said Breck, his hand gingerly on the cuff of the pants.

"Leave it," said Dev. "You can't do anything anyway and I think I'll pass out from shock if I see what I think I'll see. Just turn off the light for now." Each word reverberated with pain.

"Wait," said Taylor. "Should we film a . . ." By the look on her face her words had not trailed off for lack of a concluding thought. She appeared all too aware of what she wanted to say.

Breck nodded. "How about we just say we're going to document what's happened?"

She gave him a half-smile and brushed the hair from her face. "Okay."

Breck started recording.

"My name's Taylor Landon." She stopped and signaled to Breck. "What's everyone's name?" she asked. "Everyone."

Breck told her and she closed her eyes, her lips moving quickly and silently. When she opened them she tapped on the camera and began with her arrival and the decision to investigate whatever it was they had seen on the film. How Crosley, or Crosby in her version, had gone ahead without a trace and how they were ultimately and gruesomely reunited. How dark it was and cold, and how scared they were now. Her words watered as she discussed the present and ceased when she was about to broach the future.

Something moved behind her.

Taylor jumped as Breck rose, camera still rolling, and they collided. She fell backward onto Dev's leg and the torture in his cry momentarily pushed all fear aside. Her focus turned to him and she sobbed through an almost incoherent profusion of apologies. Breck sat up and as he put the camera down the light shut off.

"Turn it back on," said Taylor. There was a fierceness in her command.

"I didn't turn it off."

"Man . . ."

Breck found her and pulled himself close. They sat together in shared helplessness.

"I think Dev passed out," said Taylor. "What should we do? Should we do something?"

"What? Being awake is no prize right now."

Minutes crept on. "Are we going to die?" she asked. When Breck didn't answer, she told him, "You're supposed to say 'no.'"

"Why?"

"Because even if you're wrong—"

"No."

"Thanks."

By the time the first trickle of dawn appeared, Taylor had succumbed to exhaustion. Breck eased her head off his leg and onto the ground. They couldn't run now, at least not all of them. He had spent the last couple of hours contemplating his ability to leave his best friend behind. He wasn't eager to sacrifice Taylor for his own survival, but he didn't think that choice would haunt him to the same degree. He could rationalize her away.

He stood and took out his phone. His decision was made, maybe always had been, but he felt he owed Dev one more try. The poor guy was delirious with pain and hardly making any sense now.

No signal.

He walked off a few paces. Nothing. A few more. He faced each direction, held the phone high and low, switched hands, shook it. Finally it appeared. One solitary bar. One lifeline.

That tiny white rectangle that could save their lives.

Bright white pain flared up at the back of his head, then all went dark and quiet.

There was no way to know how long he had been out, no way to know what had happened. He was on his back, that he knew. He couldn't move his legs or arms, couldn't feel them. It was midday, he guessed, the sun overhead bright and warm on his face. He ran his tongue over the salty, coppery paste around his mouth. He was bleeding and sweating and something was moving closer to him.

He smelled it again as it approached, the putrid musk. It stood over him now, bigger than he had feared and not at all like any of the descriptions he had read. Everyone had always described it in human terms, but this was not a primate in the same way it was not a reptile. It was taxonomically a *monster*.

Breck wasn't scared. He was too far past emotion. His only thoughts as the creature closed over him concerned the luminous corona about its head as it eclipsed the sun. He wished he had his camera. It would have been a brilliant shot.

EDITED BY ERIC S. BROWN AND A.P. FUCHS

A FOREST OF MONSTERS

BY

GIOVANNA LAGANA

IF SOMEONE SCREAMS in the forest, are their cries heard?

Even though Jacob knew the answer was no, he continued to contemplate that very question for the umpteenth time this hour as he checked his gold pocket watch. Two hours had passed since he last heard the warrior cry from the beast, the cry that signified it would be coming for him soon.

Was it toying with him? Most certainly. The circle of huge stones surrounding him and the smaller rocks scattered about were a clear indication of it. Each time he tried to cross the circle barrier the creature had formed around him, it would catapult a rock his way, stoning him in punishment. Punishment it believed he deserved. "What comes around goes around" was a saying that he himself held true for over a year.

But now that he was on the other side of the coin, he realized its meaning should not be taken in context, but in broad perspective. A lot of good this revelation did him now as the hour of death approached with a blade's edge so sharp it cut away at his sanity with every minute that passed.

Combing his fingers through his grimy hair, he heard the growls of his stomach rebutting against its forced fasting. Four days had gone by since he last ate a decent meal. For all that time, he tried to eat leaves and plant roots he believed safe, and the water he drank was rainwater collected on tree and plant leaves in his prison deep in the boreal forest of Canada.

He felt weak, dizzy, and cold. The damp autumn air made his joints ache. Leaning on the hard rock behind him, he tried to distract his mind from his pain and despair. What he wouldn't give for a piping hot cup of coffee and a warm stew filled with tender beef morsels and vegetables.

The divine meal image he conjured in his mind suddenly turned to frayed, sanguine flesh floating in a pool of fresh, viscous blood. He covered his eyes and bowed his head, trying to shake the horror away.

He still suffered from the side effects even after a year. All the treatments, experiments, and concoctions he endured—and still the nightmares came back to him, whipping his psyche when he was the most vulnerable. They tormented him continuously, systematically forging in him what he should never forget. He was who he was and no man or god could ever change that.

That's what he tried to show Doctor Philips time and time again, but the old stubborn scientist was blind to all his warnings and words. He belittled him in the lab each time they experimented on another subject. He tried reasoning with him that these experiments would only fail and turn against him one day, but talking to a wall would have been more effective.

He sighed. This was all the doctor's fault. If he had only heeded Jacob's warning then he wouldn't be gone now, leaving him alone with the beast in this deserted forest.

As if on cue, a whizzing sound pricked his ears. It was coming closer. Jacob rolled over, hoping to miss the catapulted object, but too late. The fist-sized rock hit him square in the middle of his back. He screamed in agony as pain shot through his upper body and the wind was knocked out of his lungs.

Tears began to trickle down his cheeks. He slowly sat up. A cry of bitter revenge from the beast trembled in his ears. With fear and apprehension, Jacob peered into the dark green foliage ahead. Red, deadly eyes stared at him with acute hatred. In the shadows they were hauntingly demonic. Their owner, a cold, calculating demon—born not from the fires of Hell, but in a sterile white room—observed Jacob's every move and anticipated a counter offense.

He could hear its rage through its ragged breathing. A chill crawled up his spine as the image of the gigantic beast with sharp fangs pouncing on him and tearing his limbs off fermented in his mind.

Pushing himself backward, he recoiled instinctively, trying to keep as much space between him and the tempestuous monster as he could without passing the stone barrier it had made.

Once he moved as far away as he could, he remained motionless, staring back at the creature while it continued to taunt him with its own observing stare. Minutes passed and each beat of Jacob's heart echoed in his ears, making his eardrums throb and pop.

As he waited, his imagination wandered onto many futile and sometimes impossible ideas of escape. The question, *If someone screams in the forest, can their cries be heard?* once again crossed his mind. Only this time, the correct answer came to him.

Yes, they could.

They *could* be heard by others. Not humans, though, for no other human remained in the vicinity, but the creatures of the forest could hear his cries and they, too, would come and beat on him as the beast was doing to him now. They'd stone him to death in justice and then eat him, for he didn't belong here.

Another whizzing sound started out as a hum and got louder. A sharp stone struck him in the knee, smashing the kneecap and opened a huge gash. Cloth, skin, flesh, and thick, dark brown hair frayed in the air from the impact. Blood spouted out from the damaged joint, staining his ripped beige wool pants from his knee down to his mid shin. He cried in pain and cursed.

Blood, so much blood. He knew all too well the scent of his blood would make the others come for him soon, as well.

Doom loomed over him like a thick, rough noose. Death's chime would soon begin to ring and either Heaven's gates would welcome him or the bowels of Hell for his damnation. Only time would tell.

And that time came faster than he anticipated as the beast came out from behind the dark foliage and charged at him with such speed he barely acknowledged its movement. It lifted its huge hairy hand the size of a small medicine ball and struck him across the face. Darkness encroached with bitter sweetness as he awaited Judgment.

◆　　◆　　◆

The far sound of pounding and glass shattering awoke him. In his grogginess, Jacob tried to focus on his surroundings. The white wall and wooden table with all the metal instruments came into view. Slowly lifting and turning his head to the side, he noted he was chained to a wooden table in Doctor Phillips's lab.

His first thought was the doctor placed him here, but he remembered the scientist was no longer there. Then who brought him here and who was it trying to break into the building? The answer to the second question came before the first when he heard the moans and grunts of the creatures outside.

They had obviously picked up his blood's scent when he got wounded and followed his odor to the lab. They soon would be upon him if he didn't break out of the confines and got out of there as quickly as possible. With all the brute strength he could muster, Jacob tried to pull his arm up and out, but the strong chain didn't break.

He attempted to wiggle his thick wrists out of the cuffs, but it only caused chaffing. Taking a deep breath, hoping another solution would come to him, he heard the door open and saw the beast walk in.

Its bloodshot red eyes still glared at him with hatred. It walked over to Jacob in a clumsy gait. It obviously hadn't become accustomed to its new bulky eight-foot-tall body. When it got close enough to strike him, Jacob recoiled, closing his eyes. He screamed, hoping part of its sane mind still remained human.

"I'm sorry I did this to you, but you gave me no choice!" he said.

It stopped and just stared at Jacob. Jacob could see rationality trying to work behind its eyes.

He continued to speak, hoping the part of its brain that still was human was listening to him. "Didn't you see why I did it? Your experiments . . . they were getting worse. Completely unethical. Barbaric. Only God has a right to do what you did . . . what you made me do. You of all people know there would be repercussions. Look at what happened to you in London. It nearly cost you your life. It certainly cost you your career."

The blood-red eyes widened as if its memory was coming back. Good. Jacob's reasoning was having an effect. Too bad it wasn't fast enough. How many minutes did they have before the creatures got in and came after them? If they got to them before they could escape, things would get ugly, most definitely bloody. The image of shredded, bloody flesh floating in a pool of fresh, viscous blood once again returned to his mind.

Jacob wanted to scream, but what good would that do? Taking a deep breath and adding a desperate tone to his plea, he said, "Look, I had no way of knowing what was in the vial I gave you. I thought it was a sedative, certainly not the new strain of the experimental virus. I only wanted to knock you out to stop the experiment from continuing. It was cruel and the subject was crying in agony. You once had compassion in you. I saw it well over a year ago when you took me in, gave me a place to live and work, when I had nowhere to go after what happened. Don't tell me that compassion no longer exists in you. Look deep inside your soul and you'll understand my actions."

It remained unmoving for a few seconds more, just staring deep into Jacob's eyes. What did it mean? Jacob prayed it meant it'd unlock the chain cuffs soon and free him. But when its red eyes narrowed and it lifted a big syringe with green liquid in it, Jacob knew his ember of hope for salvation had just gone out.

He tried to scream, "Please no. No, don't do this, Doctor Phillips. I implore you!" But his words fell on deaf ears. The mutant ape-like creature that had trapped him in the forest four days ago had gone, and intelligence and vindication had turned it into a force of revenge and destruction.

It stabbed the long, thick needle into Jacob's wide bicep with such force, Jacob thought it had torn off his flesh. The hot contents of it slowly seeped into his veins as the creature tapped the needle, pushing down and ejecting the liquid into him. Heat began to spread through Jacob's limbs, making him shake uncontrollably.

He closed his eyes as pain shot through his abdomen and dizziness overtook him. His breathing became labored. His mind was overwhelmed with all the changes happening in him as the virus the creature gave him began to take effect. At least he thought it was a virus. After all that was what the mad scientist had been working on all the time Jacob helped him with his secret experiments in the lab. A virus that would change humanity's immune system and make its body regenerative. In turn it would make humans invincible against any type of injury, sickness and disease.

Doctor Phillips had started his research back in London in 1897. His research mainly involved vivisection back then, which meant cutting and experimenting on live subjects. When the interest group named British Union for the Abolition of Vivisection was created back in 1898, the backlash from its public protests made the people open their eyes to science's unethical experiments. The domino effect from these protests rendered all of Doctor Phillips's work unacceptable and immoral. His funding ceased and his reputation was ruined.

Members of the radical group even torched his home. He barely made it out alive before his cottage collapsed in a fiery heap. That's when he came to Canada, hoping to continue on with his research.

In theory, Doctor Phillips's intentions had been noble in the beginning, but all the failed attempts and creatures the virus and his surgeries turned the subjects into made his actions unforgiveable.

Even though Jacob helped him as his assistant in those secret experiments, he tried to tell him that time and again this past year. But Doctor Phillips didn't listen and look where it got him. And Jacob knew where it got himself. He was on the verge of dying. The sheer acuteness of pain shooting through his entire body, he could barely endure.

But even though the pain was excruciating, soon ice coldness started to spread through him, numbing him. It was then he realized the creature had removed the cuffs. The creature took his hand and pulled him up. It grunted for him to leave.

On wobbly legs, he turned over from the table and placed his feet on the floor. His legs felt like heavy stumps rather than his lower limbs. He half-expected himself to falter and fall to the floor, but he braced himself against the wall and made his way to the door.

A loud crash followed by shuffling sounds came from the other side of the room. The creatures had made it into the building and only a white-tiled wall stood between him and them.

Jacob expected to hear the beast—his old friend—following him out, but it didn't. He slowly turned to look at it and saw it standing next to the table. It stared at him with wide eyes. Its eyes were no longer bloodshot, but brown. Doctor Phillips was transforming from the hybrid Bigfoot creature back to his human self.

Could it be . . . ? he wondered. Apparently, the new virus strain's effects weren't permanent as with the past strains that transformed the human subjects into the same huge, primitive Bigfoot creatures that now hunted them down. Those creatures thirsted for blood. They could smell the scent miles away. The fact they had tracked Jacob down after he wounded his knee and bled was a prime example as to how susceptible their sense of smell was to the scent of blood.

His blood. If he was still bleeding, they would still be able to track him. He'd never be able to escape them. He gazed down at his knee and saw the wound had begun to heal. The huge gash was slowly closing in on itself, and the blood seeped back into the skin's pores.

No . . . it couldn't be. The doctor had found the solution to regeneration and he had injected him with it!

He gazed once more at the creature, shocked. It nodded, acknowledging his guess was correct and signaled he should leave before it was too late. The sound of the creature's approach was getting louder every second.

Reluctantly, Jacob nodded and made his way to the door. His legs' weight had lightened and the numbness was beginning to fade.

Once he got to the door, he reached to open it a crack and peeked out, but before he had a chance to do so, he spotted a creature outside. Lucky for him, it had its back to him and didn't see him before he closed the door once more, locking it behind him.

The lock wouldn't keep them out, but it gave him a sense of security just the same.

He heard a grunt behind him and turned to see the creature half-beast, half-human now, motioning for him to get into the tall metal cabinet beside it. Jacob hurried over there. His legs didn't wobble any longer nor did his gait waver. Jacob's huge feet seemed to move in a heavy brutish-like fashion.

When he got to the storage cabinet's door he scrunched up and squeezed inside the cabinet as far as he could. He tried to make as much room for Doctor Phillips as possible, but the doctor shut the door on him just as he heard the door to the lab crash open.

The creatures had entered the room.

Holding his breath, Jacob listened acutely to the fracas coming from inside the room as his heart drummed in his chest. From Doctor Phillips's cries he understood the creatures were eating him alive. Jacob knew all too well they loved fresh blood the most. The viscous texture of it, the scent.

Yes, umm, oh yes. He began to salivate and his head turned and turned. Something in his brain started to change. He could sense it, but didn't understand it until . . . the smell of freshly-spilt blood coming from outside the storage cabinet entranced him.

Then he knew what was happening and he relished it with all his heart and soul, for the order in nature would soon be balanced once more.

All the wrongs Doctor Phillips and he had committed this past year would all be eradicated. Soon the creatures in the other room would be no more and he could go back to his past life.

Retribution at last, was his last human thought as he reverted back to his beastly origins.

Jacob—Bigfoot—hit the metal door with a powerful blow of his bent arm, making the door fly to the other side of the room. It gazed at the mutant ape-like creatures as they feasted on the fresh remains of the human.

It took a deep inhale and smelled the scent of blood and its stomach churned in yearning. It wasn't the spilt human's blood that interested the beast. No, it was the fresh pumping blood in the creature's veins that got its fancy.

With a howl of dominant proclamation, Bigfoot made its ground by taking a deadly strike at its first victim.

REVENGE OF THE BLOOD CREATURES

BY

FRANKLIN E. WALES

"I'M TELLING YOU it can't miss," Danny said, shaking his trade paper. "These two guys, Lewis and Friedman, have broken new ground and made a mint!"

Carl took the paper. The two of them were sitting at Carl's kitchen table, a bottle of cheap Scotch between them. He scanned the article.

"It's almost 1964," Danny said, "it's time for guys like us to get a break."

"Will you pipe down?" Carl said. "I'm trying to read, here."

"What's to read? You've dreamed about making a movie for years and this is the time to do it. Those two guys have invented a whole new field of motion pictures. They are calling it the gore movie. We don't need a great script, nudity, or even great actors. Just some really good bloody effects."

As the vice president of Klaxy, a small self-contained studio specializing in television commercials just outside Detroit, Carl had made it his business to master all aspects of the industry, from setting up shots to developing and editing to sound overdubs. During his decade-long tenure, he kept copious notebooks of all he'd learned in hopes of someday gaining the chance to shoot a full length motion picture. A loner by choice, he had never shared this dream with anyone until he met Danny, a small time hustler with a gift for gab and a thirst for whiskey, one night two years back in a bar. "I'm an idea man," Danny was fond of saying. His ideas always seemed to revolve around the next big thing . . . so long as no real work was involved.

As much as he enjoyed Danny's dream-weaving yarns of better things to come, Carl realized quickly he would be supporting their drinking habits and recommended they get together at his house.

"Look," Danny said, "the studio shuts down tomorrow for your three-week vacation between Christmas and New Year's. Let's do it. Let's pack your microbus full of equipment and film, and head south to

Florida. I'll swipe a few mannequin parts from the warehouse I'm night-watching now and we're in business."

"Well," Carl said, unsure, "do you have a script?"

"It's all in here," Danny said, tapping his temple. "It's called, Terror Of The Missing Link. I met a guy who works the carnival circuit who spends his winters down in Florida. His gimmick is a damned fine costume of a half man-half gorilla."

Danny droned on, but Carl barely heard him; he was too absorbed in the article. The movie was panned by critics as cheaply made with shoddy production values, mediocre acting and unnecessary violence, but it was making a ton of money in the grindhouse circuit. Rumour was it cost next to nothing to produce.

"And you think we could do this?" Carl asked.

"Why not?" Danny said. "Somebody is going to. This is a whole new world in motion pictures. We should get in on it before everyone else does."

He considered it for a moment. With three weeks of vacation and no family to spend the holidays with, he had the time. As cold as it was in Michigan, Florida sounded good, too. At the studio they had just taken their year-end inventory and since he controlled the inventory itself, he could hide any missing film stock until he could replace it.

"Can we shoot this thing and be back in three weeks?" he asked.

"We can shoot it and be back in nine days," Danny said. "I've got it all worked out." He tapped his temple again.

"And you're sure we could make money?"

"Did you read the article? Lewis and Friedman are making a mint, and it would get our feet into the door to make another picture."

Carl poured two shots from the bottle and passed one to Danny. "Let's do it, then," he said raising his glass in a toast.

The following evening they returned to the studio after midnight, loaded up two cameras, sound equipment and enough film to shoot a seventy-minute feature—if they didn't waste any—into Carl's Volkswagen microbus and headed for Florida. True to his word, Danny did know a man named Ringo Gessetti who owned a sideshow attraction that proclaimed to have the living "Missing Link." Carl was not impressed. The costume might fool a country bumpkin in the backwoods of Maine, but it didn't look too good close up. Danny insisted if they kept their camera angles tight, they could pull it off.

The biggest problem was Ringo wanted to be paid. Danny struck a deal that gave Ringo ten percent of the movie if he would bring the costume down to the swamp for shooting. The man countered by requesting two females by the names of Abby and Ginny to be cast in the picture. Danny told him to pay them out of his percentage now that he was part owner in the picture. With Danny taking the reins, Carl felt his production beginning to slip through his fingers.

When Danny had finished his high finance negotiations, Ringo, Abby and Ginny loaded a suitcase each into the microbus and they all continued south. At least in all the hubbub it came out that Ringo had a Florida map that showed swamp locations, something neither Carl or Danny had thought of.

By the time they stopped for a late lunch in a little town that, according to the map, should not have been too far away from the entrance to the swamp, everyone was hungry. Carl knew he would soon be lightening his wallet even more. After ordering, Danny walked up to the bulletin board near the door. He came back holding a half-slip of paper.

"Look at this," he said, shoving the note in front of Carl's eyes. "I'd say we stopped at the right place."

Carl studied the note. In large block handwriting it proclaimed, STAFFORD BROTHERS SWAMP TOURS AND HUNTING EXPEDITIONS. "There is no phone number," he said.

Flipping the note over, Danny showed him the crudely-sketched map on the back. "Shouldn't be too hard to find," he said. "It looks close by. I'll ask the waitress."

"No," Carl said. He had already figured out the best way to shoot anything was to keep it unannounced if possible. The minute people learned there was a movie involved they saw dollar signs and thought they should get a piece of the action. "We'll find it." He let that set in before adding, "After we eat, let's shoot a few scenes of the girls around the town talking. We can dub the audio later." He had to shoot something and the girls were the only cast he had so far. Once again Carl found himself longing for the cold of Michigan.

About an hour's drive out of town, Carl took the dirt turnoff marked with a sloppily-painted sign that read STAFFORD BROS. complete with an arrow pointing to the right. He maneuvered the microbus down the quarter mile of dirt road that ended at a dilapidated little house surrounded by several old cars on blocks and a boat with a tree growing out of it.

"Looks like a trustworthy place," he muttered.

"Easy," Danny said. "We need someone to take us out to the swamp for some pick up shots of the girls and the Missing Link out there."

Carl sighed. "And how did the girls get there?"

"It will come to me," Danny said.

A shirtless man wearing bib overalls in his thirties came out the front door carrying a shotgun. "Help ya?" he called out, running his fingers through his blond hair.

"Oh this looks promising," Carl said.

"Quiet," Danny whispered. "This is why I'm the producer and you're the director." He rolled his window down and poked his head out. "Looking for the Stafford Brothers," he said. "We're looking for a trip into the swamps."

The man with the shotgun squinted, looking in the microbus. "All of ya?"

"Yes," Danny replied, "and some movie equipment."

"I'll have to ask my brother," the man said. Looking back to the shack he called out, "Willy, come on out here." He looked back into the van. "Name's Phil."

Willy came out, the spitting image of his brother right down to the shirtless-overall fashion statement. "Yeah?"

"These folks want to shoot a movie in the swamp," Phil said.

Willy looked at the sky. "Getting dark," he said. "We can't go until morning." He looked into the microbus. "Ya'll gonna make a movie?"

"We are," Danny said.

"Danny," Carl whispered.

Ignoring him, Danny said, "Why? Would you and your brother be interested in being in it?"

Willy looked at Phil, who nodded. "Maybe," he said. "What would it pay?"

"What would it cost us to all go out in the morning before sunrise?"

"Take two trips," Willy said. "Cost you . . ." He paused, thinking of a proper amount. "Two hundred dollars ought to do it."

Carl stiffened. He was the one funding this operation. Danny touched his shoulder, quieting him.

"That your normal going rate?" Danny asked. "Or did you jack it up some for movie people?"

Willy grinned. "Well, uh . . ."

Danny smiled at the man. "I thought so."

"What about being in the movie?" Phil asked.

"Do you have your actor's union cards?" Danny asked.

"What union card?" Willy asked.

Seeing the confusion on Willy's face, Danny continued. "Oh, I guess not. Never mind." He paused as if thinking. "See, in Hollywood you have to have an actor's union card to be paid for being in a feature film."

"So how do you get one of those?" Phil asked.

"It's complicated," Danny said. "Everything in Hollywood is. See you have to be in a feature film to qualify for getting a union card."

"Huh?" Willy said, scratching his stomach. "That don't make sense."

"It does in Hollywood. You have to intern in a movie. Everyone knows movie stars get big money, so you have to prove yourself by interning in a feature film first."

"So we can't be in the movie?" Phil asked.

"We can't pay you," Danny said. "You could intern."

"Intern," Willy said. "That means work for free?"

"Pretty much," Danny said. "And I know you're not interested in that."

"But then we'd get them union cards and could get big money?" Phil asked.

"Well, yes, and next time you are asked to be in a movie you could pretty much name your own price."

Carl rolled his eyes as Danny strung the two brothers along.

"What next time?" Willy said. "We ain't seen no movie people before you."

"Good point," Danny said. "I can't vouch for the rest of Hollywood, but our studio is pretty excited about this movie. They are already talking about making a part two."

"And we could be in it?" Phil asked.

"I'd say so. The roles I'm considering you two for are the heroes in this picture. You'd have to be in part two." Danny reached down on the seat and grabbed the notebook he'd been jotting notes on. "Let me see if I can work some numbers . . ."

From his seat Carl could see Danny was just doodling, but he sure looked like he was serious.

"You know," Danny said, looking at his doodles, "there might be some way we can work this out."

"How do you mean?" Willy asked.

"The studio will never agree to paying you two hundred dollars to take us out to the swamp, but let's say you take us out there for fifty dollars, act as our guides for a hunting trip for another fifty dollars, and we'll toss in another fifty for something we call 'services rendered.' He looked as if he was adding up his figures. "So we could probably give you a hundred-fifty."

"What's services rendered?" Willy asked.

"You let us camp out here in our van tonight, feed us, and appear in the movie."

"And we'll get our union cards?" Phil asked.

"You certainly will, and if we get to do a part two you will be first on the list, and then you can get the big money."

Phil and Willy conversed between themselves a moment. It was obvious where they were heading.

"Okay," Willy said. "But I want it in writing that we get the first offer and the right to name our price for part two."

"Done," Danny told him.

No one was very happy at the prospect of spending the night in the van, but as it turned out it wasn't as bad as they had expected. Willy and Phil slow-roasted a wild boar they'd killed earlier and dinner was delicious. Also, by chance, besides being swamp guides the brothers were proficient in creating moonshine. Carl got plenty of footage of the roasting hog with everyone sitting around the fire, and after a little while the Stafford brothers even agreed to stage a few shots around their whiskey still.

It was over the second or third round of what Carl quickly thought of as Stafford Brother's Paint Thinner when Willy finally asked about the movie.

"It's called Missing Link," Danny said. "The story is about a carnival that comes to town and one of their freaks gets loose and runs into the swamps. You two will play the hunters that have to track and kill it. Abby and Ginny will play your wives, and they accompany you on the hunt. They will be killed and you avenge them by hunting down the beast."

"What you got for a missing link?" Phil asked.

Danny pointed toward Ringo. "That there is Ringo Gessetti, the world renowned entertainer to kings and queens. He has a costume of a half man-half ape that is remarkably realistic."

Phil regarded Ringo. "Kinda short, ain't he?"

Willy laughed. "He is at that. If he was taller he could be the Florida Skunk Ape."

Danny stopped his sales pitch. "Come again?" he said. "The Florida what?"

"The Florida Skunk Ape," Willy said. "Some folks in other parts of the country call it a Bigfoot."

"Is it for real?" Abby asked.

Willy and Phil looked at each other.

"Sure is, little lady," Willy said. "But don't you worry none. Me and Phil seen old Skunkie a couple times out in those swamps. He ain't gonna hurt you none."

"He sure ain't," Phil said. "Willy grazed him with a bullet few years back. He keeps his distance from us now."

"I would have kilt him if he hadn't move at the last minute."

"Why a skunk ape?" Carl asked.

"Because he stinks," Phil said as if talking to a child.

By the evening's end, full of wild boar, moonshine and tall tales of the Florida swamp, the cast was in no condition to care where they slept. Fearing the worst, Carl had stayed away from the liquid brain assassin that was passed around in Mason Jars.

When the brothers came to wake them before dawn, Carl was happy he had chosen to steer clear of the 'shine. His was the only head not pounding. After a quick breakfast of strong coffee and cold boar meat, the brothers jumped in their ancient pickup truck and led the way to what they called "The Docks."

After nearly five miles on rutted road in the blackness of predawn, they finally arrived at a cut out just off a road that led down to the water. As it turned out, it wasn't going to take two trips at all as two boats were tied off together. Carl had seen pictures of airboats, but he was pretty sure what he was looking at was something original: Small boats wide enough to bolt two car bench seats behind the captain's chair—which bore a surprising resemblance to a bucket seat from a Ford Mustang— with a large fan connected to a motor that had to belong to a small car in its previous life.

They loaded the girls and Danny along with half the gear into Phil's boat while Ringo, Carl and the remainder of the gear went with Willy.

Before they left, Danny changed into a plaid shirt and jeans. "If you get a chance in some of the morning light," he told Carl, "see if you can shoot us on the boat. I'll double as Willy good enough if it's not too close."

Just after the sun came up, Willy slowed his boat and allowed it to drift. Phil followed suit.

"What's going on?" Carl asked.

"You got that camera handy?" Willy asked.

"I do." He'd been shooting some nature scenes in the predawn along the way.

"Then get it ready," Willy said, picking up his rifle. He took his time drawing a bead across the water. "You got me?"

"Yes."

"Then follow my aim."

Carl turned the camera out toward the bank. It looked as if Willy had zeroed in on a large log until the shot fired and the gator flipped over. Willy dropped two more bullets into the creature.

"Got him!" Phil yelled.

"What was that?" Carl asked.

"Gator," Willy said flatly. "Your partner said we had to feed ya."

Phil maneuvered his boat over to the fallen beast and tied it to the craft.

"Did you get that?" Danny yelled. "You can't buy that kind of shot!"

As much as the sight sickened him, Carl knew his friend was right.

When they finally docked the airboats, there was still a good thirty-minute hike into the swamps with all the gear. Carl thanked God there was a well-worn path to follow. Before they left, Phil removed the alligator's tail and cut it into steaks for easy carrying and left the remains for whatever other animals needed a meal.

The cabin itself was little more than a one-room shack with cots, a cook stove and an outhouse around the back. The brothers had cleared a good fifty feet around the front, at the center of which was a large cooking pit. Picked clean bones littered the area.

"Got a nice tree stand up there," Willy said, pointing to a tree at the side edge of the clearing. "You could take your camera up there for some good pictures, I think."

Carl looked up at the sheet of plywood nailed into the tree some twenty feet up. It was a great place for a camera. He could see the entire clearing from there. "Looks good," he said. "Once I catch my breath."

"Hollywood folk don't have much get-go, do they?" Phil asked Willy with a laugh.

Phil built a fire in the pit and prepared the steaks while Carl and Danny assembled the cameras. "Hope ya'll don't mind the fire," he said. "We keep it going the whole time we're out here. Helps keep the skeeters away."

After lunch, Danny shot some scenes of dialogue created on the spot between Abby, Ginny, Phil and Willy. Carl got some pickup shots of cypress trees with snakes dangling down, marshy waters and various forms of animal life around, all with Ringo in his half-and-half costume, wandering like an ape between the trees.

Near dusk, Carl realized he hadn't brought any lighting equipment. "Willy?" he called out. "I see some floodlights on the cabin and a few of these tree stands. Do you have electricity out here?"

"We got a generator," Willy replied. Turning to his brother, he added, "Phil, fire up the genny. Seems these Hollywood people didn't bring everything they needed."

"It's getting dark," Danny called up to Carl. "We need to shoot the Missing Link entering the campsite." When Phil had returned from starting the generator, Danny turned to the brothers and the girls. "I need you all to sit around the fire, guys facing the woods." He pointed to the woodpile at the side of the house where he'd concealed the second camera. "When I give you the sign, Willy, you grab your gun and get up."

By the time Carl had secured himself and the equipment in the tree stand as best he could, the sky had already turned to gray. "Ready when you are, Ringo!"

Ringo headed out of view into the bush. "Let's hurry," he said. "This place gives me the creeps."

"Hey," Danny said, sniffing the air, "what is that stink?"

Ginny's face twisted in disgust. "Is it the Skunk Ape?" she asked.

Phil laughed. "No, honey. It's most likely a dead possum or something upwind, but it sure does stink."

"Hey," Carl yelled, "I'm rolling here and we are wasting film!"

Danny stepped up. "Ready, Ringo?"

Something scampered through the underbrush to their left. Willy stood, grabbed his gun and fired into the bush. A high-pitched screech filled the air.

"What the hell was that?" Danny said.

"I don't know," Willy said, "but I got it." He carefully advanced toward the area where the thing appeared to have fallen. Using the barrel of the gun, he pushed the brush aside. "What the—"

"Whatta ya got?" Phil asked, heading in that direction.

Looking through the camera, Carl watched as Willy pulled out the limp body of something that looked like it might have been a monkey . . . or a fur-covered child.

"What is it?" Danny asked.

"Dunno," Willy said. "Looks like some kind of monkey-kid."

Ringo, the man-ape, came running out. "Hey, you could have killed me." Looking at the limp creature in Willy's arms, he said, "Let me see that!"

Even from his high vantage point Carl saw the oddity of Ringo in costume holding the creature. It looked like father and son. "Danny!" he yelled down. "Get a close up of Ringo and that thing."

"Already on it," Danny said.

"I'll give you a hundred dollars for this thing," Ringo told Willy.

"Make it two," Willy said.

Looking at the ape-child, Ringo decided quickly. "Two it is."

"What are you going to do with it?"

"Stuff it," Ringo said. "It will look great in my exhibit: the Missing Link's child." He was already seeing it as it would appear, and the extra price of admission he could now require.

Abby, Ginny and Phil all moved closer to see the thing. "Eww," Abby said. "It stinks."

"It does," Ginny said, sniffing the air. "This whole place stinks, if you ask me."

A loud forlorn wail filled the air, drawing all eyes to the trees surrounding the area.

"What was that?" Abby asked. "Was it that Skunk Ape?"

"Don't know," Willy said. "Could be. I reckon we've never seen one."

"But you said you shot one."

"It's a story we made up to scare tourists," Phil said.

The wail echoed through the air again. Willy grabbed his gun and looked up. "You see anything?" he shouted to Carl.

Using the camera lens, Carl scanned the trees. "No. I can't see anything." Down below he heard the others coughing and choking. "What's going on?"

"The air," Ringo yelled, "it's gone sour!"

Willy drew his rifle up and scanned the woods ahead. Something was thrashing about. A moment later, Carl saw the unbelievable as a two legged creature nearly seven feet tall covered in matted fur came crashing into the opening. Upon seeing its dead offspring the beast tipped its head back and roared, spittle flying from its jaws. By the look of its breasts, it was a full grown female version of the thing Ringo was holding. Screaming that terrible wail of sorrow, it charged forward.

Willy drew a bead and fired directly at it. The she-beast flinched back as blood suddenly exploded outward near its shoulder. Before he could get another shot, the beast reached his space and yanked the rifle from his hands. With its elongated arms it drew the rifle back and hammered the weapon club-like into Willy's temple. Even from his place in the trees, Carl heard the sickening sound of a melon exploding on impact with a baseball bat. Willy dropped to the ground, his brain leaking from his shattered skull.

The mother-beast turned her attention to Ringo, who stood panicked and frozen. She swung her arm around and simply removed his left ear, cheek and his nose with her claws. As his head spun with the impact, her paw came around and removed the other ear and half of his face. Now faceless, Ringo stood for a moment, screaming, before she grabbed what remained of his head and twisted his neck clear around with an audible crack.

Grabbing her lifeless offspring, the mother-beast turned her gaze on Phil and the girls who had backed up to the fire pit.

"Get to the house!" Phil yelled a moment before a half dozen adult-sized creatures entered the clearing from the sides, cutting off their line of retreat. Through the camera lens Carl saw Danny creeping from the woodpile toward the cabin door. He had nearly reached his destination when one of the beasts saw him and closed the distance between them in four lunging steps.

"Danny," Carl said. "Behind you."

Danny turned. The creature's mammoth paw swung toward his head. He tried to counter the blow with his arm, but the beast caught it mid air. With one mighty wrench, it pulled Danny's arm from his body and turned it on him, beating him to the ground with it. Carl watched his friend fall as his life bled out.

The creature tossed the arm to the side and drove both front paws into Danny's stomach, ripping the soft flesh apart with one pull. Once it had opened its meal, the beast dropped to all fours and buried its snout into Danny's innards.

Phil fired at the beast, hitting it in the back.

"Behind you!" Carl yelled just before another member of the tribe grabbed Phil's head and plucked it from his body as easy as popping the head of a dandelion from its stem. It looked at the head a moment, as if wondering where it had come from, before throwing it into the fire.

Left alone and surrounded, Abby and Ginny held onto each other, screaming as four of the beasts fell upon them. Even through the camera lens Carl saw little more than fur-covered bodies mobbed over the girls. A moment later an arm flew from the middle, followed by another. The sounds of the girls screaming suddenly went silent as their heads were tossed from the pile.

The lights went out when the hum of the generator died. Illuminated now only by the fire, the beasts became mere silhouettes of movement in the dark. Still, Carl tried to focus the camera as best he could. At first he was actually glad for the lack of clear vision. It was only when the sounds of animal snorting and the tearing of meat filled the stillness that he wished for the rattling sound of the genny.

After what seemed like hours of wet chewing sounds, Carl heard the beasts leaving back through the underbrush. He offered a silent prayer that they either couldn't climb trees, or couldn't smell him through their own stench.

Much later, when the sky began to lighten, he started the camera back up and used the lens to scan the area. Below him was a nightmare of pure carnage; bodies without limbs, limbs without bodies and blood soaked ground everywhere. He had never seen the aftermath of war, but realized it must look similar to what he recorded from his bird's-eye view. Every body had been torn open, its innards removed and eaten.

When the sun was full up, he finally dared venture down to the ground. There was no way he could remember what he had or hadn't touched. Nor could he just leave Danny's body out for whatever swamp creatures should decided to feast on it. He'd had enough time in the tree to know what needed to be done. Collecting the bodies and body parts into the center of the clearing by the fire-pit, Carl doused them in the kerosene he'd found in the cabin. Watching the funeral pyre, Carl began planning his next steps. His was the only footage ever shot with such clarity, the only real proof of the existence of the Bigfoot creature. And not only Bigfoot, an entire tribe of them. He would be famous.

◆　◆　◆

It took nearly two hours to haul the film equipment from the campsite to where they had docked the airboats, and several more hours yet before Carl managed to maneuver Willy's boat to the point where they had parked the microbus. By the time he arrived the smoke from the swamp had stopped. Should anyone ever venture out that far, a burned out cabin and a mass of bones was all they'd ever find.

After loading the van, he drove nonstop, living on a diet of truck stop food and black coffee until he reached the studio in Detroit. Upon arrival he went straight into the developing lab.

By the time he had screened all the footage, he was sure of two things. On one hand he had the only footage proving without a doubt that the Bigfoot race existed. He would be heralded as a modern-day Columbus.

On the other hand, with a bit of editing and a little narration, he actually had enough footage for a feature film. He could say he bought it from a struggling filmmaker; that happened all the time. He'd have to add some bogus names for everyone involved, including his own. He wouldn't be famous, but if *Blood Feast* could raise the kind of money it did, he could be rich. The acting was not good, the story was weak, but you couldn't beat the realism of what he captured on film for effects.

He'd need a better title. Danny may have been an idea man, but *Terror of the Missing Link* was horrible. He thought of the carnage he'd seen for a few moments.

Revenge of the Blood Creatures had a nice ring to it.

THE THING UNDER THE HOUSE

BY

R.J. SEVIN & ROSALIND SEVIN

FOR A WHILE, the rain on the windows and the thunder rolling through the mountain air were the only sounds. I sat on the couch, my knees drawn to my chest. It's what you do in situations like this. You huddle. Huddle or pace.

Seth paced. I wanted him beside me, his arm around me again. He might have wanted the same, but he paced. He clutched the shotgun and he walked back and forth, his work boots thump-thump-thumping on the hardwood floor, on the rug before the couch. Hollow thumps.

"What the hell is it?" I'd probably said the same thing ten, twenty times since morning, I don't know. I wasn't counting.

Seth stepped to the window, his face tight. Raindrops fat as your thumb struck the glass. Thunder boomed.

The thing under the house screamed.

♦　♦　♦

It had been raining off and on all week. Light rain, nothing to get too worked up about. Friday evening, we drove Jacob to my mother's house. Mount Hope is about an hour away. Two hours coming and going, the price we pay for quiet weekends. Jacob didn't mind. Mom had a giant-screen TV and a Playstation, just for him. And probably a little too much chocolate.

We were halfway home when the rain really started coming down. It sounded like a thousand fingers rat-tat-tatting on the roof of the truck.

"Did you check the weather?" Seth asked, clicking the wipers into high gear. We didn't have television. We had a TV, yes, but no signal, no cable. We had a DVD player and a VCR and quite a few movies, but there was no idle channel-surfing in our home. Another reason why Jacob loved Mom's.

We got our news and weather from the internet. We had a laptop and a semi-reliable dialup connection. And no, I hadn't checked the weather.

When we got home, I did. The forecast called for more rain. There was a question as to whether or not a low pressure front was going to stall. That evening, as we lay together on the couch, the weather worsened, went from heavy raining to all-out storming. Now the only question was when the damned thing would *un*-stall.

I called Mom and checked on Jacob. He was watching one of the *Star Wars* movies on his grandma's freakin' enormous TV. I told him to watch his language, that it was almost bedtime. He told me "freakin'" wasn't a curse word—Dad used to say it all the time. Furthermore, it was Friday. He didn't have to go to bed early Fridays.

"Ten," I said. "No later."

"Midnight."

"Are you crazy, young man?"

"Oh, please, Mom?"

"Jacob." The warning in my voice sounded more like restrained laughter.

"Please?" The "e" was several miles long.

"Eleven. And that's final. Okay?"

"Okay."

We swapped I love yous and hung up. Seth and I resumed lounging. The rain tapered off, intensified, tapered again.

We drank too much wine and made love like teenagers and fell asleep and slept in. We woke at eight in the morning. It was dark out. As dark as dawn—and storming.

I could tell by the look on Seth's face we were thinking the same thing: the roads. In weather like this, it's common for sections of the road to wash out. There was a lot of road between here and Mom's. Like our place, her house was built a few hundred feet uphill. Barring a serious mudslide, they'd be fine. If they stayed put.

"We have to go get Jacob," he said, pulling on his pants and wiping the sleep from his eyes.

"He'll be fine," I said, trying and failing to ignore how worried I sounded.

"I'll call him."

The line was dead. I pressed the button on the receiver a few times, a habit I'd picked up from the movies. The line stayed dead.

We looked at one another and sighed.

Ten minutes later, wet and shivering, we drove down the dirt road leading from our property to 64, which lead down into Pax and onto Mount Hope. I adjusted the heat, wiped my arms and hair with fast-food napkins from the glove box. Rain pelted the windshield. The wipers couldn't keep up. We crept along. The world outside the truck was a gray smear.

We didn't get far. Mud and debris blocked both lanes.

The road might not have been washed away beneath it. We turned around.

"He's going to be fine," I said.

"Yeah," Seth said, one hand on the wheel, the other kneading his eyes into the back of his skull. Too much wine.

For the rest of the crawl uphill, neither of us spoke.

The truck rocked, the back tires lost traction a few times and kicked up dark fans of mud. The rear end fishtailed. The road leading to our property was steep and winding. Trees clustered on either side.

Thunder ripped a hole in the sky. I winced.

We reached the yard and I released the breath I'd held forever. I eased up on the door handle. The yard was a fairly level shelf on the side of the hill, large enough to hold a shed, a picnic table, and the truck. The steep incline continued. Our house loomed, the front half perched upon pylons ten feet above ground, the back half scooted right up against the hill.

We stepped into the rain. It stung my face and arms.

The sky churned. Lightning struck. It was deafening. It was close. Splashing toward the steps, Seth said something I couldn't understand.

At the top of the stairs, he fumbled with the keys. He grew up in New Orleans, where you locked the door when you left. Even in the middle of No Crime, Nowhere, old habits die hard.

Something moved in the corner of my eye. I looked back and down. I might have gasped, I'm not really sure. At some point I became aware of Seth standing beside me. I looked at him. He looked like I felt.

"Is it . . ." I began, blinking. "It's not a bear, is it?"

His head wobbled once—left, right. "No."

"What the hell is it?"

"I don't know." He licked his lips, beads of rain chasing one another down his face. His hair was in his eyes. "I'll get the gun." He took a step backward, tugging my arm.

The thing—whatever it was—stood between the trees behind the shed, massive and black and heaving. Formless in the rain haze, it staggered toward the house. It seemed to buckle over like a person punched in the stomach. Then it stood erect and crept forward.

I could not get my mind around what I was seeing. It was tall. Water dripped from matted brown fur so dark it was almost black. Perched atop what might have been massive shoulders was what seemed to be a small head. A head, shoulders—normal enough, right? But the limbs . . . were there more than there should be? Four long legs? A tangle of arms?

I could smell the thing. A nasty, wet zoo aroma lurking just beneath the clean scent of the rain.

I heard Seth in the bedroom, cracking the barrel, sliding the shells into place. I stepped back, out of the rain. Lightning ripped through the air. I winced, blinked. Howling, the thing rushed the house.

One second after I slammed the door, the thing struck the siding that skirted the pylons. Since we got the place five years ago, Seth talked about converting the space into a work shed or a storage room or a playroom for Jacob. He never got past talk, and it remained dirt and dead leaves down there. The skirting was little more than garden lattice. The thing tore through it with ease.

Seth stomped into the living room, gun raised, eyes wild.

"It's under the house," I said. The thing screamed again. I jumped. Seth tensed, pointed the gun at the floor.

I touched his arm. "No."

This close to the source, without the wind and the rain between us, the sound of its ragged voice was like nothing I've ever heard. It sounded like fear and pain and teeth. That doesn't make sense, but there it is.

"What the hell is it?" I sounded like a broken record.

◆　◆　◆

And that's how it was for a while. Seth with the gun, pacing. The rain on the windows. The thunder and the lightning. The thing beneath the house, moaning and screaming and then falling silent for long stretches of twenty, thirty minutes; Seth pacing, saying he was going to go down there and shoot it; me telling him not to, grabbing him, telling him to put down the gun and sit down.

"It just wants out of the rain," I said at some point after the electricity had flickered into darkness.

His back to me, Seth stood framed in the window. Lightning flashed. He was a gun toting shadow. "It'll leave when it stops."

"You might be right," he said, stepping away from the window. Setting aside the gun, he sank into the couch beside me, slid his arm around me.

The thing moaned.

"Sounds hurt."

"I think it is."

"Hopefully it'll die down there," he said, smirking. Man, I loved that smirk. "I'm sure we can make a few bucks off the Mothman's corpse. Sell it on eBay or something. Get on *Coast to Coast*, at least."

"I don't think it's the Mothman," I said. There was no humor in my voice. "It didn't have wings." I thought of the confused jumble of limbs. "I don't think it did."

"Maybe it's a drunk kid in a bear suit?"

I might have laughed. I don't remember.

Thunder, lightning, rain; the thing screaming every fifteen or so minutes, falling into a pattern, intensifying, like the storm. Thunder above, thunder below. Eventually, Seth rose, picked up the gun, resumed pacing. I nodded off once or twice, snapped awake each time the thing under the house cried out. Seth stomped the floor and screamed for it to shut up.

Lather, rinse, repeat.

The screams stopped. When the silence held for an hour, then two, we figured the wounded whatever-it-was had died. We thought we heard a faint mewling, a whimpering. We weren't sure.

I closed my eyes.

"Oh crap." Seth's voice, waking me.

Vibrating. The lamp on the end table, the glasses in the kitchen cabinet—everything vibrating.

I opened my eyes. The world rattled. A wall of sound swelled, crashing and churning. I had time to note two things: the rain had stopped, the sun had risen. Then the mudslide slammed into the back of the house. It was as if the thunder had come down from the sky and swallowed us. A black curtain was drawn over the front of the house, blotting out the dawn.

I felt Seth's hand on my arm.

Then the world slid creaking and snapping into darkness.

I spun and rolled, was slammed against and slammed upon. I came to rest on my side, mud and debris pressing down upon me. I gasped and wept and struggled to move. For a long time there was silence. Then the sound of shifting wreckage.

Strong arms pulled aside the section of wall pinning me to the ground. I blinked into the early morning light.

The thing stood over me.

I was right about the massive shoulders and the fur and the small head, wrong about the rest. It had two thick arms and two long legs. Long fur—matted and mud-smeared—covered most of its body. Its chest and biceps were bare, the brown skin covered in ornate and symmetrical scars. Its face was an ape's face. Its cheeks and forehead were also scarred. Its eyes were small and wise. It pursed its lips, blowing once, cheeks puffing out: *hoof.* Utterly dismissive.

Looking away from me, it tore through the wreckage. I wish I could say that I called for Seth, that I looked for him. I can't. I didn't. I watched the massive creature sift through the dripping remains of the house until it found what it was looking for.

When it pulled the other creature up from the debris, I understood. Four legs, a tangle of arms. Not one but two, huddling against the rain. It's what you did in situations like that. You huddled.

He—not it—knelt before his fallen mate. She held something to her chest. He eased it free. Pink skin and black down. Small limbs twitching. It cried out, its tiny fingers closing around its father's fur. The big male placed the child upon one of its massive shoulders. It held fast, its small hands clutching its father's thick fur.

Gathering its dead mate into its arms, the big male stood.

I watched it leave, watched its large footprints in the dirt fill with muddy rainwater. It didn't look back.

It didn't take me long to find Seth. He was cold and still. I wasn't strong enough to pull the section of roof from him.

Collapsing onto my knees, I wept. When I could weep no more, I screamed. When I could scream no more, I rose to my feet and, turning my back to the scattered remains of our home, stumbled down the hill.

There was a lot of road between me and Jacob.

I didn't look back.

Yéiitsoh

BY

SUZANNE ROBB

CARL HUDDER AND Jake Miller stood in front of the cave entrance elbowing one another.

Carl nudged his friend once again. "You go in first."

"Come on, you're just chicken. Get in there, we got a job to do."

Carl nodded his head and edged his way into the cave. Images of his slain family flashed in front of his eyes.

Two days ago his sister and mother were working out in the field, the sun bright and warm, the sky a perfect blue. An otherwise perfect day until the screaming started.

Carl ran as fast as possible, the screams of terror pushing him on, his father lagging behind him.

◆ ◆ ◆

Elaine Hudder and her daughter, Tori, picked strawberries for after dinner. Elaine looked up at the sky, thankful they had a large harvest this year. A noise off to her left caught her attention; she looked over but saw nothing.

"Tori, did you hear anything?"

Her daughter cocked her head to the side. "No, I didn't." She went back to picking the small fruits.

Elaine didn't feel reassured by her daughter's answer. She knew something watched them, she just didn't know what. She casually stood and went for the shotgun her husband insisted she have at all times. In these parts bears, wolves, and coyotes were known to attack.

As she reached for it, a large furry hand reached out and grabbed her, the claws so sharp the beast cut right through her skin, tendon and bone. Looking up, Elaine didn't have time to scream.

The creature raised its other arm and sliced its claws across her neck. The head flew off and landed on the ground next to Tori. When she turned to look at what happened, she saw her mother's face looking at her, a silent scream formed with her lips.

* * *

Tori screamed. As she turned to see the beast, she watched in horror as it ripped apart her mother's body. Limbs were tossed to the side, the internal organs swallowed whole, and then with one swift motion her spine violently ripped out, intact.

She continued to scream as the beast turned its attention to her. She was too frightened to move and was all too aware she would die soon. The thing, taller than a man by at least a yard, with jagged and sharp teeth, scared her like no other animal she'd ever seen. The claws reminded her of razors. The beast's body was covered in dark brown fur, now matted with her mother's blood.

It growled and hovered over her. Her mother's spine hung from its left hand. She knew hers would be the next one collected. As she looked up into its dark eyes, she let out one final scream before it sunk its hand into her abdomen and began to eat her alive.

* * *

When he reached the scene, Carl had never seen so much gore, not even in the rooms where the cattle were slaughtered.

Puddles of blood liberally formed under different bits and pieces of body parts. His mother's torso lay in the center of the strawberry patch, emptied out. Tori's head was missing entirely.

An arm still held onto a basket half full of strawberries. He couldn't tell who it belonged to. Carl saw long, deep scratches along a leg and back of his sister's torso.

A gorge rose in the back of his throat when he saw her spine had been ripped out. The flies started to buzz around, and a dizzy sensation kicked in. He had to turn away from what remained of his mother and sister while he emptied his stomach.

"What happened here?"

Carl stood and looked at his father. The man remained there, staring. How he could stand to look at the massacre in front of him was a mystery.

"What did this?" Carl, still dizzy, needed to focus on something other than what lay behind him.

His father didn't respond for a long time. Carl thought he might not say anything, then glanced over to see tears falling from his fathers weathered eyes. Though he knew he should be doing the same, the tears weren't there. All he felt was anger and hate.

Fifteen minutes later, Carl finally got a response. "I have no idea, son, but do you see those footprints? Whatever did this had to of been huge, and—it'll sound crazy—but it walked on two legs."

Carl started to feel better. He had something to focus on, had something to hunt. "We need to tell the others, then go get this thing."

"I know how you feel, son, but you're only sixteen. We need to get the sheriff to come and take a look at this."

Carl followed behind his dad as they headed back to the farmhouse. They saddled up two horses and rode into town as fast as they could.

Thirty minutes later they hitched their horses to a post in front of the sheriff's office. Carl's father laid a hand on his chest before they went in.

"Let me do the talking," his dad said.

Carl nodded as his father pushed open the hinged doors.

◆ ◆ ◆

Sheriff Daniel Burton looked up when he heard the creaky hinges protest. He saw Jeb Hudder and his son Carl. He knew bad news when he saw it.

"What can I do for you, Jeb?"

"There was an attack out at my place, you need to come see it. Bring some others, too. Think we might have to put together a hunting party."

Daniel leaned back in his chair. He knew animal attacks were common in this part of the country. People settled here about ten years ago and friction remained between some of the locals and the Indians.

"What kind of attack are you talking about here?"

"I don't know, something big. Will you just get some men together and come look? I can't put it into words, please don't make me describe it." The last part was spoken so softly Daniel barely heard it.

"All right. I'll grab George and Harry. Give me ten minutes to round them up and saddle the horses. We'll meet you in front."

Jeb and his son walked out. The boy's eyes were empty, as if what he had seen took the life right out of him.

Forty-five minutes later, Daniel stood in front of one of the most horrific scenes he had ever seen. His two best deputies were off to the side looking for clues as to what might have caused this.

Jeb had been right: there were no words to describe what happened.

What kind of animal rips out a spine and takes it with it? The footprints were too large for a bear and, as far as he knew, it was the largest predator in the area.

"Sheriff, we need to move now. The trail's fresh, we can track it." Jeb held his Winchester, and his face wore a look of determination.

"All right, sure we'll load up on supplies at your place and head out within the hour. Carl, I'm going to give you a note to take back to the sheriff's office letting them know we're heading out."

"But I want to go, too."

Jeb turned to his son. "You will not be coming with us. I already lost a wife and daughter to this beast. I'm not going to lose my son, too. Now do as the sheriff told you, and bury your mom and sister before anything else gets at them."

◆　◆　◆

Carl cowered under the angry tone his father used. He watched as they loaded up ammunition, jerky, bread, and cheese before they rode out. When they were out of sight, he mounted his horse and went back into town.

Dusk approached and he didn't feel safe, but he had to deliver the note for the sheriff. Once he reached the office, full dark had set in.

He hitched his horse to the post and went into the office. He saw Mr. Miller there, his friend Jake's dad.

"Hey, Carl, what are you doing here?"

Carl held out the note as he spoke. "Hi, Mr. Miller. The sheriff went out with a couple of others and my dad to hunt an animal that killed my mom and sister this morning," Carl said as tears started to form. He forced them down and focused on his anger.

"Geez, Carl, I'm sorry. Is there anything we can do? Why don't you stay in town tonight, you can keep me company and tell me about what happened." As he spoke, he unrolled and read the note.

"No, sir, I should be getting back." He turned to leave.

"Hold up. It says here they don't know what they're hunting and to alert the other townspeople to be careful. Stay with us tonight, please? Jake would love to see you."

"I should go home. My dad wanted me to take care of my mom and sister before the scavengers got them."

His face went sombre. "I'm going with you."

Carl shrugged his shoulders and walked out front. He untied his horse and got on.

A few minutes later, Mr. Miller came round from the back. "Let's go."

* * *

John Miller had never seen someone remain so silent and wear such a vacant expression. He figured the kid had never seen violence before.

When they arrived at the farm, he watched as the boy dismounted the horse, took the saddle off, and sent the animal out to pasture.

The kid went and collected burlap sacks and some shovels. John had no idea what the sacs could be for.

"Can you carry the lantern, Mr. Miller?"

"Of course. Just tell me what way to go."

Carl led them to the middle of a strawberry field. At first, John didn't know what they were doing, then he saw the body parts. He understood why the kid had grabbed the bags.

* * *

Carl was happy Mr. Miller kept quiet as they collected all the parts they could find. Every now and then he would stop and pull a Colt, pointing it in the direction of some noise or another.

Carl felt the hairs on the back of his neck rise a few times as they gathered the blood-soaked parts into bags. He knew they were being watched, but what it was that had its eye on them, he didn't know. There were so many things out there hungry for flesh, it could be a rat or bear. They wouldn't know until it attacked.

A noise stopped them both cold. Mr. Miller had his Colt Revolvers out and ready in a second. Carl nodded, impressed. A snarling noise got closer. Carl ran to the lantern and held it up high enough so Mr. Miller could aim properly.

Carl's hand shook so he reached up with his other to hold the lamp steady. He looked at Mr. Miller and noted he had a straight face, totally focused. He wasn't reassured by this.

The snarls grew louder, turned into growls. An animal leapt out of the brush. Mr. Miller fired two shots and took it out. They both approached it slowly.

"It's a coyote, nothing to worry about." Miller kicked it back into the brush.

As they worked, sweat trickled down Carl's back, but turned icy after a few seconds. The coyote thing had scared him, though he wouldn't admit it.

When they had gathered all the parts and moved them to the family plot, he felt a minor sense of relief being closer to the house.

They worked quickly and efficiently, and within an hour had the bodies buried together. Carl didn't want to have to go through the ordeal of separating them. If he had to sort through the bits of his mother and sister that were left, it would be the last straw. His ability to control the flood of tears would shatter and he would be of no use. He would be weak, and he needed to be strong for them, for his dad.

"Thanks for the help, Mr. Miller. Do you want some lemonade or food? I'm not sure what my mom had in the kitchen."

"A drink would be great, but I'm not really hungry."

Carl smiled at the end of the comment. He hadn't been hungry since this morning either. As he walked into the house he heard Mr. Miller follow close behind.

He used the lantern to illuminate the kitchen, then lit a few candles and an oil lamp. He went over to where his father hid his bourbon stash and grabbed the bottle.

"Here." Carl handed over a bottle and a relatively clean glass.

"Thanks." The glass was filled three quarters of the way and swallowed in one healthy swig. "I need to get going, want to get home and see my family. I'll tell Jake to come see you soon, and if you need anything just come into town, okay?"

"Yes, sir."

Carl shivered as he watched the man leave. Throughout the day he felt himself getting colder and colder.

◆ ◆ ◆

John Miller rode with a Colt cocked and ready. What he saw tonight would haunt his dreams for a long time to come. He couldn't imagine what Carl was going through.

A light breeze swept over him; upon it came a peculiar smell. He slowed the horse down and took a look around, his eyes slowly adjusting to the darkness.

The smell carried with it a scent of copper. He racked his brain as to what it reminded him of. A rustling off to his left caused him to aim his gun. He waited, holding his breath to see what would reveal itself. A moment later the tall grass separated and revealed a raccoon. He chuckled.

Something suddenly grabbed his leg and pulled. He was quickly lifted off his horse and tossed through the air, his leg ripped from his body. He screamed in agony. The animal came slashing at him with razor-sharp claws. He felt the warmth of his insides as they spilled out of him in a bloody mess.

The beast lifted its hand and with a snarl drove it into his chest. John remembered what the coppery smell reminded him of—blood. The animal yanked his spine out through his upper chest, catching the heart along the way. Before the darkness came, he saw it beat one last time.

◆　◆　◆

Carl sat in the kitchen and watched the door with a blanket wrapped around him. At some point he must have fallen asleep because Angus, their rooster, woke him up just before sunrise.

A noise outside made him jump. Something scratched at the ground outside. Carl got low to the floor and crawled over to one of the drawers. He reached up and grabbed a knife, then went to the door.

He braced himself as he stood, prepared to fight whatever was on the other side. The scratching noise again, then a sniffle sound. Carl reached for the handle and opened the door. It was his father's horse.

He carefully looked around, wary of an area covered in shadow. He slowly approached the horse, and as the sun rose he saw blood matted in its fur and splattered across its saddle. His father's Winchester still in its holster. He didn't even have time to draw his weapon.

Carl dropped the knife and stroked the horse's nose.

The tears flowed freely. The sight of blood spattered on the animal in front of him shattered his control. His whole family slaughtered. His dad now dead, most likely ripped apart like his mother and sister. Carl howled in rage as he held onto the horse.

"Good boy, you're a good boy," he said over and over again.

◆　◆　◆

Jake Miller woke to screaming. He turned over in his bed and hoped his mother would get his little sister to shut up. Several minutes later the screaming stopped…and the stomping began.

From downstairs: "Get down here now, young man."

Jake sat up and sighed. The sun had only been up for a couple of hours, and since he didn't have school to worry about, sleep should be allowed. He hated this town—too darn loud.

He threw on a shirt and grabbed a pair of work pants. Stomping down the stairs to announce his annoyance he stopped short when he saw his mother crying.

"Mom, what's wrong?"

"Your father never came home last night. They just found his horse on the eastern edge of town. Then—" His mother burst into tears and held tight to his baby sister, Lisa.

"Then what?" he asked.

"Deputy Ken just came over and told me a couple of horses returned covered in blood. No sign of their riders. Right now they think some kind of monster is on the loose. No one is supposed to leave the town limits until they kill it."

A sick feeling rose in his stomach. "Where's Dad? They found his horse, so where is he?"

The look his mother gave him was answer enough. His father had been *killed*. He didn't know what to do.

"Who's going to kill it, Mom? All the best trackers are dead now."

"Jake, just stay in town, okay?"

"Whatever."

Jake left the room and went into his father's office. He knew his dad kept an extra gun and ammunition in there. After finding it and the bullets, he threw it all in a bag and tossed it over his shoulder. He would go to where they found his father and track the animal himself.

He snuck out his window and headed east. After an hour of walking he came across an area covered in a thick brownish substance.

When he bent down to examine it, he recognized it as dry blood. A body lay not too far away, missing a leg and both arms, the spine ripped out. Jake recognized his father's hat several feet away from the body, the head still inside. The meagre contents of his breakfast were on the ground in front of him before he realized he'd thrown up.

He spared another glance at his fathers' head and ran after a crow that landed on it and pecked at a milky colored eye. Three feet from the head the reality of the situation hit him and dizziness kicked in. This couldn't be happening. His father had promised him a trip out to Logan's Lake, just the two of them.

He jumped when a voice said, "Hey, you're not supposed to be here, kid. Get a move on."

Jake ran off before the deputy recognized him, fat salty tears stained his face. His friend Carl lived out this way; he'd know what to do.

◆　◆　◆

"Carl, you okay?"

Carl looked up, surprised to see the sun high up in the sky. He had been standing there for at least three hours, even the sun had not warmed him. Then he looked over to find his friend Jake who had an odd expression on his face, something between concern and a scowl. The puffy red eyes did not go unnoticed.

"Jake? What are you doing here?" Carl stepped away from the horse.

"What happened to you? You're covered in blood and dirt?" Jake asked.

Carl looked down at his soiled clothes. "I forgot to change after burying mom and Tori. Did your dad send you here?"

Jake stared at the ground. He could barely get the words out. "My dad's dead. Something killed him last night west of here."

"Sorry. I think it got my dad, too. This was the horse he left on, got blood on it and his shotgun."

"Well, let's go hunt it then. We'll get it." Jake's voice rose as he spoke, but the pain in it resonated with Carl.

He took a good look at his friend. "Are you insane? Whatever this thing is, it took out my mom and sister, a hunting party, and your dad within the space of a day. We don't stand a chance," Carl yelled, his voice broke toward the end as he remembered burying his mother and sister.

Jake opened his mouth as if about to say something, then shut it. He went over to the porch and sat on the steps.

"Then what, Carl? You can't stay here on your own. They're going to put you on the orphan train when it comes through town, and you know what happens then. You'll end up working in some factory in the city."

Carl ignored him. He looked toward the west and wondered what they could do. They were too old to be kids, and too young to be men, but if they had some help . . . . If a real tracker showed them the way, they might be able to do it.

He thought back to his father talking about a Navajo reservation a few miles from their place. At first, it had made the family uncomfortable, but his dad had made a deal to supply them with food as long as they left him alone.

Carl had gone along on one of the deliveries. They might recognize him. If he told them what happened they might be willing to help. He figured he had nothing to lose.

"Jake, I'm going to the Navajo reservation to see if they'll help. You can come with me, or stay here, I don't care."

Carl went into the house and grabbed some bread and jerky from the cupboard. He didn't change his clothes—the clean smell of newly laundered linens would give him away immediately. They needed all the advantages they could get if they stood a chance at hunting this beast. On his way out the door he grabbed a rag and wrapped the food.

Jake stood on the porch, a desperate look on his face. "I want to go with you, but I don't have a horse."

"I'll get one from the pasture, you grab the saddle from the barn."

Within moments they had a horse ready and saddled for Jake.

"Are you sure you want to do this? My dad said the Navajo can be mean," Jake said.

Carl shook his head. "My dad and them got along, don't worry about it."

He led the way and within two hours they were in Navajo territory. Two large men appeared before them. Carl noticed Jake shrink back a bit.

Carl stopped his horse and waited for the two men to approach. His father said something about showing respect. As they neared he hoped finding this animal and killing it would make him warm again.

"What do you want?"

Carl spoke clear and with authority. "You knew my father. He helped feed you for the last seven years. Yesterday, something killed my mother and sister by ripping them apart then stealing their spines. My father went to hunt it with some other men and they were all killed. I need your help."

The two men spoke to one another in their native language. They seemed to be arguing about something. One got angry and turned away, the other stayed and eyed Carl with dark eyes.

"This thing that attacked your family, do you know what it was?" the man asked.

"No, I don't."

"Take me to the place where it killed them."

Jake sighed. "Are we going to go back and forth all day or actually do something?"

"Do you have a better plan?" Carl asked.

He turned away and led them all back to his home. The Navajo inspected the place where his mother and sister were massacred. In the light of day, without the body parts, Carl could tolerate looking at it.

"Have you heard of Yéiitsoh?" The Navajo asked in such a low voice

Carl barely heard him.

"No, but that sounds like one of your words. Does it translate?"

"It would be 'big god' in your language."

"More like Big Foot."

Both Carl and the Navajo turned to look at Jake. He had a foot in one of the "big gods" prints, and it was obvious the print was well over six times the size of Jake's.

Jake looked back at the man next to him. "What's your name?"

"Call me Wolf. They call me that because I can track anything, but even I would not be stupid enough to track Yéiitsoh."

"Wolf, tell me about big god. How do I kill it?" Carl asked, his tone level.

Wolf laughed, then stopped when he realized Carl meant it.

"You are barely a man. You cannot kill something like this. He is huge, twice the height of you, and strong with claws so sharp they cut through anything. You won't know he's there until you're dead."

Carl thought about this, but refused to believe it. "But if you could, what would be your plan?"

"I would find where it lives and try to slay it while it sleeps, but you will never find his cave."

Carl looked at Wolf and wanted to shoot him right then and there.

"How do you know it sleeps in a cave?" Jake asked.

"You know where he lives, don't you? You and your people think of him as some god, that's why you don't hunt him. He preys on us and leaves you alone. We're just collateral damage so you can sleep at night."

Wolf smiled. "Better you than us."

"Show me where his cave is. You at least owe me that."

Wolf sneered. "I owe you nothing."

Carl shook with anger. "Then do it for my father, my mother, and my sister."

The smile fell from Wolf's face. "Fine, I will show you where he sleeps, but do not expect me to help you."

"Whatever. Let's go." Carl got on his horse and waited for the others.

Wolf led the way, stopping hours later, the sun just above the horizon.

"Over there, the rock outcropping, underneath is a cave," Wolf said. "He sleeps there."

"Thanks." Carl motioned his horse forward: Jake followed behind.

"You are fools, riding to your death. You know not of the big god's power."

Carl ignored the Navajo and headed for the cave. He would either kill the big god or die trying. He didn't have anything to live for, and no one would miss him, but Jake....

"Jake, are you sure you want to do this? You have a family to think of."

Jake brought his horse even with Carl. "This Bigfoot thing killed my dad, too. I want to do this."

Carl nodded. "Okay then, we go find the cave, but I think we're better off waiting until we know it's inside. We can use a torch to throw off its vision, and animals generally don't like smoke. As soon as we see it, start shooting."

Jake looked straight ahead. "Sounds like a plan."

The teens got off their horses, grabbed the food and guns from the saddle-bags and set up a mini camp. Carl led the horses away from the cave entrance and slapped them on the rear. They both took off in different directions.

Jake walked up behind him. "What did you go and do that for?"

"The smell. They've been sweating all day. That thing would have found us in seconds. As it is, I'm not sure he won't find us."

Carl walked back to their camp and sat down. The sun finally set, all they could do now was listen for the big god. He grabbed a piece of bread and jerky, then handed the rest over to Jake.

They stopped moving when rustling arose from the bushes. Neither one breathed. The rustling got louder, and they saw an opening appear in the bushes to the front of them.

Carl reached for his father's Winchester, quietly pulling it out. The opening got wider. A snarl rose on the air. A second later they heard a voice shoo away a horse, then saw a tall man come through the opening.

As the man approached Carl recognized it was Wolf. He put a hand on the rifle in Carl's hand and pushed it down.

Wolf sat down across from them with an odd look in his face. "Why do you do this? You know you will die?"

Carl shook his head. "I lost my whole family to this big god of yours. You might worship him, but he's nothing but a murderer to me."

"So you want vengeance? You think it will make you feel better, fill the emptiness inside?"

"Shut up. Why do you even care? Go back to your reservation." He went to stand up, but Wolf grabbed him.

"I will help you. He is not in there. He is on the hunt. He will return soon though, then we go in."

Carl just snorted at the Native, not trusting him in the least. Jake sat there eating bread and jerky. Carl looked down at his food and realized his appetite had yet to return.

The three sat there staring at one another. As the moon rose they could make out more of the landscape around them.

Carl kept his eyes on the cave entrance, and it paid off. He saw something almost as tall as a young bear. The thing was massive, at least four feet wide. He wondered if perhaps Wolf was right and this big god *couldn't* be killed.

The creature sniffed the air, stopped, turned to look in their direction. He looked closer and noticed it held several long items in its hand. He knew what they were—spines. The thing collected spines. He would enjoy killing it.

It took a few steps toward them and sniffed again. They were going to die, he thought. It could smell them. Carl knew the time had come. Just as he readied himself to fight it, he turned and went into the cave.

"He is here. Let him go inside and lay down to rest. We go in three hours, get some rest," Wolf whispered.

Carl and Jake looked at Wolf. Carl knew he wouldn't be resting with the thing a few hundred feet from him. He planned to hold the Winchester aimed in the general vicinity of the cave for the rest of the night.

After a moment of blackness, Carl shot up. "Wake up. It's time." How had he fallen asleep?

Glancing at Jake, he realized his friend had slept, too. At least they were rested. They checked their weapons, made sure they were loaded and ready to fire.

The sky was getting brighter; sunrise maybe an hour away. Carl sent up a prayer to his family to protect him and asked God to grant him the strength to kill the beast.

"Jake, you go in first," Carl said.

"Come on, you're just chicken. Get in there. We got a job to do."

Carl nodded and edged his way into the cave. Images of his slain family flashed in front of his eyes.

Wolf followed behind them, the torch casting eerie shadows along the walls.

Carl looked around, bones strewn about the floor, the smell of death and decay overwhelming.

Jake stepped behind him. He kicked a rock and in the quiet cave it sounded like a gunshot echoing off every surface.

"Be careful, you're gonna get us killed," Carl snapped.

"Sorry, I didn't mean it."

"Shh, the both of you or we're all dead." Wolf walked passed them, the light from the torch allowing them to see where they walked.

A low growl stopped them all. Wolf turned to look at Carl. The growling sound again, this time louder. Wolf looked down at Carl's stomach. He realized his stomach made the noise. He tilted his head to the side, nothing he could do about it.

Wolf shook his head and walked on. Shadows jumped out on the walls, every noise echoing like a cannon in Carl's ears. Then they found what they were looking for. The trail of vertebrae led them right to the big god.

The beast stood there, wide awake, and immediately growled at them. Wolf waved the torch at him and both Carl and Jake fired their guns, aiming for the head.

Carl nicked its ear and Jake got it in the neck. Wolf pulled a blade out of his belt and stuck it in the beast's chest.

The creature let out a howl of rage and swiped at Wolf. Carl reloaded the Winchester, and Jake kept firing his revolver. It held six shots and so far four of them had been hits.

Wolf moved out of the way, but not far enough to avoid getting deep scratches across his chest. Carl lifted the Winchester again and fired as the angry animal barrelled down on the Native. He took a deep breath and waited until he had the perfect shot.

"Pull the trigger!" Jake screamed.

"Relax, I got this." Time slowed down and Carl waited until he could see into its eyes.

He fired. The shot landed dead-center in the beast's face. Its eyes bled, its jaw hung off, a few strands of flesh and tendon holding it in place.

Jake reloaded the revolver and Wolf tried to move, but his injury prevented him from doing anything to help.

The big god let out another agonizing howl and began to swing its claws all over the place. Now blind, it wasn't as scary to the two boys.

Shrieking, Carl threw down the rifle and picked up a stick. He ran toward the thing that had destroyed his life. He struck it as hard as he could, letting out his grief with each blow. The beast swiped at him and made contact.

Carl fell to the ground, holding his arm . . . the big god's claws making ribbons of the flesh and muscle. Jake ran over to him and pulled him to the edge of the room, then put six more rounds into the beast.

Each one a hit.

Wolf crawled over to them. He took a leather string off of his shirt and handed it to Jake. "Tie this at the top of his arm, above where it was slashed. Make it as tight as you can."

Jake did as told. Carl cried, not from pain. He had not been able to kill it. "I failed."

Wolf brought a hand up to Carl's face. "It isn't over yet. We fail when we are dead. Now let's finish this."

Wolf pulled himself up with the help of Jake, and the both of them got Carl to his feet. The big god still snarled, blood dripping from the holes in its body, its lower jaw now missing.

Carl looked around the cavern, trying to figure out a way to kill this thing.

Wolf sprang into action first. He charged the beast and yanked out his knife, easily dancing out of the way of the creature's blind lunges.

Jake had six shots left and once again he made them all count. The head of the beast had taken a beating; it would not take much to finish it off.

Carl went over to Wolf and took the knife from his hand. He walked carefully toward the beast and when he stood within a few feet of the swiping arms he waited. The big god raised its ruined face and sniffed. Small drops of blood spewed forth into the air, then the head came down and Carl knew his location had been pinpointed.

A growl of pain or anger, perhaps both, emanated from the beast. It raised a beefy arm as Carl struck and plunged the knife into its abdomen and dragged it across. He split the big god's belly open the way he'd seen the butcher do countless times.

He jumped back as the big god fell to its knees letting out an ear-splitting wail, eventually falling over. A pool of blood and internal organs leaked from its body and covered the floor.

"I did it. I killed the big god."

Jake walked up behind him and put a hand on his shoulder. "We all did it, now let's get out of here."

Carl made his way down the corridor and Jake helped Wolf. When they exited the cave all three stumbled to the ground. The adrenaline wearing off and the reality of what they had accomplished sinking in.

Carl smiled then passed out.

◆　◆　◆

Carl woke in sheer agony. He looked around and saw Wolf. "Where am I?"

"You are with my people. Your friend told me you would be shipped somewhere bad because you have no family. I spoke with the elders and they will allow you to stay here if you want."

"Why are you helping me? I thought you didn't owe me anything."

Wolf cast his eyes down. "I forget sometimes you are not the one who wronged my people, and your father was a good man. He helped us many winters when no one else would."

Carl closed his eyes. He won, he killed the Yéiitsoh and avenged his family. Where he ended up now was irrelevant.

He started to feel warm again, he'd avenged his family. This time when the tears came he didn't fight them.

UNLEASHING TERROR

BY

JANICE GABLE BASHMAN

RICK STONE SLAMMED the door to his locker and the metallic clang echoed throughout the room. Propping one leg on the wooden bench in front of him, he strapped a KaBar knife to his right boot. A Glock 22 .40 S&W loaded with fifteen rounds was holstered at his hip. Two additional magazines, each also holding fifteen rounds, were secured in the double pouch on his belt.

"Get a move on it, Lawson," Rick said. "We don't got all day."

Jared Lawson finished buttoning his navy shirt and tucked it into his khakis. "So what are we doing, anyway? I know it's security, but what?"

"They didn't tell you when you signed on?"

"Just that if I broke the code and told anyone about what I was doing they'd lock me up for life, but my buddy Ronnie said it's good work and good pay, so I filled out an application when he told me his job was opening up. Had to pass a background check and all before they gave me the job, but I'm clean."

"Ronnie's your buddy? I didn't know that. How's he like his new place in Chicago?"

"He's cool." Lawson closed his locker, spun the lock, and yanked on the handle to ensure it didn't open.

"Let's get moving. The boat's already loaded."

"The boat? Where we going?"

"I'll fill you in on the way."

Stone and Lawson headed down to the dock and boarded the *Red Lion*, a thirty-three-foot steel-welded vessel capable of moving at eleven knots. The open stern was packed with boxes of fruit and vegetables and a huge pile of deer parts.

Lawson cut Stone a look that was a mix of revulsion and curiosity, but Stone said nothing. He just started up the *Red Lion* and maneuvered away from the dock, eyes fixed on the river.

Stone slapped an open palm on the wooden frame of the wheelhouse. "So what is all the food for?"

"Right before the All Countries War people all over the globe reported sighting these huge creatures. It wasn't like one or two or even a dozen. I'm sure you heard about it on the news. Some people called them Bigfoot, others called them Sasquatch."

"Yeah, I heard about it. What of it?"

From his front shirt pocket Stone pulled out two pieces of bubblegum, offered one to Lawson, who took it, and then unwrapped a piece for himself and tossed it into his mouth. He chewed a bit before continuing. "Indian Legend has it that Bigfoot sightings, or the Big Hairy Man as they called it, only occurred during times of trouble, that the sightings were messages to humans to change their ways or face disaster."

Lawson rapidly tapped his finger against the wood. "So what?"

"So, they caught a bunch of them this time. They got them in Pennsylvania, California, Arkansas and North Dakota."

"What? Who caught them? How do you catch something that ain't real?"

"Well, that's just the thing," Stone said. "They are real. Up until right before the war, no one really knew for sure. People have claimed to have sighted them for hundreds of years, but no one ever caught one before. After the Bigfoot moved in on villages and cities and murdered women and children the government had no choice, so they sent in the military.

"I don't know why those Bigfoot decided to attack people after all those years of hiding, but it changed everything. Maybe they did it because we just wouldn't listen, polluting up everything and damaging the world like we did. I can't say I blame them. We did need a wake-up call and the war sure wasn't the way to go about doing it. If we had just paid attention and noticed the messages they were sending, then maybe the war wouldn't have happened. All them hundreds of thousands of people killed for nothing." Stone bit his bottom lip. "At first the troops killed the Bigfoot, but there were too many of them so someone high up figured it would make more sense to study some of them, see what makes them tick, then go from there." He turned the wheel to the left and the boat changed direction. "I'm not saying we shoulda done what we done to them, and there's not much we can do about it now. The Bigfoot have been living like that for a decade already and I doubt they'd survive even if they were released."

"You mean they got those things locked up somewhere? Aren't they, like, nine feet tall?"

Stone cracked a smile. "Yeah, they are. You'll see for yourself soon enough."

Lawson stepped backwards until the wood pressed hard into his spine. "What? Where are you taking me?"

"To the ship graveyard."

◆ ◆ ◆

About twenty minutes later, Stone stopped the boat at the security barrier that surrounded the graveyard and punched in a pass code. The hydraulic system raised two large portions of the barrier until they pointed at the sky like rectangular missiles. He maneuvered the *Red Lion* through the passage and the barrier automatically closed behind the boat. Straight ahead was a half-submerged wooden ship listing toward the stern, portholes empty of glass, huge beams broken like twigs, algae growing along the hull. To the left was a tall ship with a twenty-foot mast. The flag of origin was tattered and torn and all that remained was a scrap of red fabric fluttering in the slight breeze. There were tugboats, navy vessels, cargo ships and more, all stripped down to their skeletons, hulking pieces of wood or metal rotting and rusting in the sun-warmed water.

"You see over there?" Stone said, pointing. "That ship, the one that's bigger than the others? You can kinda see it between those two right there. It's the one that's not half in the water."

Lawson turned his head to look.

"That's where the Bigfoot are. Once we go around these last few ships we should be there in a few minutes."

"Is that them moving on the deck?"

"It's nothing to worry about. The ship was modified before they got on board and they can't come near us. Just do as you're told and you'll be fine. I've been doing this for years."

The boat swung wide around a tugboat; gaping holes marked the metallic hull right above the water line. Stone eased the *Red Lion* next to the vessel with the Bigfoot aboard. "She sure is something, isn't she?" he said. "At one time she was top of her class. Ran the Atlantic and the Pacific in her day at top speeds. They brought *The Kirkwood* here to die, but then figured they could use her again to house the Bigfoot."

"I don't get it," Lawson said. "Why put 'em out here? Why not in a jail?"

Stone stared at the ship. "It's safer that way. If they ever broke out of jail it'd be a big problem, but this far from shore, there's no chance of that. They can swim, but we're two and a half miles out." Stone could tell Lawson was nervous by the pinched look on his face, so he shot him a smile and added, "Give it a few days and you'll ease into it."

Stone positioned the *Red Lion* and then tied the boat to the cleat on the other vessel. "We're all set. You ready?"

Lawson pushed back his shoulders and nodded. "Let's do this."

They walked to the stern and Stone tossed him a pair of work gloves. They pulled on their gloves and began throwing the deer meat into an empty lift that ran up the side of *The Kirkwood*. When the lift was full, Stone hopped on the platform that jutted off the edge of the lift and indicated with two fingers for Lawson to join him. Lawson hesitated, looked up at *The Kirkwood*, whose deck loomed above him, and then climbed on board. He grabbed onto the metal bar in front of him so tightly his knuckles turned bone-white. Stone punched in a password and activated the controls. The lift crept up to the ship's deck and stopped.

Stone jumped off, Lawson following, and moved to a hatch and unlocked it. He thrust his fingers through the steel grate and pulled up the hatch cover, then latched the cover to the two-foot-long bracket that jutted out from the wall. "Just put the meat down the hole and then we'll bring up the vegetables."

"How deep's the hole?" Lawson said as he tossed in a piece of meat. It landed with a faint thud.

"Fifteen feet. The Bigfoot access it from below. They pretty much have the run of the ship except for a few key areas, and there are video cameras in common areas, on the deck, in the kitchen and in a few of the staterooms. Dr. Roberts over at the university has been studying them since they got here. It's pretty fascinating stuff. Seems they have families and kids and everything."

"Sure, whatever." Lawson dug his fingers into the pile of meat and grabbed as much as he could and dropped it into the hole.

When they finished a few minutes later, Stone secured the hatch. They boarded the platform and lowered to the ship.

"I didn't realize how many boats were out here," Lawson said, casting his view across the water. "There's gotta be at least fifty of 'em."

"Seventy-two to be exact. Back when it was open to the public there didn't used to be so many. Kayakers rowed in here all the time to check out the ships. Anyway, six more loads should do it and then we'll be out of here. We can grab some lunch or whatever and then around three-thirty or so we'll make our second run."

* * *

When they pulled up to *The Kirkwood* at 3:47 P.M., the sun painted the broken ships around them with a pallet of rich coppers, browns and blacks along with bright greens where the algae grew on the hulls. They offloaded the deer meat first and boarded the lift. This time around, Lawson seemed more relaxed. He wrapped two fingers against the metal bar and took in the sights as they rose.

He cracked a smile and said, "You know, this ain't too bad. I can think of alotta worse jobs."

"Yeah, me too," said Stone. "It's kind of relaxing out here in a strange sort of way, that is, once you get used to the grunts and the other noises the Bigfoot make."

They hit topside, boarded the ship and began to unload the meat into the hatch. Halfway into the job, Stone heard a hoot from the left and then another followed by one more. He spun toward the noise, but it had already stopped.

"What was that?" Lawson asked, wide-eyed.

"It's nothing. The sounds they make bounce all over the ship. Sometimes they seem like they're right next to you." He reached down and threw another handful of meat into the hatch.

"Ain't you gonna check it out?"

Stone sighed. He knew if he didn't investigate Lawson would be jumpy the rest of the day and it would take twice as long to finish. "Wait here. I'll be right back."

He crossed the deck, turned the corner and froze. Lawson plowed into his back and he stumbled forward before stopping. Mouth wide open, Stone starred at the creature before him—approximately four feet tall, dark brown hair covering its body, large head, flat nose, muscular thighs, a broken pipe in its hand, and a stench worse than a landfill rotting in the boiling sun. Stone inched his hand to his waist until he found his Glock. The Bigfoot was definitely a baby, but how did it get up there? Bigfoot didn't have access to this part of the ship. And what was it doing with the pipe?

Stone and the Bigfoot watched each other in silence. From behind him, he heard Lawson's heavy breaths mixed with stifled gagging.

"Do something," Lawson whispered after a long ten seconds.

With his eyes still fixed on the Bigfoot, Stone said, "Like what?"

"Shoot it or something."

"Are you crazy? It's just a baby."

"So what?"

Stone spread his legs, waiting to see what the creature would do. At first it did nothing. Just watched him and Lawson with a mischievous look on its face. Slowly, the pipe started to swing, small circles and then larger ones. Then a guttural roar cut deep into Stone's gut. His muscles tensed and he took a step backwards, forgetting Lawson was behind him. The move knocked his comrade down, but he scrambled right back to his feet and backpedaled until he reached the corner.

In one fast move, the Bigfoot swung the pipe above its head and jumped at Stone. At the same instant, Stone pulled his gun, shot two into the creature's chest, and sidestepped out of the way. The Bigfoot landed with a loud thump and spun toward him, blood pouring from its wounds and coating its thick hair. Stone took another shot and the Bigfoot went down; the pipe fell to the deck.

Gun in the ready position, eyes darting left and right, Stone ensured the area was clear and then moved closer to the Bigfoot. Lawson still hung back by the corner.

It took at least two minutes for the Bigfoot to die.

Stone holstered his gun then took a deep breath followed by another and slowed his breathing before nudging the Bigfoot with his toes just to make sure it wasn't pulling one over on him. The creature didn't move.

"Let's go," Stone said.

"The sooner the better," Lawson said.

"Not back to shore. We need to figure out how this thing got into this section."

"What? No way. What if there's more of 'em?"

"I don't see any others, so either you're with me or you're not, but if you're not then you'll have to wait by yourself. I'm not giving you the code to the lift."

"Fine. Whatever. Let's go."

Stone and Lawson walked the length of the ship until about three-quarters of the way down and they were forced to stop. A steel wall blocked their section off from the area that allowed the Bigfoot to access the deck.

"Now what?" Lawson asked.

"It didn't come from here. Only other place I can think is back down near that small corridor we passed. There's a ventilation duct, but I'll need your help to check it out."

At the corridor, Stone eyed the duct, gun in hand, finger resting next to the trigger guard, but saw no movement. He holstered the weapon and said, "Give me a foot up."

Lawson laced his fingers together and boosted Stone to the ventilation duct. A rusted lock hung open from the latch. Stone gave the vent cover a tug and it swung open. When he released it, the spring mechanism moved it back into place.

"Darn it!" Lawson lowered him to the ground.

Stone planted his hands on his hips. "Can't say that's ever happened before."

"Well, it sure has now."

"Right. I've got a cable lock on the boat. We can use it to secure the cover. I'll get it. In the meantime drag the body to the hatch. When I get back we'll dump it down after the food."

"You're not tossing it overboard?"

"No, these creatures are smart and if they see the body they'll know not to mess with us again, though I doubt that baby got up here with the intention of hurting us. I think it just went exploring and found its way out. You know, got scared and attacked."

"I'm not staying here by myself. Not with that vent unlocked and you gone."

"Since you're not certified to carry weapons yet, I shouldn't be doing this, but given the circumstances . . ." Stone's voice trailed off as he bent down, pulled out his knife and handed it to Lawson. "Just don't tell anyone I gave it to you."

"You bet."

◆　◆　◆

It was a chilly morning; clouds blocked the sun except for a few stray rays that managed to sneak through.

"Wasn't sure I'd see you back here again," Stone said. "Not after what happened yesterday."

Lawson shrugged. "That vent is fixed, right?"

He nodded. "Yeah. The marine lock will hold it for a long time until way after we both retire, but just to be on the safe side I had it welded shut."

"How 'bout teaching me to drive the boat sometime?"

"Sure, you can give it a go, but not when we're near the graveyard. It's too risky. You might hit one of the ships. Sometimes parts of them are hard to see, especially when they're under the water like that."

"Nah, I get it."

It was slowgoing out to the ship graveyard. Stone could barely see through the fog coming off the water, thirty feet in front of him at best. At half speed, they motored their way to the graveyard and then slowly worked their way through the ships to *The Kirkwood*. The fog had lifted by the time they arrived and Stone stopped when he spotted movement on the deck.

"What are they doing?" he asked.

"How should I know?"

Stone edged closer, but not too close. He didn't want to disturb the creatures. From the distance, he counted sixteen massive Bigfoot near the rail. Two stood in front of the others and the taller one cradled the baby Bigfoot's body in its hands. The creatures let out a long, collective roar. The noise was so loud Stone and Lawson clamped their hands over their ears, though that wasn't enough to drown out the sound.

The Bigfoot holding the baby looked at Stone and their eyes met for a long moment. Stone grabbed his binoculars for a better look. Were those tears in the creature's eyes? Maybe they weren't as bad as people thought?

The Bigfoot leaned over the edge as far as it could reach and dropped the body into the water, watched until it sunk below the surface. Another collective roar ripped the air before the creatures disappeared below deck.

"Unbelievable," Stone said.

Lawson nodded. "It was pretty cool."

"What's cool about burying your kid? We killed that thing, but they loved it."

Lawson shrugged. "Who cares? They're monsters, and that thing attacked us."

"Maybe so, but it was still a kid."

"Whatever. Let's get rolling."

After tying up the *Red Lion*, they hauled the food onto *The Kirkwood*.

Stone's cell rang. He pulled it off his belt and flipped it open. "Yeah?" He listened for a moment then said, "What? You're kidding me? How did that happen? . . . Well how should I know? . . . Right, we're on it." He closed the phone.

Lawson asked, "What was that about?"

"The cameras went out all over the ship. We need to go to the control room and see what's up."

Stone led the way to the control room. They passed through a double door and proceeded down through a dark hallway lit only by faint bulbs hanging from the ceilings every twenty feet or so until they reached a T-junction. At the junction, Stone turned right into an even darker hallway. Two of the three bulbs were out, the only light a flickering faint glow at the far end. He pulled a penlight from his equipment belt and swept the beam across the hallway, but could only see about ten feet in front of him.

Inch by inch they crept down the hall with Stone in the lead. Neither said a word. Stone listened carefully to the muffled grunts and hoots of the Bigfoot. They were definitely agitated. He couldn't blame them. They just buried one of their own. And he had killed it. Shot it right through the heart. Sure it was self-defense, but that didn't mean he had to like it.

"How much further?" Lawson said.

"It's at the end of the hall."

With measured steps, Stone moved through the hallway, head darting left to right and back again. The noises ceased suddenly, and the hair stood up on his arms and on the back of his neck. He stopped abruptly, his hand on his gun. "Something's going on. Keep quiet and follow my lead." Stone flicked off the penlight and moved to the wall, flattened his back against it as much as possible, and fought to control his breathing. He watched and waited, but saw nothing. Not a flicker of movement, not a hint of a shadow. Did the Bigfoot escape somehow? What if they were waiting at the end of the hallway? No. There was no way the Bigfoot managed to penetrate the steel walls that separated their part of the ship from the rest of it. The noise must have been some grieving ritual. "Come on," he said to Lawson. "It's clear. They're just upset, that's all. Let's see what's up with the cameras."

"Are you sure? What if another one of those things got out?"

"It's impossible. Those walls are two feet thick." Using the penlight to guide them, they moved through the eerie silence to the control room. Once inside, Stone shut the door. He checked the video monitors. Nothing but static. "Either the cameras are all knocked out—and I doubt they all went out at once—or the power supply is compromised. The cameras should be transmitting to the main system in here which backs up the images before they're uploaded to the satellite and transmitted to Dr. Roberts and a secure mainframe in the city. I'll have to get our tech guy in to see what's wrong with it. Let's finish unloading the food and get out of here."

Stone opened the door and stepped into the hall. Metal struck metal; loud noises reverberated throughout the ship. They came from the left, from the right and from below. Horrifying roars and moans and grunts joined the banging, as though a million people and animals were being tortured. The noise was everywhere and nowhere simultaneously, deafening and filled with rage. The banging became faster and faster, the roars louder and louder. At first they seemed like they came from far away, but the more the noise continued the closer and louder it got.

Lawson pushed past Stone and raced down the corridor. Stone followed. When they turned the corner, sneakers skidding across the deck, the noise abruptly ceased. Stone grabbed Lawson by the shirt and they both stopped. It was so quiet he could hear the waves lapping against the hull.

"This is crazy," Lawson said.

"They're just upset. They just buried one of their dead." Although Stone said the words, he wasn't sure how much he believed them. Those Bigfoot never sounded like that. A roar and a growl here and there, but nothing like the noises he'd just heard. "Let's get the rest of the food unloaded and get out of here."

"Sounds good to me."

When they reached the hatch, Stone scanned the deck and then pulled open the hatch cover. Lawson bent down to grab a handful of meat and Stone caught movement by Lawson's leg. A hairy arm reached up from below. Before he could react, the hand clamped Lawson's ankle, nails digging deep into his skin, and pulled his leg. Lawson screamed. He fell and hit his head on the deck. The Bigfoot pulled and pulled, determined to squeeze Lawson through the hatch, whole or not.

"Help me!" Lawson cried.

Stone pulled his Glock but he couldn't get a clear shot, so he holstered it and dove to the deck and grabbed Lawson's arm. The Bigfoot reached through the hole with its other hand and snatched Lawson's left leg. Ripped it right off. The Bigfoot yanked Lawson to the left and down and he went into the hole. All except his arm, which Stone still held fast. Lawson screamed and screamed. Stone fished for his knife but he couldn't reach past his waist, not while holding onto his friend's arm.

A second later the Bigfoot severed Lawson's arm from his body and the man disappeared into the hole. Bile seared Stone's throat as he scurried backwards, his eyes fixed on the hole where he saw the Bigfoot standing on another Bigfoot's shoulders. With bloodied hands and massive arms, the Bigfoot pulled its body out of the hole. Stone dropped Lawson's arm, scrambled to his feet and raced to the lift. He jumped on and punched in the code, sucking in fast and shallow breaths. The lift moved down the side of the hull, each inch seeming like a mile.

The Bigfoot reached the edge of the deck and took a giant leap past Stone, landing with a loud *thump* onto the *Red Lion*. Stone grabbed his Glock and squeezed off three rounds. The Bigfoot went down, but then pushed back to its feet, bleeding from the shoulder. It let out a ferocious roar.

Stone took aim despite the impossible angle and fired down at the Bigfoot. The first shot went wide, but the second hit the monster on the top of the head. The Bigfoot crumpled to the deck and went still. Stone sighed with relief.

Moments later, a second Bigfoot dropped to the *Red Lion* followed by a third, fourth and then a fifth. Stone spun around and looked up at *The Kirkwood* where at least fifty Bigfoot stood. He hit the emergency stop on the lift and it came to a halt. Now what? He had forty shots left. Even if he took out a Bigfoot per shot it wouldn't be enough ammo. If he tried to jump into the water the impact would kill him or at least make it impossible to swim to shore, not that he could swim that far. Sweat clung to his shirt; his hand shook. He reconsidered his means. He had to try. Maybe they'd leave him alone if he killed enough of them.

Stone turned to the *Red Lion* and shot two Bigfoot before a third jumped to the lift from *The Kirkwood*. The impact threw the lift against the hull and it listed to one side. Stone grabbed onto the support beam with both hands and the Glock dropped to the water below. The Bigfoot roared then lunged toward him. He had no choice but to jump. He shifted to his side to gain clearance, bent his knees and pushed off, but a hand grabbed him from behind the instant he left the lift. The Bigfoot pulled Stone back onto the lift and pinned him to the platform with its paw. Its lips peeled back to reveal pointed yellow teeth. The creature growled.

Stone grabbed the Bigfoot's paw, tried to wrest it off of his body. "Please. Please, don't hurt me."

The Bigfoot bent down, scooped him up and tossed him overboard into the waiting hands of one of the Bigfoot onboard the *Red Lion*. The Bigfoot threw Stone against the wheelhouse and he felt something snap right before he slid to the deck, dazed. Stone tried to move his legs but couldn't. Only his head and arms moved and they hurt like hell. Tears ran down his face. *This is it. I'm dead.*

One by one the Bigfoot jumped from *The Kirkwood* to the *Red Lion*. The boat lay low in the water from all the weight.

The engine started up and the boat began to move backwards.

"What?" Stone said. "How are they doing that?" He spit blood and licked his teeth.

The *Red Lion* turned and headed through the boat graveyard and inched its way through the heavily-corroded ships. It banged one than another before hitting an open passageway. The boat approached the security barrier and the Bigfoot growled, a terrifying united roar that could easily be heard for miles and was met with a thousand more.

The boat stopped and one by one the Bigfoot jumped on top of the five-foot-tall security barrier and plunged into the river. After the last beast left the boat, Stone sighed with relief. Maybe there was still a chance to stop them. With his arms bent beneath his chest and his face close to the deck, Stone crawled, legs dragging behind him, to the hull. Using the gunwale for leverage he pulled himself upright and saw the Bigfoot cutting through the water with fast and bold strokes.

He felt his belt for his cell phone, but it was gone. He must have lost it during the attack. *Now what?* He dropped back to the deck and crawled to the wheelhouse, but the steering wheel and radio were destroyed. Stone grabbed his binoculars, slung them around his neck, and moved into position so he could watch the Bigfoot. Helpless to stop them and with no chance of rescue, there was nothing else he could do.

A half-hour later, The Bigfoot climbed onto the shore and fanned out to attack the city.

WITIKO

BY

BRUCE DURHAM

THE YORK BOAT surged over a large, white-capped wave, its wooden frame groaning. A speck on the waters of James Bay, the shallow craft labored under clouds the color of volcanic ash that coiled like some primordial snake. Lightning danced across the distant shoreline, chased by drums of rolling thunder.

Captain Thomas Douglas sat aft, white-knuckled hands clutching a wooden bench, rivulets of water streaming off his clean shaven face. An officer of the 35th Regiment of Foot, the Prince of Orange's Own, he was at once enthralled and terrified by the storm's sheer display of primeval fury.

He tightened his grip as another monstrous wave reared. The boat heaved, was tossed high into the air, then fell as the wave rolled past, the sensation of weightlessness unnerving before it struck the water with a solid smack. Douglas cursed, more an expression of relief. A sharp bark of laughter had him look over his shoulder.

Midshipman Mathias Leith returned the look with barely concealed dread. Lashed to the bench, his muscular arms bulged with herculean effort as he struggled with the side-mounted rudder.

A second man sat beside him, watching bemusedly. His thick arms were casually crossed, his blond beard and long hair limp across broad shoulders. Again he laughed, a bellow as deep as the persistent thunder. "The men turn green, Leith. See them clutch their oars like frightened children?"

Leith glared through the sheeting rain. "These men are soldiers, not seasoned sailors, you Scottish goat."

"But this is just a stiff breeze. Look at them. Children hugging their mother's skirts pissing at the first sign of a storm cloud, and here I thought you English were masters of the seas."

Douglas shook his head and swiped at the salty spray lashing his face. "You are full of bluster as usual, McNab. I would wager a month's pay you pray for land just like we do."

The midshipman cut in, gesturing starboard. "The prevailing winds continue from the northwest. We will be sore pressed to maintain our heading. The men tire quickly."

"The winds will change soon enough," McNab stated, "then we can lay sail. The men may rest their wee souls once we reach land." The Scot leaned close to Douglas and said in a surprisingly somber tone, "In truth, these boats alarm me. They are for navigating rivers and not crossing a hell-spawned bay. Let us pray this mission is nothing more than a fool's errand."

Douglas nodded in agreement.

Their fool's errand was a trade post on the southwest coast of James Bay, near Akimiski Island. The resident trappers were three weeks past due delivering a consignment of furs. Concerned with profit loss, the Company Factor at Fort Albany had dispatched two York boats to investigate, each piloted by a midshipman from the recently arrived *Prince Rupert*. Captain Douglas, stationed at the fort, was directed to lead the expedition and assess the situation. Initial suspicions involved a band of renegade Cree and French traders. Douglas selected a compliment of sixteen soldiers from his command. Alexander McNab, a Company clerk, was added to oversee Company interests. Now, two days out of Fort Albany, they braved the storm on the final leg of their voyage.

True to McNab's word, the winds died and waters calmed. Angry clouds thinned into wispy, rose-tinged ribbons. The sun appeared, low on the horizon, bathing the cold blue surface in a reflective sheen.

Douglas gave the order to raise oars. The boat coasted to a gentle rest. Wordlessly, his men collapsed where they sat, though some hardier souls fell to chewing hardtack rummaged from their kits.

Leith and McNab inspected for damage, their constant bickering providing the weary soldiers no shortage of entertainment. Repairs proved unnecessary.

A half hour later, a cry from Leith brought heads about. The second boat was just a few hundred feet to port. Soon both vessels joined and Leith conversed briefly with his counterpart, a man named Benson. They informed Douglas they were fit for travel.

◆ ◆ ◆

Douglas was nudged awake.

"You should see this, sir," said his second in command, Sergeant Gough.

Having gathered some much-needed rest, Douglas grunted and sat. Rubbing sleep from his eyes, he realized dawn was not far off.

Leith and McNab were already awake and attentive, peering beyond him to port.

Following their gaze, he spotted a glow on the far shore, its rusty color dancing across the silver-crested bay waters. It flickered brightly, then faded to a dull blush before flaring again.

McNab said, "Fire."

Leith frowned. "The forest?"

The Company clerk shook his head. "Too local. Could be the outpost."

Douglas cleared his throat. "Then we steer for it, Mister Leith."

The men groaned when awakened and ordered to take up oars.

As dawn broke, the fire had dwindled to a smoldering cloud of gray smoke drifting lazily across an expanse of muskeg, populated with pockets of poplar and black spruce.

A wooden dock and two beached canoes confirmed the outpost's location. The York boats ground onto the coarse sand. Men leapt the gunwales to wade through shallow, cold water, running the vessels up the beach until free of the gently lapping waves.

Captain Douglas stepped onto the beach and examined his musket, silently cursing the moist air. Misfires were a distinct possibility under this persistently cold and blustery climate.

McNab critically eyed the weapon. "The Cree are friendly, Captain. Don't go shooting everything that moves."

Douglas shouldered the Brown Bess and quickly inspected his bayonet before slamming the weapon home in its metal scabbard. "I have soldiered far too long to assume anything, McNab." Sweeping the murky landscape, he said, "I will leave you with two men. Expect us by evening, at the latest."

Nodding farewell to McNab, Leith and Benson, Captain Douglas joined fourteen veteran soldiers standing some distance inland, their heavy wool capote coats drawn tight over their white trousers and red jackets.

Gough approached Douglas and said, "We found the remains of the outpost." He pointed beyond a stand of poplars to a series of smoldering, wooden stubs. "Wasn't hard to locate."

Douglas frowned. "We will begin there. Have the men search the ruins. Turn stones, poke at anything remotely suspicious."

Gough gave the order and the men set to.

Before long, a soldier called out. Douglas joined a man resting on his haunches beside a patch of churned ground, casually flipping a small object in one dirt-crusted hand. Near his feet lay a half-buried musket. Douglas knelt and scraped at the remaining soil, unearthing it. Under the weapon was a broken ramrod.

"Belongs to a trapper, my guess," Douglas said. "See those iron fittings? The wood ramrod? Very old." Glancing at the object in the soldier's hand, he asked, "What is that?"

The man handed over a torn paper cartridge. "Found more of them leading inland, sir. Looks like some kind of running fight. Lots of footprints, too. Something definitely happened here."

Douglas stood and discovered Leith and Benson hovering close by, McNab several paces behind.

"We saw your men rummaging about and figured we'd offer help," Leith explained before Douglas had a chance to speak.

He passed over the cartridge. "Appears the outpost was attacked." Looking at McNab, he said, "You sure your Swampy Cree are peaceful?"

McNab stroked his blond beard. "I cannot vouch for all, Captain, but they seldom give us trouble. Our dealings are generally uneventful and prosperous."

Douglas stared into the marsh, his eyes picking out the trail of footprints. "We shall continue inland, then. See what we find."

Toward noon Douglas gave the command to rest and a camp was established along the windy crest of a bowl-shaped caldera, its gentle slope leading to a field of peat split by two large ponds. The caldera formed the center of a rocky plateau, a slab of granite a mere mile and a half long with a steep incline that made for a slow ascent.

The trail had taken them through dark and muddy muskeg with few signs of animal life and less of human habitation, though they were far from alone. Horse and deer flies, and tiny black flies swarmed relentlessly about the party, searching out patches of exposed skin and irritating the men to no end. Douglas suspected the tale of trappers eaten alive by these insects was no folklore, but on the plateau the wind kept insects at bay and he found solace on a flat rock, his heavy capote lying beside him. Staring back along their route, his mood grew surly. Beyond the meager evidence discovered at the outpost, their search had revealed nothing of importance.

Two bodies blocked the sun's negligible warmth—Gough and a soldier named Blake.

Mildly irritated at the interruption, Douglas asked, "What is it?"

"Go on," Gough prodded the veteran.

Blake was wide and muscular with a square face, deep-set eyes and graying hair. Hesitantly, he said, "I thought I heard something, sir. On the far side of the ridge. Figured it best to report in case it was a Cree war party or something."

Douglas stood, his curiosity aroused. "Show me."

The veteran led them around the lip of the caldera and stopped before a partially hidden, descending path of age-worn steps. Exchanging looks with Gough, Douglas urged the veteran forward. They proceeded carefully down the path, Blake leading, their gloved hands braced against the cliff wall. The way was narrow and treacherous, a strong, swirling wind threatening every step. They reached a wide ledge and stood a long moment, admiring an expansive view of the surrounding landscape.

Gough gasped.

Douglas and Blake turned.

The sergeant stared at something against the cliff wall. "Is that human?"

Douglas felt a shiver crawl along his spine. "I think so."

Propped against the stone was a torso, its brown, leathered skin stretched taut over a withered frame. Bleached bone jutted from shoulders and hips.

A survivor of several horrific battles, Douglas had never witnessed anything quite as unnerving as this. Dropping to his haunches beside the emaciated trunk, he noted flecks of dry blood on the exposed bone. Glancing along the cliff ledge, he said, "No head, arms or legs. No decomposition." He stood. "Not surprising, I suppose, given the weather. My guess is he was a Swampy Cree."

Blake was ghastly pale. "Who on earth would desecrate a body like that, Captain?"

Douglas shrugged. He noticed Gough staring at some point further along the ledge. "What is it, Sergeant?"

"I see a cave, sir. Shall I investigate?"

Douglas glanced at the torso and then at a sky growing thick with clouds. "We have come this far with little to show. Perhaps this cave will provide answers."

Carefully traversing the ledge, they stopped before a foreboding entrance. Douglas was immediately drawn to a series of marks gouged into stone on either side of the dark opening. He traced his finger along one of them. "What do you make of that?"

Gough and Blake inspected the scoring and shrugged.

"An ancient language?" he said. When met with continued blank looks, Douglas sighed. "Come along, then."

Tentatively, they entered. Several paces in, Douglas slowed, allowing his eyes to adjust to the failing light. He detected a faint glow deep within the cave.

"What do you see?" Gough asked. His voice sounded hollow in the rough passage.

"Light. I see light up ahead."

The path gradually slanted down. The cold, northern air gave way to a thick, musty warmth along with the overpowering stench of damp fur. There was something else, a subtle odor that triggered a memory in Douglas, something oddly familiar.

The descent leveled, and several yards along he entered a small cavern. He paused, studying the interior while waiting on Gough and Blake.

The cavern was lit from overhead, a cone of daylight descending from some surface hole that illuminated rough walls, flat ledges and a half dozen openings he suspected led to other parts of the cave complex.

He grew aware of conflicting sounds: the slap of approaching boots from behind, a moaning wind swirling above, the steady drip of water from some unseen source.

"What is that smell, Captain?" Gough quietly asked as he joined Douglas.

Blake sniffed. "Smells like rotting meat."

Gough nodded. "I think you're right."

Douglas silently agreed. That was the odor he had found so familiar. Quietly, he said, "Daylight is failing faster than I expected. We will perform a quick reconnoiter then quit this place." He motioned to his left. "Blake, you circle that way. I will circle right. Gough, you remain here and watch those openings. They say bears hibernate this time of year. Still, we will take no chances."

Douglas set out and followed the wall, stepping carefully. He passed a ledge, shoulder height, its smooth surface covered in layers of dried peat. The peat appeared recently disturbed.

Beyond the ledge was an alcove. Here the odor was strong. Douglas peered into the dark recess. A sickening wave of nausea came unbidden, twisting his stomach. He lurched back, spun around and bent at the waist to vomit. Gough and Blake called out. Douglas retched again and motioned them back. The queasiness passed. Swallowing the bitter taste of bile, he approached again.

A head lay on the ground, partly stripped of skin, dried blood rimmed its empty eye sockets. A broken jawbone gave the mouth a hideous, lopsided grin. Shredded flesh about the neck suggested it had been torn from the body, and the body, Douglas discovered, lay behind the head. It was a torso, partially devoured, the remnants of one arm still attached. He backed away.

Gough and Blake watched him, fear clearly evident on their questioning faces.

Douglas motioned to the passage. "We leave. Now."

Blake swallowed. "What did you find, sir?"

"A trapper."

The veteran hesitated. "Should we not bury him, sir?"

"There is not enough left to bury. Now do as ordered. The Company can decide how to handle his remains."

A scuffling sound suddenly alerted the men and a pungent odor assailed their nostrils.

They quickly leveled their muskets and scanned the cavern.

Gough pointed. "There, Captain."

Within the shadows of a far passage stood a hulking form. It watched with close-spaced, crimson-colored eyes.

"Damned bear," Blake said and raised his musket.

The beast grunted, a deep cough, and retreated into the dark.

Douglas placed his hand on the musket barrel and pushed it down. "No bear retreats from a weapon."

A sharp sound, like the yelp of a wounded dog, blasted from the passage and reverberated about the cavern. It was answered by another yelp from another passage, followed by a third.

Blake said, "Well, sir, we disturbed something."

Douglas looked to Gough. "Out. Now."

They started for the cave entrance, with Douglas trailing. It wasn't long before he detected the unmistakable sound of pursuit. Glancing back, he saw the silhouette of some formidable bulk lumbering along the passage, maintaining a wary distance. He leveled his musket, determined to identify their pursuer and put a face to the mysterious beast. But the thing paused and then backed into shadow while issuing a series of deep grunts. Douglas waited a moment longer before resuming his way to the ledge. His thoughts churned at what it could be, then remembered a conversation with McNab on the journey here. Had the Company clerk been right? Certainly he would question the man next time they talked, for whatever lived within these caves possessed some form of bestial intelligence.

Reaching daylight, Douglas joined Gough and Blake. They faced the cave entrance with muskets trained. Seconds became minutes as the bitter wind wailed and whirled.

A shrill whistle startled each of them. It was a soldier, waving anxiously atop the plateau. Douglas ushered Gough and Blake off the ledge and up the path, remaining vigilant for signs of pursuit. There was none. Once on the summit, Douglas was directed to a thin pillar of gray smoke rising from the vicinity of the trade post.

Gough joined him. "A signal, sir? Should I assemble the men?"

"Yes," he replied. He took Gough's arm and nodded toward Blake. "Tell no one what we saw. Understand?"

The sergeant nodded.

◆ ◆ ◆

The men stood in formation, eyes alert under their capote's wool hoods, shifting from leg to leg in anticipation. Frosty breath curled and drifted upward with each exhale. Gloved hands gripped cold muskets.

Captain Douglas stepped before them. "Men of the 35th. My brothers in hell. You see the smoke and wonder what we face." Pausing, his eyes swept the collection of faces, young and old, tired and eager. "It could be Cree, the bloody French, or those buggers from the Northwest Company. But does it matter? Should we fear them? No. We are the 35th. Our history is storied. Our honors many. We are strong, our will invincible, our muskets steady. You veterans know me. We have shared battles, slain many foes. Once again it is time to prove our mettle. Are you with me?"

The soldiers cheered as loudly as the bitter cold allowed.

Douglas turned to Gough. "Sergeant."

Gough nodded and barked, "Quick step. Advance." He pointed at a young veteran. "You, Tisdale. Scout ahead, but stay within eyesight."

The boy nodded and jogged forward.

Leaning close to Douglas, Gough said, "You failed to mention surviving the massacre at Fort William Henry."

Douglas grinned. "Some things are better left unsaid."

Departing the plateau, the soldiers trudged back through the spongy muskeg. Insects quickly reappeared.

By late afternoon the outpost was close, the pillar of gray marking its location now little more than a smoldering wisp of curling smoke.

During the return trip the scout had remained in sight, musket at the ready, head scanning left and right. Now that the outpost was close he slowed, stopped and crouched, eyes fixed on something unseen through the poplars and spruce. He stood, backed a few steps, then turned and ran, looking nervously over his shoulder.

Gough raised an arm. The men halted, anxiously watching the agitated scout stumble to a breathless stop before Douglas and Gough.

"What is it?" Gough snapped.

Tisdale pointed toward the trade post. Between sharp draughts of air, he blurted, "Beyond the trees. At least a dozen."

Gough snarled and took the scout by the shoulder. "A dozen what? Cree? French?"

The scout jerked his head from side to side. "No. I don't know. Giant apes. They look like giant apes."

Douglas said, "Easy, lad." The boy slowly calmed. "Now tell me, clearly, what did you see?"

The scout swallowed. "I honestly can't say, sir. They were tall, extremely tall, covered in fur. Like great apes. Gathered around the post."

Douglas harkened back to the cave and the lumbering shape in the passage. His mouth went dry. "Did you see Baker or O'Brien? McNab? Leith? Benson?"

"No, Captain, but there were bodies. The giants were eating. I think they were eating our—"

"That's enough, Private," Douglas said, his tone heavy with caution.

A gust of wind swirled through the muskeg carrying moisture from the bay. Another storm was brewing. A second gust blew from the opposite direction, from landward. Immediately there sounded a series of deep grunts, like the challenge of some hell-spawned boars.

"What was that?" someone asked.

Gough snapped, "Silence." As the grunting continued, he added, "Form two lines. Prime and load."

The men promptly obeyed, removing their capotes and dropping the heavy coats to the round. Producing muskets, they began loading the weapons with well-practiced motions.

The grunts continued, increasing in volume. Then several hulking figures appeared in the distance, loping through the sparse forest like mighty silverbacks.

Douglas pushed the scout back to the main line and readied his own musket.

As the men finished priming their weapons, Gough shouted, "Fix bayonets." Steel rasped as blades were drawn and snapped into place.

The creatures erupted from the forest to stand not more than thirty paces from the waiting soldiers, grunting and stamping their feet in the soft muskeg. They came no further. Then another emerged. This one was larger than the others, its fur as black as night. Like the rest of its kind, it had a wide face with small, obsidian eyes that simmered under a heavy brow jutting over a flattened nose. The mouth was a lipless gash buried inside its massive blood-matted beard. One large hand clutched a thick tree limb as its followers formed a rough semi-circle behind it.

"Must be their leader," Gough said. "Whatever they are."

Douglas said, "Witiko."

Gough's voice rose. "What?"

He raised his shoulder in a half-hearted shrug. "A Cree legend McNab told me. Cannibals, he said. The Swampys live in fear of them. I remember laughing at the tale when he told me."

Gough licked his upper lip. "They hardly look like legends, sir. Cannibals, you say?"

Douglas nodded. "Apparently."

"Is that what we saw back in the cave?"

"It would be my guess. The females, perhaps."

The beast leader raised the tree limb above its head and bellowed a thunderous sound that raised the hairs on Douglas's neck. The call was immediately echoed by its companions, a deafening cacophony that swiftly peaked. A pregnant pause ensued. They charged.

Gough barked, "Front row, make ready. Choose your target." The soldiers brought their muskets to bear. "Present!" They sighted. "Fire!"

Eight muskets discharged. White powder curled from priming pans to mingle with the soldier's gusting breaths.

Three creatures jerked and dropped to the ground, slipping lifeless into the spongy peat. Another two staggered, blood erupting from the thick pelt of fur covering chest and belly, staining their black and brown coats with red. They fell heavily to their knees, howls of pain splitting the air.

Gough commanded, "Second rank. Make ready. Present. Fire."

The second volley proved less effective, most having sighted on the wounded creatures. Those hit slumped to the ground.

The deaths had no effect on the surviving creatures. They came on, dark eyes fierce with rage, their heavy legs churning the soft ground, muscular arms pumping, clawed hands flexing.

Shaken by the approaching horror, the British front rank managed a second volley, wounding two more beasts and sending a third tumbling to the ground. Three soldiers stepped from the line, panicked flight written across their ghostly faces.

Douglas dropped his spent musket and drew his sword. "Stand and fight, damn you."

Gough grabbed one of the men and pushed him back in line. He glared at the others. They meekly resumed position. "Present bayonets," he commanded. "Let's send those bastards to Hell."

Man and beast clashed. Steel met flesh, piercing thick hides. Soldiers thrust and tore with adrenaline-induced fervor. The beasts howled, their huge arms sweeping viciously, rending flesh, exposing ribs, tearing entrails. A soldier was lifted high into the air and slammed mercilessly to the ground. A massive foot ground into his screaming face. Yet another soldier had his arm torn from its socket, and while standing in shock, his head was twisted to face his back.

Douglas faced a gray-pelted creature over seven feet in height. Its ebony eyes simmered hatred. A jagged scar split its heavy facial fur from forehead to chin. A grunted snarl revealed yellow canine-like incisors dripping fresh blood. Douglas swept his sword crossways, slicing the belly, but its thick fur blunted the force of the blow. Howling at the sudden pain, it swung a thick limb. Douglas dropped to the ground as the knotted weapon sailed closely overhead, ripping off his tricorne. Desperately, he thrust at an exposed thigh. The steel penetrated, cutting deep. Twisting the blade with his wrist, he sliced up before tearing it free. Hot liquid jetted across his face as the creature pitched back, its life-blood pumping freely from a torn artery.

Douglas came to his feet, his breath coming in great gasps. Standing over the creature, he drove his sword into its mighty chest, through the heart, then dropped to his knees atop its hairy body. The Witiko released a last frenzied howl before the eyes glazed over.

Suddenly, Gough was there, offering a hand.

Douglas reluctantly allowed the sergeant to pull him up. "How . . . move!" Pushing Gough aside, he raised his sword to take the brunt of a huge limb sweeping down in a mighty stroke. The limb bit deep into his blade, its impact numbing the arm and forcing him to his knees.

It was the gigantic black Witiko. The beast roared its fury and pulled on the limb with extraordinary strength, ripping the blade from his numb grasp, pulling him forward with the momentum to land heavily on his stomach. With a quick prayer he waited for the killing blow. It never came. Rising to his knees, he saw why. The beast struggled to free the blade from the limb, working it back and forth. Unsuccessful, it howled frustration before tossing both aside. Seeing him, the Witiko advanced with arms outstretched.

Douglas came to his feet and backed away, his hand fumbling for the pistol tucked inside his waistband. The beast charged, closing so swiftly he knew he had no time to fire.

Gough rushed in cursing like a demon, his bayonet plunging deep into the beast's torso. The unexpected impact knocked the creature off balance, the action tearing the musket from Gough's grasp and sending him tumbling to the ground.

Granted those precious seconds, Douglas raised his pistol, aimed at the hell-spawned face and squeezed the trigger. The weapon discharged, its smoke obscuring his vision as the massive body drove him to the ground. Grunting at the pressure of its immense weight, he pushed desperately at the face, expecting the large canines to momentarily rip into his throat. Instead, the beast sighed, a long exhale that preceded its death rattle. The ruined face rested mere inches from his, the bullet having entered its left eye to explode out the back of the head. Blood from its ruined socket began to ooze onto Douglas's forehead.

Douglas pushed against the body. Its immense weight wouldn't shift. Worse, he felt himself sink slowly into the soft muskeg. Turning his head he gasped, "Help me."

Two bodies were quickly beside him, each man grunting with effort as they rolled the creature off him.

The captain sat up. Gough and Blake nodded, grim looks on their bloodied faces.

"The men?" Douglas asked.

Gough shook his head. "We're all that's left, sir."

Blake spit on the dead Witiko. "But we killed them. Every last one."

Douglas raised his arms. Gough and Blake each took one and pulled him to his feet. Standing unsteadily, he quietly crossed the small battlefield. The bloody remains of his men brought a thick lump to his throat. "Gather the weapons and reload," he mumbled. "Two muskets each. We will go to the beach. See if anyone survived."

He waited as Gough and Blake rummaged among the weapons. His body was stiff, his arms heavy and numb. He spotted the thick tree limb with his embedded, bent blade. Glaring at the body of the Witiko, he muttered, "Bugger cost me a good sword."

◆ ◆ ◆

At the outpost they found the partially devoured remains of the two guards Douglas had assigned to protect McNab and the midshipmen. He identified them by their white trousers. A third body lay with them, another midshipman. Continuing to the beach they discovered a York boat gone, the other a smoldered, burnt husk.

Douglas said, "Someone set this ablaze to warn us."

Blake asked, "Are we stranded, then?"

"We could use those." Gough motioned toward the two birch bark canoes.

"Will not be necessary." Douglas pointed toward the bay. Bobbing in the rough waters was the missing York boat. Two figures stood waving on its shallow deck before sitting down and taking up oars.

As it neared, Gough said, "It's McNab and Benson. Pity about Leith."

From deep within the muskeg came a chillingly familiar grunt.

"I thought we killed them all," Blake said with a groan.

Gough said, "You forget the cave. No telling how many remain."

The boat was some thirty feet from shore. Blake stepped into the cold water. Flashing an apologetic look at Douglas, Gough followed.

Douglas watched them wade toward the vessel. He couldn't blame them. The chilling cry came again. He sighed, stepped into the water, and idly wondered how he would ever explain this to the Company Factor at Fort Albany.

NIGHT STALKERS

BY

JASON HUGHES

THE FULL MOON glistened over the snowcapped ground of Pennyworth, Pennsylvania. It was rather a small town, right outside of Pittsburgh. Most were nestled in for the night. Some couples sat outside, and enjoyed the isolated and icy landscapes that stretched before their eyes. "What do you think of those murders? The ones down the road, I mean," Valley Mayor asked. She took another sip of coffee.

"Oh, ya mean the murders ya kept bringing up to ma relatives during supper? Tha ones that almost had 'em a - barfin' what they scarfed? Those are tha murders ya squealin' about again?!" Charlie Richmond blasted at her. He chugged the last of the tightly gripped, random alcoholic beverage.

"Well, I'm just worried is all. I mean, it is a small effin' town, ya know. It could be . . . someone we know even."

Just as Charlie and Valley enjoyed the beautiful winter wonderland that was bestowed before their watery eyes, they despised each other's company as well. Football and hunting meant a lot to Charlie, that was about it. Valley's semi-joking and subliminal bashings were delivered more from the heart than it sometimes seemed. She meant every word coldly, but in the most warming sarcastic tone. "Well, ya went ahead and blared out somethin' about a dang human carcass while ma parents were tryin' ta ask ya somethin' important. It was about ya schoolin'. Ya just cut 'em off while they was askin' ya where . . ."

"Shh . . . did you just hear that?" Valley inquired as she removed her index finger from her mouth and twisted her head to both sides.

"I ain't hear nothin'. You hearin' thangs. I'm outta bee . . ."

"There it was again, shut up for a second and you'll see . . . hear, I mean," Valley said as she jerked her wide eyed head behind her. "I'm . . . I'm getting kind of cold. Let's go in now," Valley said as she stood up and continued to look around in a silent tremble.

"Shoot, you can go in. I'm stayin' right here. It feels good out here," Charlie barked in a retaliating manner. He spat once into the snow and wiped his mouth, paying no attention to Valley as she turned around and walked toward the house.

◆　◆　◆

Within the city limit of Rakersville, the Fellowmont family returned from the hospital with their handicapped son, Williford. They referred to him as "Will" for short. It was also easier for him to understand and comprehend that they were speaking to him. "Will, it's almost time for your bed-bed," Jill Fellowmont said as Craigory Fellowmont looked down in a shroud of descending emotion. He knew somewhere ahead that Will's time was short. He was wheelchair bound and barely mobile on four wheels. Craigory kept in the hopelessness buried deep within the shunned tombs of his aching heart.

"Bed-bed?" Williford asked in a nocturnally-charged daze of wonder.

"Six more bodies were found in Rakersville. Each of them seemed to be torn to pieces . . . ripped to shreds. Police have not found any leads to these grizzly attacks . . . which seem to head toward Pittsburgh. One entire and once peaceful town is now covered in a blanket of fear. A killer is lose and wandering around . . . in their neighborhood. I'm Brian Bakerson, Channel Thirteen eyewitness News," the Reporter announced in a droned tone of synthetic sympathy.

"Did you hear that, honey? Those killings . . . . Oh, let me help Will to bed. I'll be back. We can talk about it then. That's scary to think of," Jill said as she turned around and wheeled her weakened Will away. Craigory looked at the two of them with a hollow sigh. "Good night, Will," Craigory said with a wave and drizzling tear.

"Night," Will replied as he was gently reclined and rolled down the hall. Jill gave him a lift, tuck-in, and kiss before exiting the dark bedroom and closing the door.

◆　◆　◆

Williford began to drift into a horizontal trance. He could not move, but he was aware of what was going on around him. He could see clearly out of his windows and hear through the echoing and amplifying thin walls. The snow caked on the window on this particular night and usually season made the vision a blur. At the same time, Will's parents' voices carried throughout the half empty house . . . loud and clear. He could hear Jill's muffled voice on several occasions. Sometimes the words would chill him to the bone. "You could never do that," she would repeat, but no one would answer her back. Williford often wondered what she was saying and who she was talking to.

The present conversation included Craigory's airborne, echoing whispers. "They just found two more. It's showing it live on television. There's barely anything left of her. The reporter said that her body seemed masticated to almost nothing. They're broadcasting live," Craigory said as Jill re-entered the living room. "Where did they find these?" Jill asked in a flat-lined tone of concern.

"They found her over by the woods. Her clothing ripped to pieces, just as the flesh from her body and bones," Craigory replied.

"Don't say that, Craig."

"Well, I'm just saying," Craigory replied with a chuckle.

"I hate it when you say that," Jill said in a playful tone and sarcastic giggle.

◆　◆　◆

"Just let me alone and deal with your own problems!" Charlie wailed on the other side of the small town, barely introduced to the map. He had just about had it with Valley's verbal attacks of belittling sarcasm. "I thought you were going to stay out in the effin' cold weather for all you cared or something to that effect. Isn't that what you said, Charlie?" Valley snapped as Charlie shut the fridge with a chilled one in his hand.

"Yeah, yeah . . . sometimes you almost force me to wanna become whoever Channel Thirteen is talkin' 'bout here on ya. Can't let a man relax for tha life of ya, can ya?" Charlie said as he spat into the kitchen sink.

"Don't spit in the sink!" Valley screamed in an uncoiled strike of venom hissing anger.

"I'll spit in your face, girl," Charlie replied in a seriousness that almost repulsed Valley to no end. She would clench her fists and grind her teeth when she would hear Charlie use this biting tone.

"Ladies and gentlemen . . . we cannot believe what we are hearing. Six more bodies have popped up within the last few nights, the station has just reported... one within the last hour. This is surely a sudden shock to the small town of Rakersville. Authorities are baffled by the savagery and intensity of each faceless attack that has seemed to haunt this community. Doors and windows are being locked and bolted in what seemed to be . . . a peaceful and tranquil place to reside. His savagery seems to have no age limit or traceable method of operation. We know that whatever he is using to chew up these helpless victims is one or many sharp objects. Axes or large knives are what some believe are the murder weapons in this particular, yet unfamiliar case. The bodies seem to be masticated . . . or chewed . . . in an overly savage manner and method. There are several lacerations to the flesh and some of the victims seem to be scalped. This is the worst crime the area has seen in as long as the residents can recall."

"I just heard some rustling in the woods over there. I didn't think nothin' of it. Woke up the next morning, my neighbor was sprawled out in the front of his hut, bleedin' everywhere and stuff. My kid found him layin' there. He was paid fer, I tell ya . . . paid fer," local interviewed resident, Herman Maypalm said through a grainy picture and fuzzy voice, each of which were transmitted by a coat-hanger as a metal rod of makeshift bunny ears.

"Someone's out there. I'm telling you, Charlie. I'm effin' scared. What if he's close to here? You wouldn't protect me! You don't care at all!" Valley snarled as she stomped into her bedroom and slammed the door in an instant violent rage.

"Stay in there!" Charlie yelled with his head straight forward. He continued to watch the news as the Reporter continued to explain the body count unfolding practically in his own backyard. The number of the mutilated was mercilessly piling, inducing mind shattering and contagious fear and dread among the frightened citizens.

Something clattered outside of Charlie's window. He jumped up in a skillfully quick swivel and pivot. He was in a semi-blasted, drunken state of incoherence and blissful ignorance. Another crash clattered through the yard outside. Charlie slowly walked toward the door. A large human-like silhouette passed the window as Charlie half blindly made his way toward the front door. He slung it open with a bravely fueled jolt of energized adrenaline. "Who's *out* here?!" Charlie screamed in anger driven impatience. He scanned the front yard and wooded area across the street with his eyes. He could not see past the forest at an eye level. Right at the edge of the perimeter was a large hole embedded in the snow.

He could hear the reporter in the background as his waving vision attempted to lock in on the pit in the frozen ground. "We are certain that the killer is armed and extremely dangerous. Do not leave your homes after dark, not even in groups. A town wide curfew has been placed into effect as of now. The victims have been away from their respected homes, at the times of every remorseless attack," the Reporter repeated.

The once grimly crimson glazed crime scene that was a few short blocks away, had been recapped and coated in frost white sheets of freshly fallen snow. Charlie looked around and closed the door. A mammoth sized, human-like shadow passed by the window behind him as he stumbled back to the couch and planted his dizzy shell back to a comfortably padded oblivion. His body started to shut down at a rapid pace. The huge human-like shadow stood at the window and watched Charlie as he dozed into a forcefully spinning slumber. The room would not sit still or stable around him. He could feel it in his head and stomach. The dark figure outside of the house was visibly breathing heavily and hunched down in a slight crouch. It raised its large right hand.

◆　◆　◆

"I'm afraid for Will. He's defenseless. What if he . . . he can't protect himself from someone like that? How could someone be such a . . . a monster.? How?" Jill asked Craigory in a mental state of swirling paranoia.

"We are going to protect him. You know we can. We were meant to meet and conceive Williford. We must and we will protect him. He is our son and you know that just as well as I do. We will protect him."

Williford could not sleep. He overheard his mother and father's entire conversation. About three hours of listening slugged by and eventually died away.

Later that night as someone savagely walked the streets, Will could hear Jill talking . . . but no one would respond to her. The subliminal tone in Jill's voice made her son's bones quiver worse than the cold weather seeping through the screen. Will could hear everything that happened outside as well. He heard movements. There were shadows outside of his window as well. He had never encountered outbursts of any kind. He was very intelligent for his unfortunately accidental outcome. It was not his fault. He understood that brutal fact. "It . . . is not . . . my fault," Will would cerebrally say to himself every night as he lied down alone to eventually sleep. He repeated it to himself as many times as he could when his mother would start talking with no response. It was the best he could do.

◆　◆　◆

Rachel London was an attractive twenty-one-year-old. She lived most of her nights on an edgy and wild side. Most men of Rakersville knew who she was . . . or knew the buzzing name. "I'll meet you outside, around the back a little later," Rachel said to another nameless face as they vanished into the darkness. She had just made arrangements with Charlie after her current meeting. He was waiting in a cold sweat for the time to arrive. The time seemed to crawl by at a torturous pace. The clandestine meeting was to be the following night at midnight. Until then, Rachel had other business to attend.

"Most of the residents of Rakersville are terminal shock and despair. Stay tuned as this story unfolds," the Reporter said on the motel set at the Rakersville Inn.

Rachel rolled over and pulled herself out of bed. She was in quite a post orgasmic stagger as she made her way around the room. Her occasional friend was gone. Rachel gathered her purse, clothing, posture and thoughts and walked outside. She left the television on behind her. She returned the key and walked off through the parking lot. She had so much swimming through her skull and her mind's eye was drained and fuzzy. She looked around as she stumbled down the street. Without a warning, she fell, face first into a large snow pit. She raised her weary head and looked around. It was something much weirder than a pit . . . and much worse. Something moved behind her . . . something not human.

◆　◆　◆

"I don't want him here sometimes," Jill said as the silent air filled the empty space in which Craigory's response would usually reply. Craigory was not there. He was in his bed, out cold and sound asleep. Jill was standing in the hallway, outside of Williford's bedroom. Her palms were sweaty. "It was my fault. I shouldn't have done it," Jill replied to herself a little while after the strangely lurking dead silence. As these dark wishes whirled through her head, something else lurked outside of her home. They were watching the family through the windows, from deep within the woods which surrounded their home. Four sets of inhuman eyes watched the Fellowmont family as they slept. She was lost in a scatterbrain sense of insomnia injected and delusional sleep deprivation. Jill was talking and replying to no one, but herself. She was speaking upon her own dead ears. She cracked open the bedroom door and looked in on Williford as he laid still in bed. Someone she never noticed was creeping on the other side of the window. They were inching their way closer to the Fellowmont castle. They could smell the warm blood inside of the wooden and glass encasement. Through their starving vision, the family was a home shaped happy meal. Multiple breathing began to circle the home from the shrouding night sky. Sniffs and growls in the wind began to close in on the sturdy wooden structure. The family was unaware and without a clue as to what closed in on their home on this cold and snowy night. Jill closed the door and walked into the living room. She sat and watched television. Breaking stories were continuing as a commentary to the macabre string of homicides happening around the area. It seemed to reach further than Rakersville.

"Whoever is out there is extremely dangerous. We repeat, he is extremely dangerous and savagely vicious. Everyone is ordered to their residential domains as darkness falls. This is a mandatory request by the local law enforcement."

◆　◆　◆

"Psycho . . . outside . . . I'm not . . . afraid . . . of some . . . ffffruity little hay-hhhhay truck driver . . . that landed on his cranium as a baby. Come . . . over . . ." Charlie mumbled in a dying slur of drool and sputtering words.

He could barely comprehend his own coined language of incoherent babble. A loud slam outside sprung Charlie to his feet and a firm attention with almost a sharpened military precision. "Who's there!?!" Charlie screamed as Valley slept through the vocal rampage of regurgitated and slithering words. "Who's that outside!? I'm comin' out with a bat . . . no a . . . a freakin' gun!" Charlie threatened with as much force as he could verbally muster up within his gut and throat. Charlie could not control his masculinity as his voice trembled and quivered into a crumbling block of scrambled, cracking octaves. Whatever was out there had moved much closer to his home and within comfort zone. Two huge corneas could be seen through the falling snow and frosted window against the nocturnal backdrop. A sinisterly squinted brow draped over the beady night prowling eyes.

◆　◆　◆

Rachel scanned the premises and noticed the oddly shaped indention into which she had stumbled and fallen. She felt dumbfounded in disorientation until her reflexes and instinct finally took control and commanded her to react and look behind her. She gazed up from the hole in which she was suddenly embedded. Heavily panting snarls were closing in from all around her. She could hear them howling throughout the brutally nipping breeze. The pressure and force of the flake laced wind made Rachel's eyes water with an uncertainty of what lied two steps ahead or behind her. She knew someone had her surrounded. It sounded like multiple large men hacking in the night air. The only difference was their nostril inhalation. There was something a little different about the way he . . . or they breathed. Rachel could hear their chainsaw-like snorting through the heavily raging winds.

Something was not right. It could have been someone from her past that she did not want any confrontation with, there were many. She had been threatened before. Whomever it could've been kept getting louder and closer with every forceful, beastly inhuman breath. The sound resembled that of a large, hungry dog or wolf that had not eaten in a week. It was too loud, too solid . . . to be human. She knew it wasn't Jolie, her neighbor's home protection, a Boxer half her size. This sounded like ten of them amplified into a roaring pack, a hunting pack that was out for flesh and blood. Still, it could not be the sound a human would make. No man could possibly produce such a ghastly nasal inhale. Their breathing patterns began to sound somewhat along the lines of a feasting lion, chewing on a freshly severed leg of lamb or deer.

◆ ◆ ◆

"Mom . . . Momma! Mom—*momma*!" Williford screamed from his bedroom in a shriek of deafening terror. "Help! It's a ba—a bad . . . muh-*man*!" Jill's firmly snapped initial reaction was to immediately check on her child. He had never displayed such behavior that either of his birth givers could recall. Craigory and Jill were smacked into a rude awakening in the middle of the night. They both met each other at Williford's bedroom door as he continued to wail in a screeching fit. "Someone's outside! Someone's . . . out . . . outsiiiiide!" Williford hurled in a glass shattering tone of fearful excitement and sweat pumping fury.

"What in the world is *wrong* with him!?" Jill shouted in a halfway aggravated hiss.

"I . . . I don't know. Let's go in and find out, okay?

"There's bad . . . man outside the window! Bad . . . bad man, window!" Williford screamed as he pointed at the window in a possessed trance of emotionless fright. Half of Jill knew her son could not have been as crazy as some of her darker personalities. The obscured extremities inside of her were fighting to get free somehow.

"What is it?" Craigory asked in a calm manner."

"Someone's . . . outside!" Williford replied in a tantrum of torment.

"There's no one out there, Will!" Jill bellowed in hatefully verbal gore.

"Jill!" Craigory forcefully spewed at his loving wife.

"Well where is he, Craig? Huh? Under the bed, in the closet? Where, Craigory? There's no one out there, Craig," Jill proclaimed as she pulled the curtains closed. Craigory comforted Williford until the certainty washed over him that he had calmed down enough to settle and fall asleep. A dark, human-like figure shifted and shuffled across the white cloth tented wooden frame behind Jill. As she met Craigory in the hallway, the silhouette had already made its way out of sight. She looked behind her one last time and closed the door.

Williford was alone again. He could still hear the stirring around outside. The shuffling around in the trees were subtle, yet to Williford, sounded like a set of razor sharp rusty nails on a chalk board. He could hear Craigory and Jill talking in the hallway as their voices eventually made their separate ways. The silence crept into Williford's bedroom once again, like a disturbing stench that would not go away. Something was outside of his window. Whatever it was, it was not his parents. He was not much of the social type, so that marked out any friends wanting to scour about in the night, especially with someone that could not make a quick getaway, much less an escape at all. Williford looked through his window and saw a large man-like hand. The nails on the fingers were too long to be human. Williford began to shake horribly and clench onto his bedspread pulling it up, over his face. His mother had planted in his head that he was seeing things. This was no hallucination. There was no scary man outside of his window. There was no serial killer. There was no human being on the other side of the cloth draped glass. That was all that stood between Williford . . . and a monster. Williford's mind started to battle in a bout of believing his mother that it was all in his mind, or come to reason with what he saw with his own two eyes.

◆　◆　◆

Charlie Richmond moved closer toward the door in a panic ridden stumble of toxicity. He had a Louisville gripped in his right hand and the other extended toward the front door. "You ain't killed nowhere near as many deer as I have, you dingbat psycho!" Charlie screamed as he reached his hand toward the door knob.

He slowly turned the knob and pulled on the door. It was locked. Charlie reached down, unlocked the door and flung it open in rage. He stepped outside and onto his front porch. He looked around, and deep into the quilt of darkness that was knitted over his straining vision. He jumped off the porch and into the yard and began to walk around, keeping his head swiveling like a sprinkler. His bat was raised high above his shoulders in a combat stance.

He heard heavy breathing coming from the trees . . . a sinisterly powerful and starving pant. "Who's back there?! You don't come out n' you're a paid fer sum . . . . Hey! Who's back 'er?!" Charlie yelled as synthetic sense of alcohol fueled bravery swept over him. "You out *here*?! I don't see ya nowheres! I got ma buddy with me! He, he wants ta give ya' a lil' *kiss*!" Charlie shouted as he continued to move his head around.

Subtle head jerks seemingly turned into nervous spasms before too long. The breathing was closing in from the dark woods. Charlie proceeded to make his way toward the outskirts of the wooded perimeter. He looked down to his feet and took a deep gasp. He had never seen anything like it before. A miniature crater. Charlie bent down and pulled in at a closer glance. He realized what he was standing over was no crater caused by a rock of any kind. This massive part missing from the earth was caused by none other than a foot. Something had left its mark and it was not of the human race. Charlie knew this by all of the animals he had hunted growing up with his father. The footprint almost looked somewhat human, only three times in size. A foul odor began to burn and singe Charlie's nose hairs. He glanced over at a tree stump a few feet away and almost gagged in sickened disbelief. His glance locked into a solid stare. He had seen many animal paw prints in his days, but nothing this large.

"What . . . in . . . tha . . ." Charlie said as he glared at the most massive pile of bodily waste he had ever seen. He knew right away that no human alive could produce something this enormous, let alone devour what it would take to produce what massive pile steamed before him. "Holy . . ." Charlie gagged again before he could finish the commonly used and perfect occasion fitting phrase. He could feel someone . . . or some*thing* breathing down his neck. He looked up into the jaws and gaping pie hole of a beast like he had never laid his eyes on before. It was massive, hairy, hungry and reaching down for Charlie.

He grabbed the baseball bat and hit the beast in the ribs. This feeble attempt only upset the creature. He let out a huge roar and smacked Charlie to the ground with a swift swipe of his gigantic hand-like paw. Charlie screamed in fear as he felt something warm slide down his leg in the freezing climate. He had too much pride to openly admit to himself what had just happened. He looked up and covered his face. "Noooooooo!" was the only word Charlie could force through his shrilling vocal chords as the beastly hands grabbed and pulled his limp body upward.

A mouthful of razor sharp and blood spattered teeth began to gape wider as Charlie screamed in waste excreting agony. His girlfriend, Valley, slept peacefully in her bed without knowledge of Charlie's gruesome dismemberment that took place in the patch of woods that overlooked their home from across the street.

◆　◆　◆

Rachel snapped into a quick sense of reality and looked around. The heavy breathing was all around her, and getting closer with each pounding footstep. "What do you freaking people want?!" she screamed with a spastic back and forth motion of her whipping head and hair. She made her way from the mini hole in the ground and took off without an instinct to see what or who was following her. She could still hear the many footsteps that trampled behind her in a solid stomping and killing pace. As the ground raced beneath her feet, she noticed several large footprints in the snow, much like the hole in which she thought she had fallen into a few sprinted yards behind her. She suddenly tripped, face first in the below negative degree snow. She could hear them getting closer with each pounding trample. She jumped up and limped as fast as she could and was not about to pay attention to who was relentlessly on her trail of attempted escape.

Rachel was painfully aware that there were more than one after her. She also knew they wanted to do her harm in a severe way. No matter how close they were gaining behind Rachel, she was blind to the fact that they were extremely far from the human species. The sharp pain in her right ankle slowed her down as her heart defeated her pace by miles. She took off her high-heeled boots and began running in the inches of penetrative snow. The pulsating pain in her right leg did not help her game of tug-of-war with struggling speed and descending physical stability.

"Just leave me alone!" she cried into the storming winds that scraped against her face like a thick wall of whirling bewilderment. There were no vehicles or signs of life for miles. Everyone was faithfully abiding to the curfew laid down by the law. Even the police force had more than one reason to stay indoors. This included the rough weather conditions on the icy streets, not to mention a nameless killer in which they were clueless to where or who he would strike next.

Rachel's ankle gave out with a sudden pop. She was embedded in the snowy ground once more. The sky beamed ray of moonlight that somewhat guided her was divided by huge human-like shadows as they surrounded her. She could not scream as she realized who had been following her from the motel. They did not want her money. They did not want to assault her . . . they wanted her for a late-night snack. Rachel was reaching her final breath. She was about to become the link to a food chain in which she never knew existed. This was no serial killer, but Rachel was about to become another marked statistic, all the same.

◆　◆　◆

In the meantime, Williford noticed the large silhouette at his window as it raised its hand and put it against the glass with a quaking thud. The monstrous hand lowered as the long nails scraped against the frost tinted bedroom window. He noticed another giant figure standing behind it. "Mom-ma! There . . . monsters outside of . . . the window! Monsters! They are mon . . . sss-teeeeers!" Williford wailed in what seemed like a hopelessly doomed moan of despair to a child in his condition.

"There he goes again," Jill announced in a deeply battered sigh of agonizing defeat. "Can you go check on him this time?" Jill asked as she barely raised her head.

"Yeah . . . I'll . . . I'll do it," Craigory said in a completely submissive manner.

"Good," Jill stated in a dead utter as she rolled over and drifted back into dreamland.

"Local authorities have just released the news that more than one perpetrator is involved in this horrific case that seems to stalk our once silent . . ." the Reporter announced on the television as Craigory grabbed the remote. He turned off the announcement, mid-sentence on the way into the hallway as he rubbed his adjusting eyes.

Williford wasn't "crying wolf" in the least bit as his mother may have expected. He was truly screaming for dear life. Something was outside of his window and he knew it was not make believe. His imagination could not drum up something so terrifying and nerve shattering. The fear was all too real.

As Craigory opened Williford's bedroom door, the lingering shadows began to leave visible sight of the window. They spread out and around the house. Williford was screaming on the floor, next to his bed. "Will! How did you get down there?! Are you okay?!" Craigory asked in fearful curiosity.

"Bad . . . people, out—ssss-side! They . . . going to get me!" Williford shouted as Craigory reached down to retrieve his son and set him back onto the bed.

"It's okay, Will. There's no one out . . ." Craigory began to say as a loud bang came from somewhere in the hallway.

"Craig! Someone's outside the window! Someone is watching us!" Jill screamed bloody murder from her bedroom. Craigory was caught between his grieving child and suddenly ballistic wailing wife. He was beginning to have second thoughts in Williford's shrieks. Just as he was debunking his son's possible overactive imagination, Jill's ear blasting screams reconfirmed both Craigory and Williford's realization that this was no figment of mental frailty. The other four eyes of the home were certain of what Craigory's own two had not yet witnessed. He was instantly cradled in his family's contagiously shared fear. He took Williford into his arms and ran into the bedroom.

"What happened, Jill?!" Craigory asked in panic as he looked into the room. Jill was right next to the door, on her way into the hall. A muffled snarl greeted Craigory through the glass, along with large salivating teeth. It was truly a monster, indeed . . . a beast-like, sasquatch creature. There were more than one of the hungry and vicious growlers of the night searching for prey. There were several, and a small group had found their way to Craigory's humble abode. The mammoth creature let out an angry roar as its paws came crashing through the window. "Take Will and run!" Craigory yelled to Jill as she jumped up in shock.

Craigory grabbed his rifle from the gun case by the wall. He had always kept one loaded in case the unfortunate call of home security should ever rear its ugly head. He did not know what to think of this particular occurrence, but knew he did not have time to do so. His first reactions were to aim the deadly double - barreled steel and pulled the trigger. Along with a whining yelp, he did just that. Another crash of shattering glass came from the living room. A roaring growl accompanied the unnerving clatter that arose down the hall. The beast went flying backwards, through the broken and jagged glass. Just as one of the beasts was taken out by pump action, another was entering the home through the living room. Jill fled in that fatal direction with Williford screaming in her arms, just as the front window served as a second entrance. A second blood and snow caked sasquatch was in the living room, and looking around for something to eat. Jill froze in her tracks and let out a terrified shriek of shock. The beast came charging for her just as a cold, steel barrel extended over her shoulder. Craigory shot the inhuman intruder in the head as he fell backwards, onto the coffee table. There was a constant pounding on the back patio door, until finally, an inevitably (and collectively) dreaded shatter followed. Another creature had made its way into the family's once secured space and somewhat cozy comfort zone. The glass and wooden structure was no match for the four hundred pounds of fur, power and fury. A group of unwanted visitors avidly wanted a warming welcome and forced entry into the home. Craigory, Jill and Williford had no idea how many were out there. The cringing family was certain that they wanted into their home. Nothing seemed as if could stop their appetite for intrusion and quench for human delicacies.

Craigory could hear the kitchen being ransacked as he made his way toward the living room-to-kitchen entrance. A lonesome growl could be heard in the darkness. Craigory pulled the trigger in a n early, overreaction, but nothing happened. He was out of bullets. He could feel warm air as it huffed and puffed on his face through the darkness. He reached into his pocket and pulled out two more bullets with his quivering hands. He loaded the gun in the dark and flipped on the light. There, standing two feet in front of his face was a third blood thirsty hairball with sharp teeth and huge hands, feet and nails. It growled ferociously as it grabbed Craigory, lifting his feet from the kitchen tile. The face and mouth of the man-like monster were covered in blood and leftovers of the helpless victims from earlier in the night. These were the poor souls mentioned on the Channel Thirteen evening news.

Craigory knew that he not only had to protect himself, but his trembling family bloodline as well. Their lives and wellbeing meant more to Craigory than his own. They were all he had to hold onto. This was his family. Craigory wanted to scream, "leave me and my family alone!" like so many of the Horror movies he had seen that had the bargaining option. He knew somewhere within his fight-or-flight state of mind, that these attackers would not understand a single word. To these beasts, the family was one thing and one thing only . . . brunch. Craigory knew that if he didn't do something in a heartbeat that he would be eaten alive in his own kitchen and in front of his wife and son. They would more than likely be next and it was the last thing he wanted to happen. Craigory screamed as he pointed the barrel straight up and firmly against the chin of the hungry mouth that could possibly consume and digest him. He pulled the trigger, shooting the beast at point blank range. The last snarling threat to his family's lives was dead within his own castle, along with three others. Craigory ran for the phone to call the police and notify them of who . . . or what, he had just encountered.

◆　◆　◆

Charlie's shredded body was found the next morning. There was barely anything left of him. The unseen predators were walking into the rising sun. Several gigantic sized footprints left paths out of Rakersville and Pennyworth, and into the neighboring city of Pittsburgh, Pennsylvania.

THE LORD HELPS THOSE . . .

BY

TONIA BROWN

BUTCH LOVELACE HAD seen a Bigfoot.

There was no doubt in his mind, however small it might be, that he'd seen the Sasquatch live and in person. Well, live and in *Sasquatchedness*. It happened one night, when he was shifting hay from one field to another, getting ready for the oncoming winter—from the signs and portents, it was going to be a bad one—when he saw it. There, at the edge of the fence that bordered his cow pasture, stood the tallest, hairiest, ugliest thing he'd ever laid eyes on.

Butch didn't know what to do, so he just sat there in the high seat of the Deere, shining his spotlight on a surprised-looking beast, who just stood still and stared at him in return. Slow as rising sap, comprehension dawned on the old farmer, and he opened his mouth and let out a strangled shout of astonishment.

It sounded halfway like, "Bigfoot," and halfway like, "Lord, help me!"

Either way, Butch's cry startled the thing and it took off like a shot into the woods beyond the field. All arms and legs and stringy hair as the beast was, he expected it to scramble across the field willy-nilly in its effort to get under cover, but he never supposed that something so big would move so fluid and precise. It shifted in clean, easy glides as if its joints were made of pure oil, its body fueled by sheer grace. It was a wonder of nature just to watch the thing lope off toward the tree line, where it disappeared into the inky night without a hint it was ever there.

Now it didn't do his story justice that he might or might not have been a little tipsy from too much corn liquor. Nor did he win any sympathy when Gertrude let it slip he was supposed to wear prescription glasses that would better suit the base of a glass soda bottle than his ugly mug. In short, no one believed him. Not even his wife. But he didn't right care what others had to say on the matter. He knew what he had seen. Folks might think of Butch as a boring old coot, but he'd seen lots of interesting things in his life.

Once he helped a heifer birth a two-headed calf.

One time he watched a lightning strike split a ten-foot spruce in two.

And in his heart of hearts, Butch knew he had seen a Bigfoot.

He just wished he'd kept his fat trap shut about it.

"Hey, Butch!" Jimmy yelled just as Butch was settling into his usual seat in his pew one Sunday morning. "You gonna ask the Lord to protect us from the Bigfeets?"

The usual gentlemen's Sunday school crew laughed at that. Oh, yes, they had themselves a fine time at Butch's expense, and had been doing just that for almost three weeks now. Three weeks of poking and prodding and joshing and jesting, and, Butch figured, any moment now, he was due to blow his top. Surely the Lord would understand if he took Jim out back and taught him a lesson in manners? With his fists? Surely?

"It's Bigfoot, you ninny," Butch answered, instead of taking Jim out back. "Ain't no such thing as Bigfeets."

"That's what we've been saying!" Jim shouted.

The men had another good round of laughter.

Jim slapped his knee and snapped his fingers. "Come on now, Butch. If they's Bigfoot by themselves, what's a flock of 'em called?"

"Flock?" Dale asked. "Sure they don't travel in herds?"

"Or maybe schools," Joseph chimed in. "Like fish?"

"Or maybe soles," Jim said, then cackled. "Get it? A sole of Bigfeets?"

Again, everyone laughed. Butch just ignored them. He knew what he had seen. That was all that mattered. Still, if there was just a way to make other folks believe him . . . . As it turned out, Preacher Pruitt had the answer in his sermon, "The Lord helps those who help themselves."

The following lesson promised to be a pleasant one, but Butch didn't hear the rest of the lecture. Instead, his mind latched onto those first seven words, focusing on them with a surprising amount of clarity for a man who couldn't remember his own wife's birthday after thirty-five years of marriage. He plucked those seven words from the very air and held them under the bright church lights. Turned them about. Scrutinized them. Discovered an answer in them that, just minutes before, he never hoped to find.

The Lord helps those who help themselves.

Butch decided the only way he was going to get folks to believe him was to help folks believe him. He had to convince Jim and the others that Bigfoot was real, and in order to do that, he had to show them what he'd seen. He had to show them a Bigfoot. In a flash of inspiration, he knew just when and where and how. To save his reputation, not to mention his sanity, he had to turn them into believers, even if it meant stretching the truth a little bit in the process. Butch reckoned the Lord would forgive a little lying in the place of outright fist-fighting because if Jim kept up with his mocking, one or the other was bound to happen.

After the sermon wound down and the members filed out of the church and back to their cars, Jim stopped Butch to ask, "Ya ain't still mad at me, are ya?"

"Naw," Butch said. "I ain't mad."

"Good. 'Cause you know we're just kiddin', right?" Jim smiled wide.

"Right."

"You coming to Sal's for the big 'un?"

It was less a question and more a plea for reassurance. Every man worth his salt as a hunter would be at Sal's Feed and Seed next Friday afternoon for the official start of deer season. And so would Butch. But not for the deer. No, sir. Not this year.

"I wouldn't miss it fur the world," Butch said, then smiled with Jim for the first time in weeks. A plan was forming inside his thick skull and the more Jim grinned like a monkey at him, the more the plan seemed like an awful lot of well-deserved payback.

At first he thought about ordering a costume on the Internets, but that would mean employing one of his grandchildren to show him how to order the thing, and that would produce a witness, and then the costume purchase and subsequent delivery would provide a paper trail. The last thing Butch wanted was evidence of his deeds, whether in the form of people or paper. This had to work smooth and simple, with no evidence that led back to him as the instigator.

The alternative was simple in theory, but proved to be a whole lot of work for just one man and two short weeks. All day Sunday he sorted through the various skins and pelts of animals he had trapped or hunted over a lifetime. Nothing was suitable. Nothing fit the memory of that loping, hairy giant. He needed something with long hair, not fine or silky, but a great gathering of thick knots. A bear pelt would've been perfect, but it had been a number of years since he'd seen or even shot a bear.

Butch plopped onto the couch in the den and slid off his shoes to lie down for a nap, when the answer appeared right under his nose.

The den carpet was a throwback from Butch and Gerty's glory days. Back when Gertrude was a little less conservative in her décor, and he had a little more say about what went on in his own home. The result was a thick shag carpet that, by some grace of a higher authority, also happened to sport a dark brown color. Butch looked down between his bare feet and ran his toes through the gnarls of knots. Gerty often said it was the ugliest carpet she'd ever seen, and he couldn't agree more.

He made up some excuse about being right tired of the old carpet, so tired in fact he yanked it up from baseboard to baseboard without so much as an idea of what they would do for a replacement. Gerty made a few overtures like she might get mad about it, but in the end, she couldn't hide her joy . . . or her affection.

Butch slept real good that night.

The next few days were a flurry of clipping and sewing and gluing and stapling. For a while, he worried he wouldn't be able to pull it off, that an almost-retired dairy farmer wouldn't be able to create a convincing Sasquatch costume from scratch. Yet he did. After two weeks of hard work—not to mention avoiding Gertrude and her ever-prying eyes—he was done. The Thursday before the big day, he drew his weary body to full height, pulled on the poorly constructed but passable mask consisting of a squashed metal bucket with some holes punched through and the carpet glued all around, and stepped back to take a look in the bathroom mirror.

By and by, if he didn't look sort of like the thing. Not a lot, mind you, but just enough. Enough to fool Jim and the others? Perhaps. If it was dark enough, and he was a good distance off from his intended target, he reckoned he could just about pass for a Sasquatch. Yes. This was going to work.

The first day of hunting season arrived with all the appropriate fanfare that a small mountain town could heap upon such an event. Butch packed the truck to the brim with his gear, said his farewells to Gerty and set out for Sal's. As usual, all the men of the town were there, as well as a few young ladies who forsook the duties of home to take upon themselves the work of men. Some of the fellows scoffed at this addition, but Butch was nothing if not tolerant. He wouldn't mind giving the young girls as much of a scare as the old boys. Yup. Everyone was going to get their comeuppance. Tonight.

Butch and the fellers got their paperwork in order, stocked up on bullets and beer, then headed deep into Dale's back forty to camp and drink and shoot at whatever moved. They set up camp in the same place as always: the base of a hillside just at the edge of a small brook. It took the better part of the day to get everyone settled in, and after pitching four tents and drinking three cases of beer between them, they all decided to leave off hunting for the first night. Meanwhile, Butch had been pouring his beer in the bushes all night and making sure the others got good and soused.

"Well, boys," Butch said once the others started to sway with drink. "I think I'm gonna turn in for the night."

"What?" Jim said. "You can't go to bed. We just got started."

"I'm an old man. Let me get my sleep."

"You won't get none," Joshua said. "We're gonna be at it all night."

The others hollered their agreement. Jim even howled his.

"You can have all night," Butch said. "I'm gonna lay down a bit."

"But what if that Bigfeets comes about and you ain't here?" Dale asked in a drunken slur.

The boys kicked up their heels, laughing.

Butch narrowed his eyes at Dale. "What makes you think that?"

Dale, sleepy-eyed and red-nosed, shrugged. "Why not? You got a mononopopoly on Sasumasquatches?" The man never could hold his liquor.

Butch ignored the jab and stomped away to his tent, leaving the heat of the fire and embarrassment behind him. Let them laugh it up. Let them have their moment. They wouldn't be laughing no more once the whole town thought they were as crazy as him.

After going through the motions of retiring, Butch cut his lantern and lay awake in the dark, waiting. At it all night? He knew better. The only thing men his age could rightly claim to be at all night anymore was staring at the inside of their eyelids.

Sure enough, the boys dropped off one by one, crawling back to their tents to sleep off the first drunk of hunting season. When the final zipper sealed the last tent, Butch leapt into action, rising from his tent to gather and empty everyone's guns. The last thing he wanted was to be mistaken for a deer or a bear and get himself a bellyful of buckshot. By the time they realized what he was supposed to be, and what kind of prize bagging him would fetch, he planned on being long out of the costume and back in his tent. No time to load the weapons and give chase when the mysterious beast had simply vanished into the night.

Butch grabbed his homemade Sasquatch skin and hiked a little bit up the hill, which he supposed was really the crest of some unnamed mountain. A plump harvest moon dominated the clear night sky, full of seriousness and bright light, both of which served his purposes. When he reached the top, he slid into the costume, amazed at how easy the whole plan had been to execute thus far.

For a moment, alone at the apex of Dale's unnamed hill, he was left to wonder at how truly dimwitted his so-called friends were. He turned his mind for the briefest of moments to himself. Could it be possible that his own Bigfoot sighting was a setup by the very same folks who had been laughing at him the whole while? Naw. They weren't clever enough to make a costume, much less catch him at just the right time in the dark like that. No one else could have known he was moving hay at two o'clock in the morning. Just he and a jug of white lightning had decided on that impromptu moment of labor.

In the silence of the night, Butch thought he heard the snap of a twig breaking to his right. He could almost feel the pressure of eyes on him as leaves crunched underfoot from someone approaching. More likely *something*. A loud snort in the darkness confirmed this. Great. Just what he needed—some deer to wander into his path, then kick up a fuss and ruin his plans. But no, nothing sprang out or skittered by. Still, Butch couldn't shake the feeling he was being watched. Not that it mattered. Let some half-crazed possum or raccoon ogle him 'til the sun came up. Whatever it was, it was probably wondering if Butch was a real Sasquatch, which filled him with even more confidence.

Dressed and set, he watched the campsite from his higher vantage point, perhaps two hundred yards or so from the tents proper. He waited not in idle pause, but for something specific. Something one could all but set a watch by.

Jim's weak bladder needing relief.

Sure enough, at ten after midnight, Jim Walker crawled fully dressed from the confines of his cavernous tent and stumbled toward the bushes to do his business. Even at a couple hundred yards, Butch heard the steady stream of Jim's relief hit the ground. Just as Jim zipped up and returned to crawl back into his tent, Butch drew himself up as tall as he could, moved out into an open space between the trees to let the moon backlight his performance, raised his arms to the sky and growled loud and proud.

Jim snapped his head up to where Butch stood a-growling and a-raising a ruckus. The man stared in silent shock for half a second, then proceeded to holler blue murder. "Holy jumping jehosephats! What in tarnation is that?"

It was a scant moment before the others, also fully dressed, rolled out of their tents to find out what all the hoopla was about. Joshua held aloft a lit Coleman while Jim continued to babble to all the heavens and hells about what he was seeing. The quiet night carried their delicious words of worry right through the bucket's ear holes.

"What's with all the screamin'?" Dale asked as he rubbed his tired eyes.

"Yeah," Joshua said then yawned. "What's wrong?"

"What is that?" Jim asked in a yell.

"What?" Dale shouted back.

Jim raised a shaking hand to the monster on the hill. "That!"

Dale and Joshua turned as one to face Butch. Jaws dropped. Eyes went wide. Butch was even prepared to bet that underpants were just bricked.

All three men were quiet for a moment, but not for long.

"I think it's one of them Bigfoots!" Dale yelled.

Eureka! That single phrase made the whole thing worth the effort of two weeks spent slaving over a piece of work that no one could ever know he had made.

Jim said, in a voice so low Butch almost didn't hear it, "Well I'll be a monkey's uncle. Butch was right."

Butch was right! Butch was right! Butch wanted to rip off the mask and scream:

"I told you so! I told you I done seen a Sasquatch. You were my friends. You were supposed to believe me!"

Now it should be noted Butch's original plan was to duck down once spotted, slip out of the costume, creep back to the campsite and sneak back into his tent. In the confusion of looking for the Bigfoot, he supposed he would have plenty of time to make it back and pretend to have slept through the whole sorry affair.

But instead of ducking low and sneaking off, he got greedy. Greedy for more attention. Greedy for additional praise. Greedy to make them feel as sorry as he felt for the last three weeks. Instead of stooping, he stood his ground, growling and waving his arms. *I am Bigfoot Butch,* he thought. *And I was right!*

Dale was the first to scramble for his rifle, setting the thing to fire with an eerie and empty click. "What?" He paused and popped it open to look down the chamber. "I thought I loaded this thing."

"Give me mine!" Joshua shouted. "I know for a fact it's loaded." With a disappointed howl, he discovered his was just as empty.

"It's okay, boys," Jim said with his usual air of confidence. "I got Sweet Bessie, and she's always loaded." He reached behind him to the band of his jeans and pulled forth a pistol.

A .45 revolver, to be exact.

Sweet Bessie was a gift Butch had given Jim years ago.

Time seemed to stretch paper-thin as Butch caught the glint of blue steel under the bright harvest moon. A pistol? Who brought a pistol on a deer hunt? Jim Walker, apparently. Butch tried to crouch, but it was too late. Jim whipped the pistol around to an aim and fired before Butch realized things had gone far beyond his control.

The revolver cracked the night wide open with a loud report. Pain bloomed in Butch's gut. He stumbled back then forward, and before he could catch himself, he tumbled the whole two hundred yards down the hill, trailing a wide streak of blood and gut juice all over the moonlit trail behind him. Once at the bottom, he groaned and moaned and rolled about, clutching at the site of his now-gushing belly wound.

"Gee gosh," Dale shouted. "You hit it!"

"'Course I did," Jim said.

"You shot me," Butch groaned. In the muffled tin of the bucket, in which he'd drilled ear holes and eye holes but not a mouth hole, the words came out as part grumble, part growl.

"Good hit," Joshua said.

"I never miss," Jim said.

"I can't believe you shot me!" Butch yelled. Nothing but pained moans came out of the bucket mask.

"It sounds pissed," Joshua said.

Butch writhed at the edge of the camp, wishing the guys would stop fooling around and figure out it was all a game and get him out of the costume and into an ambulance.

Before anyone could do anything, a wild roar thundered from the top of the hill.

"What was that?" Jim asked.

Butch struggled into a sitting position as he held onto his belly and tried very hard not to die. He wanted to get the mask off, but the bucket must have suffered some damage in the tumble because it was now stuck fast on his head. He tried to motion for them to help him, to recognize how stupid and lame his costume was, but the other men were far too distracted by the new noise. The roar came again, this time followed by the crack of snapping tree branches and the rush of something approaching the camp.

Something very large, very strong, and very angry.

"Holy bananas," Joshua said. "Look at that . . ."

"There's another one!" Dale yelled.

Butch swiveled his head about to catch a sight he never expected to see again.

Bigfoot, or rather, Bigfeets. There must've been five or six, maybe even more. It was hard to keep count once they started pouring out of the tree line.

Three weeks back, in the dark of the cow pasture and from a respectable distance, the lone Sasquatch looked almost friendly. But here in the woods with the orange glow of a smoldering campfire and Dale's lantern, they were the most frightening thing Butch ever seen.

Each Sasquatch boasted a mouthful of madness: twisted, yellowing razor-sharp fangs they didn't mind presenting to the four frightened men. An easy eight feet apiece, they leapt across the campsite until the scene was saturated with Sasquatch. From the growling and roaring and great gnashing of teeth, Butch could tell these bad boys weren't here to ask for a cup of sugar.

They were here to kill.

Jim tried to raise the pistol, but the beasts were far too fast. Three pounced on him, tearing the man limb from bloody limb, tossing aside body parts and organs, which landed in a wide circle about the fray with a wet slop. A gurgling scream accompanied his slaughter, like some horrific soundtrack, until there were no lungs or throat or vocal cords left from which Jim could scream his death call.

Dale stood his ground, clutching his empty rifle and reciting the Lord's Prayer, but the beasts took to poor Dale in much the same manner they did Jim.

Ever the brave one, Joshua acted on natural instincts and tried to run like hell. The beasts were too quick and too good. One leapt upon Joshua's back and sank his sizable fangs into the man's neck and down they went together. Joshua screamed for three seconds before all went quiet.

Then there was one.

Butch trembled as he held his gut and squeezed his eyes shut and waited for the end. Instead of the end, a great snorting rose up about him, as if several dozen nostrils were taking in his smell. Part blood and fear and sweat and crap and piss, the costume was a miasmic mix of human stink and animal reek and who only knew what else after rolling down that path. Yet still the nostrils sniffed and snorted. A moment later, Butch left the ground as many hands lifted him then carried him Roman-style into the forest beyond.

Many big hands of many Bigfeets.

Was it the stink of his twenty-year-old carpet that saved his life? Or was it simply the look of the costume? Butch couldn't be sure about any of that. He could only focus on one question: What would happen to him once they realized the costume was just that, a costume and nothing more? A costume sheltering a human.

Thinking back on the preacher's sermon, and those seven words that got him into this whole mess to begin with, Butch decided he had to take matters into his own hands. With a wince, he released his tight grip on the belly wound, then stretched his arms out wide, almost reveling in the feel of his warm life fluid seeping into the depths of the filthy costume.

What would happen when the Bigfeet found out he was a man and not one of them?

With any luck, and the Lord's blessing, he prayed he would die before he was unfortunate enough to find out.

IN THE FORESTS OF THE FAR LAND

BY

CHRISTINE MORGAN

"I SHOULD HAVE brought my harp," Thorkild said as we sat by our fire, the dark woods gloom-shadowed and ominous around us.

"Your harp?" Fenbjorn snorted with scorn. "To kill with your singing what you couldn't kill with a spear?"

Ingolf and Guthdar laughed at that insult, and for a moment I almost laughed as well, but I stopped myself even before Fenthris elbowed her brother hard in the ribs. I did this not to win favor with proud and pretty Fenthris—well, not only that reason—but because Thorkild was my friend.

He might have been no great hunter—thin and scrawny and clumsy as he was—but he had still come with us, had proved himself brave enough, braver than those others of our friends who had stayed home to look after the fields and flocks, to fish and do farm work.

We six, we were the sons—and one daughter—of warriors, not farmers and fishermen. Our fathers had fought in great battles, been in the shield-walls and given slaughter to their enemies, before taking to sea in the long ships to seek this far land and make it their own. We had been raised from the cradle on tales of blood and plunder, swords and glory.

"A song would be nice," Fenthris said. She smiled at Thorkild, her golden hair gleaming. "Every hall must have a skald to sing and tell the stories."

"And is this our hall?" I asked, gesturing around.

It was no hall, of course. Not even a shelter. Just a camp we had made in a clearing, scraping away deep layers of pine needles to find bare earth, then making a ring of stones to pile branches and kindling at the center. We had logs to serve as benches, and our spears stuck in the ground so they stood jutting toward the star-pierced summer sky.

"If it is," said Guthdar, "which of us is the lord?"

That stirred some argument, good-natured though it was, with each of us putting forth their own right to claim. Ingolf was the oldest, already boasting a reddish fringe of beard. Fenbjorn had brought down the most game. Thorkild's family was wealthiest, as he reminded us by showing off the chain of silver he wore around his neck. Guthdar was the biggest, wide across the shoulders and stout as a barrel. I, Wulfric, was the quickest . . . and, some said, the cleverest.

"You cannot be lord if you're to be the skald," Guthdar told Thorkild.

"Well, he won't be skald in *my* hall," Fenbjorn said. "His music will curdle the milk and set all the dogs to howling!"

"You cannot be lord if Fenthris is to be the lady," Ingolf said. "She is your sister!"

Fenthris scowled. "Why must I be lady of the hall?"

"Because you are a girl," he said.

"So?"

"So, you will spin and weave and—"

She bounced a pine cone off his head. "I am a sword-maiden!"

"You don't have a sword."

"I have this." She drew her knife, which had a wide leaf-shaped blade, sharp-edged and tapering to a good stabbing point.

We argued a while more, coming to no conclusions but enjoying ourselves, passing the time while we roasted one of the hares over the flames, and ate it dripping with greasy juices, and chunks of bread torn from a loaf we'd brought with us.

The hunting trip had been my idea. Not because we needed the game, but because we were young and impetuous, chafing under chores and weary of having our elders looking over our shoulders. And they, for their part, were just as glad to have us out from underfoot.

"I don't want to be a lord," Guthdar said, gnawing at a bone. "I will be a warrior."

"Ah, you will not," said Fenbjorn. "You'll be a blacksmith, like your uncle."

"I'll be a blacksmith *and* a warrior," Guthdar said.

"You'll make horseshoes and cooking pots," Ingolf said. He made a rude noise and spat into the fire.

Guthdar bristled. "Swords and spear points, axes and mail coats!"

"For what?" Thorkild asked. "To bring battle to no one?"

We fell silent for a while at that, finishing our meal, handing around a skin of weak and watered ale.

What Thorkild said was true enough, we all knew. There were no kings here, no mighty war-lords to lead great armies or fleets of beast-prowed ships. We had no enemies.

Here, there were only us, and the skraelings.

I shivered, though I did not mean to, and had no reason. It was as if some strange foreboding passed over me, but I pushed it from my mind and ignored it.

"I'll sail," Guthdar said at last, as if pleased with himself for thinking of it. "I'll sail back to the countries of our grandfathers. I'll become a warrior there."

"I wouldn't mind having my own ship." Ingolf stirred the embers with a stick, watching the sparks fly. "I'd go wherever I liked, trading and raiding."

We had news sometimes, when men hungry for it—or hungry for the sea, old friends, fresh places and faces—took loads of lumber and furs to trade for other goods. We had visitors sometimes and new neighbors when more folk chose to follow and settle.

Only once, that I could recall, had a ship come to the river-mouth of our valley that, instead of spilling forth men eager to trade and talk, had spilled forth men eager to kill. I had been a lad of eight then, too young to do anything but go with my mother when she and the rest of the women took the children and fled up into the wooded hills.

I remember, though. I remember watching from that distance as the strangers came with their swords and spears. I remember my father in his bright helm, how fast he was, how agile, how shining a warrior when I had foolishly thought him a sedate old man with strands of silver in his beard.

I remember the fathers of my friends, likewise seeming young again, and gleeful. I remember their shields and their shouting, weapons jabbing and slashing, and how I had seen the red blood spurt high into the air, how I had heard the screams of the dying.

Later, when the work of men was done, our mothers led us back down and we helped with the stripping of the corpses and their ship. Fenthris had found her leaf-bladed knife then, and, though only a child, she'd used it with ruthless fury when one of the invaders proved to have some life left in him and clutched at her, begging for mercy.

I remember, too, my mother falling upon my father, her arms around his neck, sobbing. How he had held her, comforted her, even with the blood of battle still drying upon his hands. He'd given her a necklace of gold, and given me a bronze ring in the shape of a horse's head.

We might never know that battle fervor, the joy and terror. We might never seize plunder from our dead foes, and win glory and be known.

"I will have my own hall," said Fenthris, stretching out her legs to warm her feet by the fire. "I will command warriors, and reward them with treasure, and have feasts every night."

"And be a mighty *lord*," said her brother. "Lord Fenthris. Will your husband nurse the babies?"

"Who says I'll have a husband?"

"Of course you'll have a husband. Every woman has to have a husband."

"The daughters of Odin don't," Thorkild said.

"She's no Valkyrie," said Ingolf, whooping and slapping his leg.

I looked at Fenthris and thought she could be a Valkyrie, or a war-queen, but that she would certainly be no man's mild and gentle wife. It would be a waste of her.

"Well," Fenbjorn said, "you can have your small dreams, but I, Fenbjorn Fenrulfsson, will do better than any of that. I will be a hero like from the old tales. I'll fight giants and dragons, monsters and sorceresses. My name and reputation will live a thousand years after they bury me in a hall of pure gold."

When we were all done laughing at that, Fenthris glanced at me. "And you, Wulfric? When Guthdar is a warrior, and Ingolf a ship-master, when I am a lord and Thorkild a skald, when Fenbjorn is fighting giants, what will you be?"

I ran my thumb over at my horse's head ring, which I used to wear around my neck on a leather cord but could now fit upon my finger. I wondered if I would be as fast as my father. He had trained me and said I moved with his same speed and grace. But there was considerable difference between practice and the truth of battle.

"I don't know," I said, which seemed to disappoint her, disappointed them all. I was supposed to be the clever one and I could think of nothing to say, so I added the first thought that came to mind. "Maybe I'll make friends with the skraelings, and learn their ways, learn their wild spirit-magic?"

"Live among them?" she asked, teasing. "Have a black-haired skraeling for your woman and braid feathers into your hair?"

"They'll kill you," Ingolf said.

"They're peaceful enough," I said.

"They're cowards," said Fenbjorn.

"They trade with us."

"Only because they know we're stronger. They're afraid."

We did not often see the skraelings. When they did come, it was along the coast, paddling in their small and narrow boats, bringing fine furs, hides, and fish. They were broad-faced and brown-skinned, dark-eyed, with hair like ravens' wings. They had some other name for themselves but we called them skraelings for the way their words sounded, like the screeching of birds.

The fire burned low and we bundled ourselves into our cloaks to sleep beneath the high pine boughs that waved and whispered in the night breeze. I was the last to succumb, uneasy and restless, twitching to full wakefulness at every sound until at last my weariness overcame me.

I dreamt I heard my mother singing to me, and my little sister weeping. I dreamt my father stood over me, solemn and grim, as he held out to me in both his bloodied hands his sword, Ice-Wind. I dreamt of silence, and stillness.

I woke to pale dawn and Fenbjorn's snoring. My stomach felt sick, my mouth tasted sour. A nameless urgency beat within my breast, out-matching the pace of my heart, and I shook the others from their own slumber.

"We must get home," I said.

"It's early yet," said Guthdar, rolling over and drawing his cloak over his head. I kicked him in the hip and he sprang up, indignant, ready to fight, but I turned from him and grabbed my spear from where it stuck in the ground.

"What?" yawned Thorkild, his hair standing out in crazed sleep-clumps. "What is it? A bear?"

"Wulfric?" Fenthris watched me, her blue eyes wary.

I shook my head because I did not have the words, but somehow she understood whatever mood had possessed me, for she nodded and helped me break the camp.

We all shook the pine needles from our clothes, fetched our game from where we'd hung it so no scavengers could steal it, and set out through the woods toward the green river valley of home. Guthdar grumbled, and Fenbjorn protested the quick march I set, but a glare from Fenthris shamed them and they followed with no further objections.

The woods grew thinner as we neared the coast, morning sunlight trickling through the trees like golden honey. Soon, I smelled the salt air of the sea, and heard the raucous cries of gulls.

Many gulls.

"A storm must be coming," Ingolf said.

"The sky is clear." I pointed eastward, where no clouds loomed.

Fenthris tipped her head to one side. "The sky is very clear. Where is the smoke?"

We looked, and saw no smoke rising from the valley. No smoke from cook-fires and the ovens where bread was baked. No smoke from the smithy. No smoke at all.

Then we came closer, and saw the cluster of huts and houses that had been our village was now a butcher's yard, where the gulls feasted on the slaughtered corpses.

None of us moved. We just stared, the six of us in a line, eyes wide and mouths hung open, our spears dangling half-forgotten from our hands. There was a meaty thump as Fenbjorn let the carcasses fall.

And we stared.

Men and women. Children and animals. The grass and earth were dark with blood beneath their strewn bodies. Some were torn to pieces, some gutted so that flies buzzed thick over the heaps of their entrails.

There was another meaty thump, this one as Guthdar fainted. Thorkild whimpered like a child, and Ingolf spun away, heaving. I thought Fenthris might scream like a girl, but she only gripped my hand so tightly I felt the bones grind together.

The nearest gulls kept their oily black gazes upon us but continued feasting. I grimaced as they dipped their skinny, hooked beaks to pluck eyes from sockets, or plunged into opened bellies to pull out long strings of gristle. They threw back their heads, and their throats worked as they swallowed their gruesome morsels down their fat, insolent gullets.

"We have to help them," Thorkild said. "There might be survivors, wounded—"

"Oh, don't be a fool!" Fenbjorn shouted. "Survivors? Look around you. They're dead, every one, all of them, dead!"

He was right, but we did not want to believe him. We rushed into the village, running from house to house, calling the names of our parents, our family, our neighbors, our friends. The gulls flapped away shrieking and settled again in our wake, too greedy to leave even when we hurled stones at them. Theirs were the only answering voices, theirs the only movements besides our own.

A madness fell over us, one of anguish and grief and terror and rage. I cared nothing for what the rest did, conscious only of my own house and what I found there. The door had been wrenched loose, the furnishings thrown asunder in a terrible violence. The bodies of my mother and little sister were crumpled in the corner, broken like eggs. My father lay by the cold hearth, his head crushed, his limbs twisted at strange angles. He had died in his loose linen sleep-shift, bare-footed, and had not even had time to don his helm or seize his shield. His stiff dead fist held Ice-Wind's hilt and the sword's fine blade was stained with blood.

He had died defending his home. He had died a warrior.

I knelt and reached out, seeing the horse's head ring on my finger, and took Ice-Wind from his grasp. A numbing calm replaced my panic.

They had come in the night, those who did this. Come in the night while the folk slept. Come and killed them. Not raided, not raped, not robbed. I saw untouched valuables, and undisturbed food-stores. I saw livestock that had been killed in their pens and byres. Even our faithful hounds had not escaped the carnage, but nothing had been plundered nor burned. Our two ships were as they had been, drawn up on logs on the shore of the sandy cove, where we kept them when not planning a voyage.

Eventually, one by one, the others came to join me at the flat-topped stone the men had used for their witan-meetings. They looked as I felt: their eyes bleak and hollow, their faces stunned, their color ashen.

"All dead?" I asked, already knowing the answer.

"All dead," Fenthris said.

"Murdered," said Ingolf.

"It was the skraelings," said Fenbjorn, his voice ragged. "The cowardly bastard skraelings did this!"

"Then where are their dead?" demanded Fenthris. "Our fathers were warriors. Our fathers would have cut them down like stalks of grain."

"My father injured one," I said, showing them Ice-Wind's blade.

"They must have taken the bodies of their own with them," Ingolf said.

"You told us they were peaceful," Guthdar said to me.

"They were," I said.

"They murdered our folk!" He clutched a silver bracelet I recognized as one his mother wore. There was blood crusted upon it. His lower lip trembled. Despite his size, he was close to crying.

"Why?" asked Thorkild, plaintive. "Why attack us? Why attack us and take nothing?"

"And how?" That was Fenthris again. "With their stone-flake knives and arrowheads?"

"By treachery," Fenbjorn said with a snarl. "They came slinking in the night like curs and vipers to destroy us all."

I said, "But they reckoned without us. We lived. We *live!*"

"So . . ." Thorkild looked up at me, his cheeks wet from tears, holding the pieces of his harp. "What do we do?"

They all looked at me, expectant.

In the end, we realized we could not bury them. There had been more than fifty men in our village, and their women and children, as well as some slaves. We could not dig so many graves nor could we build a big enough pyre. It would have to be one of the ships.

We spent the rest of that day, the longest and hardest day we had ever known, gathering corpses. It was grisly work, and terrible. We carried them. We dragged them on sledges. We placed them in the belly of the larger ship, which was called *Sea Thunder* for the great cracking sound her oars made when they struck the rough water. We put staves and cudgels with each man so he would not go weaponless, but we saved back their swords, their axes, their bronze-tipped spears. We put tools, toys and other grave-goods into the ship as well.

Then we stacked the *Sea Thunder* with firewood and roof-thatching, and pushed it down the rolled ramp of logs until it floated in the cove. The sun had nearly set by then, making the whole of the western sky blaze with its own flames of crimson, orange and gold. We brought torches, lit the pyre, and said nothing as the tide swept the burning ship out into the vastness of the sea.

"If they see it," said Fenthris, "they will know they missed some of us, and return to finish it."

"Let them come," Fenbjorn said. He hefted an axe. "Let them come and die."

"You want to fight them?" Thorkild squeaked the words like a mouse.

"Vengeance," said Guthdar, who now wore his mother's bracelet on his own wrist. "We must have vengeance."

"Or die ourselves in pursuit of it," Ingolf said. "We'll die anyway left alone, the six of us."

"We won't . . . will we? Wulfric?" Thorkild looked to me again.

"We could survive a while," I said, sweeping an arm to encompass the empty village. "We have the food-stores, the shelter of our houses. We could even become farmers and fishermen." They made faces at that, and I did not blame them, for the words were sour on my tongue. "But we have no livestock, and Fenthris is right. Sooner or later, they'll return."

"Even if they don't," added Ingolf, "there's not much future for us here with one girl among the five of us."

Fenthris hit him.

"The four of us, I mean," he said, rubbing his arm where her fist had struck. "Since she *is* Fenbjorn's sister—"

Fenthris hit him again, splitting his lip against his teeth and knocking him down.

"That's enough!" I stepped between them, giving each a harsh glare. "We're not here forever. Traders have visited before, and other ships—"

"Yes!" Thorkild nearly danced in his excitement. "Other ships, or . . . we have the *Wolf's Jaw*! We can go away from here—"

"The *Wolf's Jaw* needs a crew of a dozen at least," I said. "If we set out in her, we will drift until we starve or sink."

"And if we must die," said Ingolf, wiping at the blood that had run into his sparse beard, "better to die in battle as our fathers did."

No one could disagree with him.

"We will not die tonight," I told them. "We will arm ourselves, and bring food, and hide in the woods again so we won't be found. Tomorrow, in daylight, we'll decide what to do next."

They did as I said. I found my father's mail coat, but it was large enough for two of me and heavy, so I did not wear it. His bright helm, I did take, and the belt and scabbard that went with Ice-Wind.

Soon, we were ready. We had food and weapons, and we buried a hoard of the most valuable items—gold and silver, amber and ivory, jewelry adorned with precious gems—deep beside the witan-stone. Then we went into the woods to hide, with no fire and with each of us taking watches in turn while the rest slept.

While the *others* slept.

I did not. There seemed no sleep in me, even after all the day's grief and hard labors.

Fenthris sat with me when her own watch was done, and we listened to the wind in the trees, and to Fenbjorn's snoring. Finally, she spoke and asked me if I did think it had been the skraelings who'd done the slaughter.

I shrugged. "You were right about their stone knives, and our fathers. How could they have done it?"

"Spirit-magic?" she said.

I loosed the breath I had been holding, and my shoulders slumped.

"You don't want it to be," she said. "You like them, the skraelings."

"I like them," I said, "but if they did this, I will finish what my father started, and kill as many of them as I can before I fall."

"You won't fall. You have us." She leaned over to press a quick kiss against my mouth, astonishing me so I could not put two words together. Then she was gone, back to her sleeping-place.

Thorkild, whose turn it was at watch, saw the kiss and grinned at me so widely I thought he'd pop like a pine knot in the fire. I made a show of scrubbing my hand across my lips, but in my secret heart, I was delighted.

Morning did come, though the sky was hazed and the sea was sullen. We returned to the edge of the woods to look out into the valley, finding it a still-dismal sight with the corpses of our animals being fed upon by the gulls and more scavengers. There was no indication that anyone had gone back there during the night.

We began a search for some sort of track or trail despite knowing if it was skraelings and they had traveled by their narrow boats we would, of course, find none.

But we did find tracks at the north end of the valley where a hill-stream flowed into the river and the ground was soft and damp.

Tracks. Not the pawprints of a bear or wolf, not the hoofprints of a horse or deer, but foot-tracks, long and five-toed, unshod, tracks like any of us might have made going barefoot through the mud.

Except . . .

"They must grow some big skraelings," Thorkild said after a few moments had passed, unease lending a tremor to his voice.

"Some very big skraelings," Fenthris said.

"Or giants," Fenbjorn said, and this time nobody laughed.

How could we laugh, when the tracks here measured more than twice the size of any of our feet, even Guthdar's? They sank deep, too, drawing puddles from the wet earth.

I turned to my friends and once again they all looked to me, and for that, in that instant, I hated them.

If I chose to abandon this and huddle in wait for the next visiting ship, they could do so, even with relief, and tell themselves they had only been following my lead. Any shame or cowardice or reluctance would be mine. The failure to avenge my father and mother and sister, ignoring my blood-duty, would be mine. Men might excuse it and say I could hardly be blamed—I was a mere boy, no warrior yet—but it would hang over me for the rest of my days, a stain on my reputation.

Fear crawled over me, like a host of living vermin between my skin and clothes. I shut my eyes, saw in the darkness behind them my father's dead, gray flesh, and opened them again.

"We go on," I said, touching Ice-Wind's hilt.

So we went on. The tracks led us up the hill-stream and into rougher country, where the brush was dense with brambles and the soil choked with stones. We found places where the bushes had been bent aside or forced apart. We found scraps of dark, coarse hair clinging to the thorns. There was a lingering stink to the air, a musky bestial reek that wrinkled our noses and churned our stomachs.

Then we found a skraeling.

A dead skraeling.

He was a boy even younger than Thorkild, ten or eleven at the most, and he had been broken like a child's doll made of twigs and twine. His body lay half in the stream, headfirst and facedown, so that his raven-black hair rippled in the water and his lifeless arms moved as if waving to us. He wore just a leather breechclout and wrappings around his feet. The splintered remains of fish-traps littered the stream's bank.

We found the skraeling camp next, or what was left of it. Their shelters of animal hides and long poles had been flattened, racks of drying meat smashed, baskets of nuts and berries overturned. More bodies, brown-skinned and half-naked, sprawled upon the dirt. Most of them had fought, but it had not saved them. Some wore head-bands of cloth they had gotten from us, woven cloth dyed in bright colors, for which the skraelings had a great fascination.

"Do you still think it was them?" I asked Fenbjorn in a harsh whisper.

He held his axe and shook his head, then pointed at more of the huge tracks stamped deep.

"Do you remember the story old Njalthan used to sing?" Thorkild spoke suddenly, louder than he might have meant to, and startled us. "The one of the king and the hall, and the monster and its mother?"

Fenthris, kneeling beside a skraeling girl of her own age, nodded. She had picked up the girl's knife, a chipped flake of stone with a handle made of antler, tested its edge, and discovered it sharp enough to bring a bead of blood to the pad of her thumb. "And the hero—"

A shrill cry and a rustle interrupted her before she could finish. We all spun as something came crashing through the brush. Fenbjorn was quick to bring up his axe, quicker than I expected, but I was quicker still in staying his hand, for I saw it was a woman. A skraeling woman with a baby on her back. She wore a doeskin dress, fringed and beaded. Her black hair hung in braids over her shoulders. She was unarmed, and frightened.

Sobbing and babbling, she rushed at us. She threw herself against Guthdar, who was closest and biggest. He twitched with shock but embraced her, as he blushed—she was wide-hipped and very buxom—and stared pleadingly at us for help.

We calmed her, or Guthdar and Thorkild calmed her, Guthdar patting her shoulder uncertainly while Thorkild attempted to speak to her in what few words of their tongue he had learned while helping his father in trading. The rest of us stayed on our guard.

"She ran when it happened," Fenthris said. "Ran and hid and got away."

"How do you know?" Ingolf asked. "You can understand her?"

"No, but she did. She ran to protect her baby."

We looked at the baby, which looked back at us, nothing to be seen but dark owl's eyes in a dark face framed by the rabbit fur that made up its carrying sling.

"What is she saying?" I called to Thorkild. "What did this?"

"Was it giants?" asked Fenbjorn.

He hushed us with an irritable flap of his hand and continued talking with the woman. Finally, he urged her to sit on a stump and she did so, rocking her baby.

"I think her name is Nittawowsew," he said.

We blinked at him.

"Nittawowsew," said the woman, touching her palm to her chest.

"And it was a hunt-camp," he went on. "They came to fish and hunt and gather food to take back to their settlement, but then they were attacked."

"So who attacked them?" I asked.

"She just kept saying the same thing," Thorkild said. "Saeaskewatta."

"What?" Fenthris furrowed her brow.

"Saeaskewatta." He uttered it slowly, clearly, but it still made no sense.

"Saeaskewatta," said the woman, bobbing her head.

"But what's that?" Fenbjorn asked. "A person? A name?"

None of us knew.

"Saeaskewatta." Nittawowsew pointed at the dead and at the tracks. Then she snatched up a clump of coarse hair like the kind we had found stuck to a thorn bush, and shook it in our faces. "Saeaskewatta."

A terrible roar shook the forest. Birds took flight, shrieking. We felt the ground shudder as if many horsemen were charging, and heard the snapping of branches. Again, we spun toward the noise, and this time it was no frightened skraeling woman.

This time it could only be the saeaskewatta, for they were like no other creature I'd ever seen or imagined.

I counted four of them as they thundered toward us, but there were more than that. Eight, or even ten of them came bursting through the trees.

My body seemed to turn to ice, as if the whole world froze in that instant, one I knew would be forever in my memory . . . if I lived to have a memory.

Each of the great brutes stood far taller than the tallest men in our village, and thick-slabbed with muscle. They ran upright, but not in the way that some animals reared up on their stubby hind legs. The saeaskewatta ran upright on long legs like ours, ran with a lumbering, loping stride. They had long arms as well, with enormous long-fingered hands. They were covered head to foot in pelts of coarse hair, dark and shaggy, matted, filthy and snagged with burrs. Their faces were lumpy and hideous, as if half-formed out of dung and mud and moldy bread dough. Their eyes were yellowish, wild with fury.

I thought of war-stories my father had told of the berserkers, men swallowed up by a battle-frenzy. I thought of legends of cursed men who became bears by moonlight. I thought of the tale Thorkild and Fenthris had mentioned.

Then I thought no more, because the nearest of the saeaskewatta was upon me. There were ugly, clotted wounds upon its body, and I knew with no doubt this was the very one who'd slaughtered my family.

I thought no more, because Ice-Wind thought for me.

Ice-Wind leaped and slashed, and my arm went with the sword.

A blow rang my head like a smith's hammer. If not for my father's bright helm, my skull might have split open from the force of it. I ducked and dodged, danced and darted, while Ice-Wind stabbed and cut and stabbed again. Blood sprayed. My foe roared his hatred at me, roared it into my face on a hot and rancid gust of breath.

I drove Ice-Wind straight into its stinking, gaping mouth. The blade scraped along teeth and sank into the back of the monstrous throat. More blood gushed out, a torrent of red, a flood, soaking me. I shouted with triumph as the giant toppled. It thudded to the ground, gurgling and choking.

I looked to see how the others fared and my triumph turned to dust.

Ingolf struggled in the grip of one of the saeaskewatta. I saw him slam his own forehead into the monster's face, its thick arms bunch and squeeze. I did not hear the crack of his spine but I imagined it, then Ingolf went limp and the beast shook him like a dog with a rag and flung his corpse aside.

Thorkild . . . I did not want to accept what my mind told me it was seeing. Thorkild lay on the ground; he should have been facing away from me, but his head had been twisted around on his shoulders so his wide eyes stared surprised into mine.

Nittawowsew wailed, cowering, clutching her baby to her bosom. A beast swept its gigantic hand but Guthdar was there, protecting her. I saw his mother's silver bracelet flash in the hazy sunshine. The skraeling woman ran away into the forest. Guthdar rammed up with his spear. The sharp bronze point gouged through hair and flesh, and the saeaskewatta bellowed. It caught him by his silver-braceleted wrist, and gave such a wrench that Guthdar's arm tore off at the shoulder, just as the hero in that old tale had done to the monster that raided the king's hall.

I saw Fenbjorn with his back against a tree trunk, two of the saeaskewatta trying to get at him, but he chopped hard with his axe each time they reached near. Chunks of their severed fingers plopped into the dirt. He was bleeding from a split scalp, turning his fair hair to a sodden scarlet mess. I gave a loud shout and raced to help him.

Fenthris leaped upon a beast as if she meant to ride it, clenching its shaggy sides between her knees. From each of her fists sprouted a knife, her own leaf-bladed one and the chipped-stone dagger she'd taken from the dead skraeling girl. She plunged both into the sides of the beast's neck, screaming with rage. It reached up and over, snared her by the tunic, and with its last ebbing strength hurled her headlong into the same tree her brother stood against.

I heard the crunch, and saw how the life fled from her, scattering, like a flock of startled sparrows. Fenbjorn howled her name. He became like a berserker then, his axe madly hacking at the saeaskewatta, his injuries ignored. I joined him and we fought them together in a red fury until suddenly there was nothing left to fight.

Four of them lay dead around us. The rest had retreated to the cover of the trees and waited there, hunkered low, wounded, watching to see if we were done for.

I went to my knees and on one hand. My head was down, hair hanging sweat-tangled in my face, my breath hotly heaving in and out of my lungs. I felt the painful jab of broken ribs and could not even remember being hit. My helm was gone and I could not remember losing it. I still held Ice-Wind, as if my fingers might never unclench from the hilt.

Fenbjorn collapsed near me. He looked at me, began to speak, vomited up a river of blood. A moment later, he died, his eyes still on mine.

The saeskewatta stirred, and crept closer.

I sank to the ground, kissed Ice-Wind's sticky blade, and closed my eyes. I mourned for my friends, but it was a grief mingled with pride. We had proven ourselves. We had avenged our families. They had died as warriors, and I—

I would not be following them just yet, because I heard another noise and rustle from the woods, and knew even before I turned my head and opened my eyes what it was I would see.

The skraelings had come. A fierce band of them, men armed with bows and stone axes, their brown skin painted with marks of red, yellow, and black.

Stone-tipped arrows sang from bowstrings. The shriek and screech of their war-cries filled the air as they brought battle to the saeaskewatta.

There were women and wise elders with them as well, led by Nittawowsew. They lifted me on a length of hide stretched between poles, and carried me away to their village. They tended me and healed me.

My friends had died as warriors.

I would live among the skraelings a while longer.

RONALD REAGAN VS BIGFOOT

BY

ERIC DIMBLEBY

RONNIE WAS APPREHENSIVE of the woods that surrounded them. The crickets chirped, but in a hesitant tone, as if the storm had not yet passed. Except for the occasional cricket, it was quiet. *Real quiet.* Sneaky, even. Like the Ruskies. Whenever you stopped and blinked for even a moment, they were upon you, breathing on your neck and cutting off your head without warning.

"Mr. President?" asked Paul, his new—and hopefully not temporary—head of security. "Do you still hear it out there? I don't hear it anymore."

"I'm eighty-five years old, son. I don't hear much of *anything* anymore," Ronnie replied, clutching tight to his father's well-oiled- and perpetually-cared-for- shotgun. His father, Jack, had never built up enough heart to actually use it during a hunt. It had become a sort of badge of honor that he preserved the gun for the Perfect Moment, one that he would never live to see. His hunting comrades had always nagged him for that, but it only made his resolve on the matter that much stronger. In fact, Ronnie was almost positive the thing had never been fired before, not by anybody, let alone his father. No time like the present to see what his daddy's Winchester was made of. It would most likely fart into the air, leaving Ronnie and his last remaining security guard easy pickings for their nightmarish visitor, but there was always a good chance the old girl had some fight left in her.

His father had always talked about that one Perfect Moment. The Perfect Moment, as far as Ronnie was concerned, was upon them, staring them in the eye. And it was pissed. They had stepped into its domain, and it was not happy.

I should have listened to Nancy. He repeated this to himself over and over again, a mental mantra to get him through whatever lay ahead. She had advised against his impromptu vacation. He had only just begun his autobiography, and so getting away from it all, to be only in the warming arms of his own mind, had been a prescription for progress. *Should have listened to Nancy. I'm such an old fool. My biography's going to end with my head on a platter. That thing is going to rip ol' Ronnie to shreds.*

He looked over at Paul, who was hunched beside him and trying to hold his composure. The room was void of light, only the shards of illuminated runoff from the moon darting through the trees. They were mostly pines, like most of Maine. Georgie Boy—interminably recommending visits to Maine, no matter who he spoke with—had recommended a cottage just a couple hours north of Baxter State Park, which was the last stop to No Man's Land, also known as Aroostook County. Ronnie would find tranquility, Georgie had said, in the thick of nothing, in a potato-farming town without a name. When you got far enough north, they stopped bothering with the naming of towns; they just designated them with random numbers and letters, everything but a bar code. Nobody would know him that far north. The locals barely were lucky if they had running water, let alone Wikipedia. He could go unnoticed for the entirety of his writing sabbatical, which was originally planned for four short weeks. He had brought along several notebooks and a typewriter. Nancy had recommended one of those new-fangled laptops, but when Ronnie had informed her he would be without electricity, she gasped. "Why would you torture yourself like that?"

Ronnie had only shrugged.

It was out there still, waiting for his move. He was certain.

Ronnie felt like a child, hiding from the monster in his closet. His sweaty palms ran up and down the Winchester Model 12. Surprisingly, his usually shaky hands were staying perfectly still. It had to be the adrenaline.

Did eighty-five-year-old bodies still produce adrenaline? he wondered, but couldn't be sure, although he was positive he was holding his composure better than that tub-of-margarine Clinton would be under similar circumstances and constraints. Maybe not Carter, though. Carter could hold his own against the creatures of the night. But definitely not Ford. Ford was a certified sissy.

Only an hour earlier, his security squad had diminished from four men to only a solitary soul, that being the wet blanket of the bunch, Paul. Paul wasn't much older than a freshly-hatched butterfly, so his presence was not as reassuring as Ronnie hoped it would have been. Paul had only just become the lead security officer in the former President's detail, and he was still green around the gills, unready to take on his new role.

"You think it's still out there, sir? I don't hear anything. It was banging around in the trees before it got Johnny and Greg."

Ronnie shook his head. He wasn't sure if it was still out there, but he knew it would not forget him. It would return, eventually. The look in its eyes had said as much.

Ronnie considered Johnny and Greg, guilty he had never learned their names until it was too late, after he had witnessed both of their demises. He could still picture those final moments of their lives, replaying in the back of his brain as if recorded to a VHS tape. Ronnie wanted to unspool the tape, to smash it beneath his foot and burn it, so he might never have to relive the moment again. The moment when everything changed. The Perfect Moment. Again and again, he squeezed his eyes shut and watched their deaths on the back of his eyelids.

Johnny had run from the woods after investigating the strange noises, calling out to Greg that there was a huge bear in the woods and that it was coming for them. Ronnie could still hear the cry Greg had given in response as he witnessed the eight-foot beast trudge from the thick trees, barreling into each trunk along the way, shaking the dead autumn leaves like nervous little wind chimes. Greg barely had time to react, pulling his pistol from the holster and taking aim at the juggernaut of a shadow.

"That's no bear!" Greg had called to his partner.

Johnny had started to call toward the house, to warn the rest of the staff and their prime directive, but he had been choked out in the middle of his gurgle. "Get to the c—" He had meant to say "car," that being the black Bronco—*a truck, really, thought Ronnie, not a* car—with the tinted windows and the miniaturized American flags on the hood. Johnny would never get to the car, for the beast had torn him in half, grabbing his left arm with one of its hands, whipping the security guard around. It had used the other hand to capture Johnny's hip. It had lurched and growled into the terrified man's face. Ronnie had been in the window, watching it all transpire. It wasn't so much Johnny had been ripped in half, but that he exploded from the sudden attack on his body. *Spontaneous combustion at the hands of a brute*, a coroner might have notated. Ronnie could still picture the chaotic spray of Johnny's blood. It had been just approaching dusk then, which was all the worse. Bad things came out in the dark, but *even worse* things came out while the sun was still in play. Just like those damn Ruskies.

Greg had fallen to his knees, shaken to his core and unable to react to the approaching monster. The thing stomped upon him with its foot, pressing Greg's neck into the ground. It paused from its one-two punch of attacking his two targets. They had provoked him, and so there was hell to pay. Greg had looked into the Bigfoot's wide black eyes in the final moments of his life The beast lifted its foot into the air and stomped upon Greg's throat, his windpipe smashing into a million bits, a splash of blood jettisoning from deep inside of his gut and out from between his lips. Ronnie had cried out, disbelieving the carnage he'd just witnessed. The poor man. Ronnie had only thought of the guard's family in that moment.

Mourning in America.

The guard's eyes went to another place and the Bigfoot glared at the brown cabin. Through the window, Ronnie could swear it had been looking at him. It had taken off into the woods, as if scared. *Or as if baiting them to follow,* he had considered. To play his game. To eat the worm. But that was then.

And this was now.

"We need to make a run for the car," Paul noted in a whisper. He had also failed to notice the vehicle was not a car, that it was in fact a truck. Ronnie shook his head, coming back to reality after an instant replay of Johnny and Greg's grisly deaths. It had only been an hour earlier, but it felt like a lifetime ago. For all the temperamental and sticky conflicts he had engaged in, he never witnessed a man being killed in cold blood let alone two men in the course of twenty seconds' time. It was horrific to think such a thing could ever happen to such brave souls. They would be missed.

A touch of wetness formed at the corners of his eyes and he started to dream of Nancy. It seemed entirely possible, quite likely in fact, that he would never look upon her smiling face again. She had stood behind him through everything. The Iran Contra affair. The death throes of the Cold War. *Bedtime for Bonzo.* The assassination attempt.

Sweet Nancy. He could picture her reaction upon finding that her loving beau had been decimated at the hands of a mythical beast. The headlines alone would ruin his good name for all eternity. He was old enough and had lived his fill of lifetimes, each as fruitful as the last, but there was no way the big hairy S.O.B. outside of his cozy cabin would be the nail in his coffin. Not now. Not this way. He needed to toughen up, like he had when he declared a war on drugs.

"We're not running anywhere, kid. That thing is still out there, I can feel it in my bones. And it knows we're holed up in here. I saw its eyes. It isn't the big dumb galoot you think it is, trust me. It's waiting for us. It knows we'll try and run like yellow-bellies, and when we do, he's gonna kick our heads off just like he did to Karl."

Karl had lost his head soon after the initial incident with Greg and Johnny. He had warned Ronnie and Paul to stay near the window as lookouts and to arm themselves for whatever was coming their way. By the time Karl had built up enough courage to inch his way out of the cabin, the sun was fully gone, blackness pervading the wooded glen around them. The Bigfoot was nowhere to be seen in the copse of trees and dead grass, but that was expected at such an hour. He could have been anywhere. Behind a tree. Beneath a rock. Right outside their window.

Stepping from the front door, easing his way across the rickety porch, Karl had descended the steps. He looked toward the Bronco next. The keys were in his pocket and there was no reason he couldn't start the thing up, signal for Ronnie, and be halfway back to the heliport in Bangor by midnight. He had reached into his pocket while Ronnie and Paul stared intently from the window. Karl grasped the keys and gave a half grin back toward his delicate assignment, giving the former President a hearty thumbs up. Each cautious step brought him closer to the vehicle, but then it happened.

It had been behind the truck, waiting in a crouched position for a bit of meat to come meandering into his path. The beast stood upright and walked around the car with a cool, calm, and collected demeanor as though he had done this a million times.

Ronnie had called to him, "Karl! Look out!", but it had been too late.

Karl had turned to face the thing and fired his pistol, which sent a bullet flying into the patch of woods beyond the Sasquatch, crackling into a tree trunk. The beast breathed slowly, rubbing its hands together. Ronnie could no longer see the thing's face, but he had seen enough fights in his day to know it was ticked off and ready for a brawl, whether Karl was a fitting competitor or not.

The beast had craned back on one leg, extending the other leg in a sweeping motion, clobbering the side of Karl's head. The agility of the Bigfoot was dazzling and unexpected. The sound itself had been dreadful. It reminded Ronnie of the husk being snapped off an ear of freshly shucked corn. Karl's head, now removed from his body, had rolled across the gravel driveway, clunking against the clapboards of the cabin. The Bigfoot looked at the window again and Ronnie was sure the thing was smiling at him. It had grabbed one of the little American flags off the front of the Bronco. With both hands, the monster snapped the flag, to which Ronnie knee-jerked a reply from between his dry lips, "You bastard."

Their deadly intruder retreated into the darkness once again, grunting in revelry.

Paul cried out, "Did he just karate-kick his freakin' head off?"

Ronnie didn't reply to this. He could only think about the head of his security team. Specifically, he could only think about *the head* of the head of his security team.

And now, in the silence of the cabin, after that grievous moment with Karl's decapitation, Ronnie felt the adrenaline rushing through him again as twigs snapped in the distance. "It's still out there, kid. You hear that one? I've got terrible hearing, but I definitely heard that. He's coming, I think."

"I heard it, too," the guard groaned.

Ronnie looked to his side and saw the gun dancing in the kid's hand like a Mexican jumping bean.

"You think that gun's gonna do any good, Mr. President?" he asked, looking at the gun in Ronnie's hands, on the verge of tears.

"We've got no choice in the matter. Sometimes, life calls you into action." Ronnie stood. His back screamed at him for engaging in such a youthful activity. It was no use having a bad back when readying yourself to battle a Sasquatch in the deadened woods. He rubbed at his lower back and propped the Winchester on his shoulder. "Get away from the window. It's not safe."

Paul complied, standing and pulling back into the deep darkness of the cabin's living room. He and Ronnie were only a few feet apart, but could not see each other through the blackness of it all.

"Let ol' Ronnie handle this one," he said, holding the Winchester up against his chest and approaching the front door.

"Is that thing even loaded?"

"My daddy always kept a box of bullets with it, and I've always done the same. Never had the need, but need just came knocking at our door. I've got one loaded. All I need is one, because I won't have time to get off a second, I reckon."

Paul smiled in the darkness.

"Please, Mr. President. Be careful," Paul said.

Ronnie felt bad for the kid, more than anything. It was a shame he was such a spineless jellyfish, but that was the way kids were today. No backbone, but lots of worthless opinions and that ridiculous Internet.

Nudging open the front door, Ronnie stepped out into the exact same path Karl had taken only a half hour earlier. He hoped to keep his head, unlike Karl, but didn't promise himself anything. He vowed to do what he could to see Nancy again and that was the best he could promise to himself, to her, and to God.

Stepping down the creaky steps, Ronnie felt his blood rushing through his veins. His finger firm against the trigger, the Winchester felt lighter than a feather. His arms were thinning and tired, as with any eighty-five-year-old man, but his will was all steel. Unbreakable. "Come out and let me show you the Reagan Method of ass-kicking." He clenched his teeth and paused, listening for the sounds of breaking twigs or padded footsteps.

Nothing.

He was only inches from the Bronco now and suddenly realized a weak point. Beneath the truck there was a blind spot. The thing could be beneath the truck, ready to grab his ankle and snap his foot off like beef jerky. How could have he been so stu—

Inside the cabin, Paul screamed, a caterwaul of blood and fear, pain and confusion. "Mr. President! Run!" Paul went silent.

Ronnie turned on his heels and jolted for Karl's headless body, fishing through his pockets for the keys, but then realized they were still clutched in his hand. "From your cold, dead hands," Ronnie whispered to himself, pulling the jingling keys free. He looked up toward the cabin, where the door was wide open.

Breathing.

He heard breathing from that layer of masked space, from just beyond the blackened door. It was there, looking at him, studying his next move. With his aching hip, he would never make it into the Bronco in time, and if he did, the Sasquatch would have overturned the vehicle or put his fist through the window by the time he had the ignition turned over.

He thought of Nancy. Of the kids. Of the nation he loved so very much, which had given him everything and had asked for nothing in return. He looked to his left. He saw the American flag, broken in two pieces, sitting in the dirt with the light of the moon gracing its red stripes and field of stars. The S.O.B. had to pay. There was no other option.

Kneeling, Ronnie took aim of the doorway. He only had one shell loaded, but that was all he needed to end this nightmare.

Paul's body, loose like a dummy, came launching from the door, landing with a dull thud in the dead leaves and grass before him, only a few feet away from his feet. It was meant to unnerve him, to disarm his senses. He wouldn't let in to those urges. He glanced down at the young man's face for a moment. He could barely make out the face. Most of it was missing. The Bigfoot had ripped it off like a curious ten-year-old did a bloody scab.

"I see you, dumbbell," Ronnie said, his voice unwavering. The actor in him took over. He was on the verge of soiling himself, but had to keep up appearances for the chess match of it all. This game was as mental as it was physical.

The beast grunted, huffing a steamy plume of breath into the chilled air.

"Come out so I can blow your dang head off."

It grunted again. A single footstep forward, calculated and precise. Ronnie saw the silhouette and the whites of its eyes, but not much else. It encouraged him to take the first shot, and then it would charge into action. The beast knew he was still far enough away that he would, by most odds, miss him completely. He was a weak old man, with no chance of getting a clean shot from afar. If it charged, then all Ronnie had to do was wait for his Perfect Moment and pull the trigger.

"Listen up, Mr. Bigfoot. I ended the Cold War. Next to that, you're nothing, *pardner.*" He had never done many westerns, but it felt good, that dirty twang dancing off his tongue. It felt macho, and effective.

But still, it refused to make the first move.

"BANG!" Ronnie called out with his voice, offering his best impersonation of firing the first gunshot. It was quite convincing, apparently, because the Bigfoot charged, growling and flailing its hairy arms. It acted as a child would on the verge of a bloody tantrum.

He waited for a moment, training the sight on the thing's head. A body shot would hurt it, but not kill it. The beast was too massive. It had to be a shot in the head. One shot, well placed.

"I'm comin', Nancy," he whispered to himself, pulling the trigger.

The Bigfoot fell without much fanfare, crunching the leaves. It did not move at first, then lurched for a moment. Again, it lay still. Ronnie felt the car keys in his pocket, which had a miniature light on them. He was certain the shot had landed in its head, but he needed to check, just to be sure.

Ronnie shined the light on the wound. He was correct. His shot had plugged the monstrosity on the left side of the forehead, right above the eyeball. It had tunneled directly into the brain, certainly killing it upon impact. The left side of its hideous head was matted with bright red blood and he couldn't help but laugh. He looked just like *Gorbie,* with the grape-jelly stain on his bald dome. He wished he had a camera, but even if he had, there was no time for that. He needed to get home and tell

Nancy the story of his brave security cache, how they had laid down their lives for him. It would make a great opening for his autobiography.

Ronnie versus Bigfoot. They'd never believe it.

He looked at the thing's yellowed fangs then turned for the Bronco. The engine started on cue, unlike most horror movies he had seen.

No, he whispered to Fate, *not getting Ronnie this time.* His Bigfoot was dead, no doubt. Good riddance.

Dropping the ancient Winchester—he still could not believe she had fired on command—and the box of shells into the passenger seat, he breathed heavily, finally feeling the panic setting in now that the ordeal was done.

Survival. That's what they call it, Ronnie. Survival.

Throwing the truck into reverse, he watched in the rearview mirror as he eased back against the house, three-point-turning himself back out toward the dirt road. The first couple hundred feet were fine, a smooth ride. He rolled down the window so he could hear the crickets, if only to feel human again. It was then he heard the sound of his tires. Hisssssssssing, losing air and fast.

"No, no, no. No! Come on, Lord. Give me a break here," he pleaded with a God who was not quite listening at the moment.

The Bronco came to a halt and Ronnie threw it into the parked position. He stepped from the door and examined the front tire with the mini flashlight. Flat. *Slashed,* actually. The beast was smarter than he gave him credit for, just like the Ruskies fifteen years earlier. He looked at the back tire next, which was more of the same. No chance of using a spare in that case.

"Mercy," he mumbled.

Twigs and branches snapped in the distance. Not from one direction, either. One to the east, another to the west, and a third to the southwest.

Ronnie reached across the seat for his weapon and for his box of shells.

It was going to be a long, cold night, and soon enough, it would be *morning in America*, and he planned on being there for that moment—that Perfect Moment—to raise his pride up the flagpole, to eat a Big Mac for breakfast, and wipe some Sasquatch blood from his hands.

To be the man that was once elected to the country's most lauded office and not the old codger he had become.

"Come and get it, you hairy Commies."

Sti'ya ha

BY

E.M. MACCALLUM

BEHIND JARED'S HOUSE was the highway. Beyond that was the vast untouched forest belonging to the Malcolm family. A very old family that had owned that land since the founding of the town back in 1876.

Jared sat in his backyard on the kiddy swing. He was almost too big for it now. His long legs cramped up and each time he swung too hard the entire swing-set threatened to tip over.

Clutching the rusted chains, he watched the cars zip past, their headlights blinding at first, but he'd force himself to stare into their glare even as they roared by. It left inky smudges in his vision as he focused on the receding red brake lights.

Palms sweaty, he adjusted his grip on the chains. Licking his lips again he nervously opened his mouth to say the word and felt his insides crawl, stopping him cold.

What if he did it wrong? What if he never found Mark? He could be dead. After all, it had been a year.

Having felt so self-assured only an hour ago, Jared began to second guess his decision. Glancing over his shoulder at the side of the house he saw the small scratch mark in its wood siding just below his bedroom window. The blood was gone at least, though its memory haunted him nightly.

Shaking his head, he gripped the cool chain until it hurt his palm, and focused on the highway. Tonight was the night. He couldn't chicken out now. The kids at his junior high school wouldn't be any kinder tomorrow. His parents wouldn't be any less distracted. His friend's wouldn't be any less missing . . . or dead.

No, tonight was the night.

The comforting weight in his pocket renewed his sense of bravado. It was his favorite pocketknife and at his hip he had his dad's fillet knife looped into his belt. It was the best he could do without raising suspicion.

He wiped his damp hands on his jeans, cleared his throat, and took a deep breath. His voice cracked as he said, "Sti'yaha."

On the highway, a horn blasted, drowning out his voice.

Grinding his teeth he abruptly stood up and stalked to the chain-link fence separating his home from the highway.

There never used to be a fence there. This had always been a safe place to live, but events spanning as far back as eight months ago had changed the face of the town. The peaceful, tiny community grew wary and untrusting. To Jared's limited knowledge, the worst that had ever happened in the tiny community was drunk driving and a few fender benders before this. No one ever died or disappeared, not since his dad was a kid. He said a tourist drowned in the river when it was high and the rapids were dangerous.

The chill in the summer air made goosebumps rise on Jared's flesh despite the sweat stains under his arms and against his back. Curling his fingers into the fence, he glared across the highway.

Further from the house so as to not wake anyone he said, "Sti'yaha."

For the past seven days, Jared had sat on the little swing and watched the highway. He wondered where his friend and neighbor, Mark Rabbit, could have gone. Mark vanished one night, right out of his bed. No sign of a struggle or hint of a prank. It wasn't like Mark to be gone so long.

His parents said they came downstairs the next morning and their backdoor was wide open and Mark was gone. There was no sign of a struggle. He didn't even take his shoes.

The phenomenon naturally gripped the small town in a vice, with gossip spewing from every corner like the time Clark Henderson knocked up Jessica Domer, who turned out to be his cousin who had been given up for adoption. The hair salons, coffee shops and stores buzzed with speculation and hearsay until Jessica's family moved away after the abortion.

The first day Mark was gone, Jared was convinced he was playing a prank.

Mark used to wander onto the Malcolm's land and start campfires, then leave them for people to discover. It was bad enough everyone thought that land was haunted. The Malcolm's had a reputation of being misers through every generation. Some folks said they could control Bigfoot to do their bidding and kill those that crossed them. And the ghosts of those who passed still supposedly haunted the acres of trees.

Jared often told the story to his little sister and her friends on sleepovers. It was hilarious when he and Mark would sneak outside the house to his sister's window and howl and snarl just to hear the shrieks and screams until Jared's mom would come racing into the room.

Frowning, Jared knew it wasn't just a story anymore. Maybe a little off, but Bigfoot was real. It had all started when they saw the drunk.

◆ ◆ ◆

Brendan spotted the man first. He was staggering half a block down from the 7-Eleven.

Nudging Mark with his bony elbow, he nodded to the streetlamp. The older man was hugging it as if it was a lover. After a heave, he vomited just off the curb. The tattered dark trench coat and cowboy hat hid his identity from view.

Mark wrinkled his nose. "Who's that friggin' guy?"

Behind them, Mrs. Donaldson hissed.

Jared kicked himself for not saying it first. Mark was always quick that way.

It was a new thing amongst the boys. Swearing or any word resembling a swear was *cool*. It was even cooler when an adult was present to cast the icy stare of disapproval. What snagged bonus points was that Mrs. Donaldson was the elderly woman who taught their grade eight English class. Her glares promised word getting back to their parents. Not that it mattered to Mark. His parents were rarely bothered by what he did, no matter how bad.

Brushing past them with obvious distaste, she ducked inside the 7-Eleven. It was the only store open this late; everyone else closed their shops at six.

Moving the slushie to his other palm, flexing his chilled fingers, Jared answered. "Looks like a new bum was kicked out of Kimberly."

Mark flashed a devilish grin. "Should we throw rocks at him and see if he can chase us?"

Brendan groaned. "I just ate that hotdog and bag of chips, man. He'd catch me for sure."

"And puke on you," Mark added before pretending to wretch on his friend.

Despite the dimness from the streetlights overhead, Jared could have sworn he saw Brendan pale a little.

The three adolescents watched as the man pushed himself off of the lamppost and stumbled into the alley.

Before Jared or Brendan could react, Mark bolted forward.

Jared fumbled, almost losing his slushie as he sprinted after his friend.

"Mark!" Brendan said, the pubescent squeak penetrating his command, making it lose all its value.

Mark didn't stop. He wouldn't even if Brendan had a booming voice like his dad.

Skidding to a stop at the first shadows of the alley, Mark squinted. "Hey, you!" he shouted. "You know you're trespassing, right?"

Trotting up beside his friend, Jared peered into the dark, allowing his eyes time to adjust. Curled up against the wall, his arms around his knees, the ragged man sat on the cold ground. The large-brimmed cowboy hat gave him away amongst the shadows.

Small pools of water from the recent rainstorm still offered a glitter or two from the lights outside the alley.

"Hey!" Mark advanced into the shadows while Brendan and Jared lingered on the fringe, still skeptical.

Brendan whispered to Jared. "I think it's Kenny Gritz again."

"No, dummy." He paused, frowning. His chance to accent his speech with a swear was tarnished. "Kenny's still in jail, remember?" He turned back to the alley in time to see Mark wheeling a foot back to boot the silent man on the ground.

Jared and Brendan both prepared themselves to run when a deft hand snaked out from the tatters of the drunkards cloak and caught Mark's foot.

With a shout of surprise, Mark lost his balance, his arms windmilling wildly before crashing to the concrete.

Brendan didn't hesitate. He took off down the street. The surge of fear almost sent Jared launching after him and if it wasn't for Mark, he would have.

He dropped the slushie, splattering it over his shoes and the pavement before darting into the alley shouting, "Let him go!" He already had a hand in his pocket, ready to wield his trusty pocketknife.

Unexpectedly, the man let go.

Mark crab-walked backwards, his expression changing from stunned to furious. Standing, he brushed himself off. "I'm wet!"

Jared reached down for his friend, hauling him up by his arm.

"You will leave me alone," the man growled in an even, slow tone. Not a single slur marred his speech as he lifted his chin. It definitely wasn't Kenny Gritz or anyone Jared knew from town.

The man was a Native American, which wasn't uncommon. The reserve was only a few kilometres to the west, but Jared knew most of them who came into town. It was a small town after all. He had never seen this man in his entire life.

Mark was about to protest when the man was on his feet. It was a swift movement, almost a blur, when he grabbed Mark, spinning him around and slapping a hand over the boy's mouth, stifling the scream.

Jared began to charge forward when the man froze him with a venomous stare. Something in the dark, shimmering eyes warned him to fall silent. If Jared hadn't glanced over his shoulder to see if Brendan had come back, he might never have known why he should keep quiet.

Across the street he could make out the outline of a very tall, broad figure. Hunched slightly with arms longer than most, it was wearing an exaggerated dark brown fur coat. It had to be the tallest—man?—Jared had ever seen. It was moving fast, wearily swinging it head from side-to-side.

Sprinting through a streetlight, Jared realized it wasn't a fur coat. Long tufts of fur covered it from head to toe, fluttering with each movement as if made of silk. Each step was calculated as if it was preparing to run or attack.

Jared couldn't do anything but stare as the figure strode quickly from his view. Its head was turned away from them, so he couldn't catch a clear view of its face, but the stature was undeniable.

Snapping his head back to the stranger, Jared whispered, "Was that *Bigfoot*?" The moment the words escaped his mouth he knew he sounded crazy.

Mark had stopped struggling, but his body was turned so he couldn't see what Jared had just witnessed, which was the worst thing that could have ever happened. If anyone on this planet needed to see Bigfoot, it should have been Mark. He had been obsessed with the beast ever since they were little. He had tons of books and videos on him.

"Let him see," Jared said, "if we get to Robbs Street maybe we can still . . ."

The stranger hissed. "You will not. The Sti'yaha is not to be toyed with. It must have hunted me here." The last part he seemed to be saying mostly to himself, his eyes wide and alert, unlike that of a drunk.

"Why were you puking back there?" Jared asked, hoping he'd release his friend. Shifting on his feet he wondered if he could kick him in the junk from here. That would release Mark for sure, though he recalled how fast the man was.

"I was running," the stranger said. "I thought I had left it behind. Get home now, and don't come out."

Pushing Mark forward, he started to turn when Mark tilted back his head and shouted to the heavens, shattering the silence.

Before the stranger could move to quiet his friend, Jared leapt at Mark and slapped a hand over his mouth. Leaning into his ear, he whispered, "I really saw it, Mark. We have to go after it. Shut up and let's go."

Mark wrinkled his forehead as Jared slowly slipped his hand away, confusion flickering on his face.

Jared wasn't sure how the man overheard him, but he responded just the same. "Do not chase it. It will chase you once it has your scent. It is a dangerous animal."

"He's lying," Mark said. "I've read all about them. Bigfoot are gentle creatures. You can't just go hunting them. Besides, if there was one in the middle of *our* town, we have to go find it!"

The stranger glowered at Mark and said, "They are not as they appear on your Discover Channel."

"Discovery," Mark said.

Waving a dismissive hand, the lean stranger continued. "The Sti'yaha is a nocturnal monster, bent on returning the world to the natural, primitive environment it once was."

Jared began to ask. "Why do you keep calling it Sti—?"

He was interrupted when the stranger jerked his arm as if to backhand him.

Staggering back, Jared held up his arms, expecting the sharp pain, but it never came. Mark gaped at the warning, though the surprise was fleeting.

"Do not say its name." The stranger hissed, eyes darting past them to the street. "You are not yet old enough."

Mark snorted. "We're not children. I'm in junior high, buddy and I'll be damned if I can't say some *name*."

The man glowered at him before spinning on his heels. He suddenly sprinted down the alley, the tattered trench coat fluttering like a cape.

Mark started to run after him. If it was for Jared grabbing his arm, he might have. "Come on. Maybe we can see it still," Jared said. Honestly, he wanted a second glimpse. Though he knew he had seen it, he was already wondering if what he saw was *real*.

Mark paused, the temptation overriding his anger for once. Turning to face his friend, he said in a lowered voice, "Did you really see something? You're not joking around, are you?"

Adamantly shaking his head, Jared pointed to the street. "It was only there a second." He tugged on Mark's arm. "Come on!"

He didn't need much more convincing than that, and the two boys took off.

After darting across the street, they skidded to a stop in the exact spot where Jared had seen it. "It was right here. It was big and hairy and—" He gagged he was so excited.

Mark remained perfectly still, his eyes wide while Jared struggled to hide his nose and mouth in his hand.

"What the heck is that smell? Did the sewer back up?" Jared asked.

Mark shook his head. Whispering, he said, "People say that Bigfoot has a bad smell."

"Wouldn't predators find him easier that way?" Jared didn't dare remove his hand. Though it didn't completely stifle the fetid stench, it reduced it enough for him to speak without feeling bile at the back of his throat.

Shaking his head again, Mark motioned up the street. "Maybe it's still here. Jared, do you know what this means?" His voice was soft, but cracking in his excitement. "We might have a real, live *Bigfoot.* We might have a—what did he call it?—*Sti'yaha.* Let's see if we can find it!" Thrilled, he was already turning in circles, searching the walls, the streetlamp, the ground.

Jared nodded though he doubted he'd be able to deal with the smell much longer.

Mark's eyes glistened in excitement when he bent to pluck the long dark hair from the sidewalk. How he managed to see it in the dim light was beyond Jared.

Holding it up, he said, "You think it's his?"

Lowering his hand from his face, Jared realized the air had cleared itself of the foul odor, and shrugged. "Or Mrs. Donaldson's."

"Ugh." Mark dropped the foot-long dark hair.

Together the boys searched the darkened streets for any sign of Bigfoot, but it never showed.

Mark used a payphone to call Brendan's cell—being the only one of them who had one—and told him what he missed. He did embellish a little, saying he had actually seen the Sti'yaha and that they were hunting it down while Brendan ran off like a wuss. They had a good laugh about it before heading their separate ways.

The next morning, Mark was gone.

◆ ◆ ◆

Three days later, Brendan turned to Jared and asked, "I was thinking last night what if that Sti'yaha thing did get Mark? Maybe it's not a joke after all."

Jared, who was still obstinate it was all a hoax, wasn't about to be fooled by one of Mark's pranks again. They had kept the Bigfoot tale amongst the three of them, not wanting to be considered complete idiots. Mark's parents reported him missing the morning he disappeared, but otherwise they didn't seem very distraught.

This wasn't the first time Mark had vanished. When they were eight he wanted to run away. He hated the town and his parents were fighting a lot. No one really spoke about his mother's bruises much. They came and went and it was only when his dad was really drunk. The AA meetings had helped a bit and his father drank less now than before.

Walking home from school the last three days, Jared kept looking over his shoulder. He expected Mark to come flying out of the bushes any minute to surprise them, but Mark never showed up.

Reaching Jared's house first, Brendan said. "Do you think that crazy man was right about those things?"

Jared shrugged, ready to go inside. He found himself staring at Brendan and his friend refusing to budge. The pause was drawn out much longer than needed, so he awkwardly asked. "Did you want to come in?"

Brightening as if this was his plan all along, Brendan nodded. "Yeah, you want to do homework?"

Jared gave a start and stared at his friend to see if he was messing with him. Brendan never did homework.

"Uh . . . sure," Jared answered. Truth was, he didn't want to do the Math homework assigned. He wanted to watch TV and eat the brownies his mom stashed in the downstairs fridge.

Resolved to be a good friend, he opened the front door and invited Brendan inside. Trailing after him, Brendan squirmed, picked his teeth and fidgeted like he had to pee. At one point Jared's mother asked if Brendan was all right, then asked Jared in private if he was high. By the end of the evening, after Brendan stayed for supper and lingered in the foyer for over a half hour making pointless conversation, he was asked by Jared to spend the night.

Left in his room, Jared eyed Brendan from his bed for several seconds before the curiosity got the better of him. He knocked Brendan's sleeping bag with his foot, hard enough to jolt his friend. "What gives?"

Brendan grunted from the floor, having shifted the sleeping bag closer to the bed from where Jared had originally rolled it out. "I just don't feel good."

Jared knew if Mark was there he'd tease Brendan about being a scaredy-cat—but he wasn't. It occurred to Jared maybe Mark wasn't joking. Maybe he really was missing, but if he was, where was he? The cryptic question made him feel uneasy so he usually left it in the back of his mind. It was finally getting the better of him.

"Do you think Mark is really missing? I mean, *for real* missing?" Jared whispered.

Brendan's breathing answered for several seconds before he dared a reluctant reply. "I don't think it's a trick anymore. I looked up the name of that thing on Google and I found out they were mean and took people in the middle of the night while others said it was really gentle. I'm scared, Jared."

Jared allowed the words to soak into his brain before propping himself up on his elbows. "Do you think Mark is dead?"

This time Brendan didn't hesitate. "Yes."

The single word destroyed the conversation.

Flopping back onto his bed, Jared fell silent and Brendan didn't add anything. Though neither said it, Jared knew they were both wondering the same thing: was their best friend dead?

It was hours before Jared fell asleep. He didn't even realize he drifted off until he heard the shuffling. At first he thought it was just Brendan coming back from the bathroom until he felt the chilly breeze brush over his bare leg, which hung over the side of the bed.

He turned his head and saw his bedroom window open.

Groggily, he rubbed his face when he heard the shuffling again, but this time he knew it wasn't coming from inside the bedroom.

It was outside.

The putrid stench made him choke at first. He vainly tried to breathe fresh air, understanding within seconds that there wasn't any.

Rolling over, his eyes snapped to the rumpled sleeping bag on the floor. It was empty.

Within a heartbeat he was scrambling out of his bed and diving for the window as the piercing voice ripped through the air. The guttural howl was almost human if it wasn't for the phlegm-like undertone that gurgled beneath.

It was close, so close, it chilled the blood in his body, bristled every hair.

He hadn't realized he wet himself until after he heard the scream and felt the warmth trickling down his leg. It hadn't been the beastly bellow of a wild animal, it was a boy's.

The house clamored awake with noise.

His father barreled into his room first, wide-eyed and frazzled. His hair stuck out in every direction with lines from his pillow still etched in his cheek. Already he was in the middle of a question before Jared simply gestured outside.

Where was Brendan? Was he out there with that thing?

He glanced down at the sleeping bag. It was kicked open. Why didn't he wake him? Why sneak outside? An image of the large, hairy creature across the street, eyes gleaming in the lamplight, made him pause.

Appearing behind his father, his mom fumbled with her bathrobe and wrinkled her nose at the stench. "What the heck are you boys doing in here?"

Without answering, his father bolted down the hallway to the back door of the house. The hallway was right next to Jared's room and he could hear him banging around in the gun cabinet.

His mother flicked on the light, blinding him.

"No!" He bolted for the switch, switching it off. He didn't want whatever was outside to see them. What if it would come for him, or his sister or his mom or dad?

Jared took off down the hallway. "Dad!"

"Where's Brendan?" His mother was hot on his heels. She grabbed his shoulder and spun him around.

Wrenching away, Jared said, "Something took him out the window!" He took off again and almost ran into his little sister, whose long dark hair was twisted in an unruly rat's nest at the back of her head. Rigid and scared, she didn't dare get in the way or offer any help, which was fine by him. The last thing he wanted was for his little sister to get hurt.

The backdoor was left open by the time he reached it. His throat suddenly closed—not just from the fetid smell, but from the terror that triggered an adrenaline rush.

A gunshot pierced the air, deafening his hearing for several ringing seconds. He stumbled outside, his mother bellowing something after him. He wasn't sure what.

His father faced the highway, where the fence would soon be erected.

Standing outside the doorway he covered his mouth and nose with his hand to save himself from the choking smell. The cold air against his soiled boxers made him distinctly aware he should have changed before coming out.

To his left he noticed the broken branches scattered on the lawn.

Inching closer, his back to the house, he reached the edge and peered around the corner to be safe.

It was only him and his dad out in the yard, but the closer he moved to the wooden fence separating them from their neighbor's yard, the more shadows there were.

He noticed for the first time the wall below his open bedroom window. In the moonlight he could make out three shallow grooves scratched into the wood paneling. Swallowing hard, he saw his father running toward the highway, shouting Brendan's name, when he noticed the ferns. His mother's beloved ferns. She had taken them from Grandma's garden after she passed away saying they reminded her of her mom. Tonight, they had been tainted.

The edge of three of them had been trampled. Something shimmered in the moonlight. At first he mistook it for a drop of water, but it was too dark; even in the shadows water didn't look like that.

Kneeling in the grass, he pulled the fern out into the moonlight. Something wet and sticky soaked his bare kneecap.

The gunshot went off, his father aiming across the highway at something on the Malcolm's property.

Jumping to his feet in surprise, he jerked his chin down to see the same blackened liquid stain coating his knee. Staggering back he heard his mother's frantic voice on the phone with the police.

The neighbors were waking up. He heard Mr. Wong cursing something in Mandarin as he staggered into their backyard, near the highway to argue with Jared's father.

Mark's parents had their lights on, but they hadn't come out yet.

His father was shouting at him, but it was as if he was shouting down a tunnel. Swaying on his feet, he leaned back against the side of the house, his heart jack-rabbiting when he saw the hand.

Nestled beneath the ferns, severed from the owner, it was a small, hairless, human hand.

His stomach twisted and he heaved at the sight. He sunk down the side of the house.

Jared's gaze swept a foot to the left and in the darkness between the house and the bushes beside the fence was a tattered hunk of flesh. He wasn't sure what it could be. It was large, bloodied . . . maybe a torso? His vision began to fade at the edges and he felt as if he was going to vomit.

He heard his name being shouted over and over in the distance, but when he tried to turn his head to look, his stomach reduced itself of its contents and everything went black.

◆　◆　◆

This time the eyes glowed with the aid of the headlights and Jared was convinced he had seen something across the highway.

What Brendan didn't mention about his research was children were admonished to ever speak the name, "Sti'yaha."

For a long time Jared and the figure across the highway stared at each other.

The figure seemed shorter than he remembered. It had been over a week; he didn't think it would have made *that* much of a difference.

After Brendan's body was found practically torn to pieces at the side of his house, he told everyone what he knew. They all thought he was crazy—his folks, the few other friends he had, the RCMP and even the psychiatrist his parents hired—but he had done his homework. Sti'yahama were like the old Indian had said: bent on making the world their own again. They were sheer evil, stealing horses and animals in the middle of the night. When children said their name, they'd snatch them away. Jared had never spoken their name, not once, until now.

Climbing over the fence, he took his time, carefully watching the dark figure. It didn't move to greet him, it didn't attack or disappear either—it just watched him, eyes glowing and unblinking when the single passing car sped between them.

Reaching the edge of the highway, Jared waited as another car approached. He could have sprinted across in time, but he wanted a better view of his foe and to gauge where it was and where to cross. His hand moved to his hip, ready to unsheathe the fillet knife.

The car zipped past and for a moment he didn't think he understood exactly what he saw.

"Mark?" he asked the dark.

It couldn't be. The boy across the road looked haggard, dirty and disheveled.

He had the same dark hair, big dark eyes. He even looked as if he was wearing the same clothes the day he disappeared. Dark T-shirt and jeans, though they had been soiled beyond anything salvageable.

"Mark!" he shouted and staggered forward. The look in Mark's eyes stopped him from coming any closer.

The fetid stench had returned, forcing him back several steps, and he whipped the fillet knife from his belt. Holding it out in front of him, he caught movement out of the corner of his eye. Swinging the knife toward the trees, he made out the tall, lumbering figure just within the shadows.

Freezing in place, he heard the thing grunt; the familiar gurgling undertone sent chills up his arms.

Mark glanced at the creature and grunted back. It sounded nearly as fierce, but something had passed between the two of them, an understanding Jared couldn't quite grasp.

"Mark, what's going on? Everyone thought you were dead."

Mark peeled back his lips and hissed.

Taking another step back toward the highway, Jared heard the car approach. It honked its horn as it roared by.

"The Sti'yaha" —Jared pointed at the shadowy figure, trying to keep his face from scrunching due to the smell— "you're living with it?" The words spoken out loud caused him to realize something: the beasts were seeking a way to revert the world back to its most basic, primitive state. Why not recruit? Mark loved the idea of Bigfoot. Brendan said the name out loud. *He* had said the name out loud. They all did.

"What happened to Brendan?" he asked Mark, caution ringing in his voice.

Mark gurgled a response, which was replied by the monster in the shadows. To Jared, Mark spoke for the first time, his voice gruff and tainted, but clear enough to understand. "Why not find out?"

Unprepared, Jared never saw the hand until it struck his head.

His world tilted and before he could protect himself, he landed in the grassy ditch on his side.

Mark was on top of him in an instant, holding him down, his knee digging into his ribs. It was as if he didn't see the knife in Jared's hand, poised to use, though Jared didn't think he could anymore.

He expected a monster and instead he got his best friend. "Mark, what are you—"

"Come with me, Jared. Come with *ussssss.*"

The way his voice hissed at the end of the word made Jared jerk and squirm to buck Mark off of him. "What? Where?"

Mark hopped off of him before he could start to protest. Landing on his feet like a cat, he hunched his back, just like the Sti'yaha in town had a week ago. It was as if he was a mini-Bigfoot in training. If it wasn't for the fierce shine to his eyes and the predatory stance, Jared might have thought it funny, though the memory of Brendan's bits against the side of his house removed any sense of humor from his thinking.

"To be like you or Brendan?" Jared struggled to his feet. His movements were slow and even awkward compared to Mark's.

"Brendan wussed out," Mark spat in disgust. "You won't though. You and me, we could be like them, Jared, and take back what is ours."

Swallowing hard, Jared adjusted his grip on the knife, sweat making it difficult to hold. He tried to imagine Mark doing that to their friend. No, not Mark. He couldn't have. It must have been the Bigfoot in the trees. He remembered the gruff howl as if it was yesterday, but Mark didn't seem the least bit remorseful. He didn't even try to stop it and now their friend was dead because of him.

Preparing himself for an attack, he said, "Y-you nuts?"

Moving fast, Mark launched himself at Jared. Crashing together they fell back on the highway. Jared stiffened his neck so not to crack his skull onto the pavement as Mark's weight pressed down on him.

The headlights of an oncoming car veered, tires skidding on the road as the vehicle barely missed them.

Mark landed on top of Jared, the air rushing from his lungs. The fillet knife had penetrated, sinking deep into his friend's stomach before either of them knew what happened. Warm, sticky blood coated his hand and he saw the terrified expression on Mark's dirtied face. Hair had sprouted on his face, hair that hadn't been there before on his forehead and the bridge of his nose.

"You were supposed to join us," Mark said.

"Like Brendan?" Jared asked. He couldn't stop the shaking in his hand as Mark rolled off of him with a groan.

The large Sti'yaha thundered from the tree line. At first, Jared was certain it was coming for him, to finish him off, but it ran straight for Mark.

Mark mewled at it, an air of trust to his cry. The beast scooped him up in its oversized, hairy arms like an infant.

Neither the Sti'yaha nor Mark saw the Mack truck as Jared scrambled for the edge of the road. The headlights illuminated their figures . . . but it was too late.

Brakes squealed, headlights flared, and Jared felt two hands grab him from behind lifting him from the ground.

He screamed and yelled until he was spun around and found himself face-to-face with the Indian stranger in tattered clothes and wide-brimmed hat.

"We must run now," he said, eyes bright with a sharp intensity. "They know your scent."

"Wait, what? I killed it. My friend . . . he could be hurt . . ." He glanced over his shoulder to see the hairy beast crumpled and bloodied on the road. Mark must have been thrown off to the side; Jared couldn't see him anywhere in the dark.

The old Indian grabbed his arm hard. "You think there is only one? You think they didn't all see? You're like me now, boy, we're fighting a battle here, you and I. If you want to survive, you'll run. Your friend is no more. He is Sti'yaha."

The Sti'yahama ululation filled the mountain air, coating the town with its foreboding message.

Pulled by his sleeve, Jared half-ran, half-stumbled with the stranger and jumped into the passenger side of the old Sedan idling at the side of the road.

His eyes rolled to the older man in the driver's seat, choking back the emotions that threatened to overtake the adrenaline.

Noticing his stare the man nodded. "Name's Terry."

Hearing his voice shudder, Jared asked. "Where are we going, Terry?"

"Hunting, boy. We're going hunting. Might as well get acquainted with each other. We're on our own now."

Jared had considered that this may be the last night he saw his family or what remained of his friends, but not like this. Wiping his bloodied hand on his jeans he fell silent as they drove down the highway. Terry said that they'd catch a hotel for some sleep and would start the next morning.

The Sti'yhama knew them and would be hunting them from now on, unless they got to them first.

BIGFOOT VS GRANDPA

BY

ERIC J. GUIGNARD

"GRANDPA, WHAT REALLY happened to your hand?" Freddy asked.

"Eh, what's on my hand?"

"No, what happened to it. Why don't you have it anymore?"

"Oh, this here? I thought you knew already. It was bit off by a Sasquatch. That was back in the early spring of 1889."

Freddy paused, waiting for his grandpa to elaborate with a colorful yarn. Grandpa didn't and went back to absentmindedly reading a Jack London novel, cover crumpled and pinched from the imprints of the old man's metal split-hook left hand. Freddy and his grandpa sat on opposite ends of a sagging linen couch.

"Dad said you had a hunting accident," Freddy announced.

"Well, I guess that's one way of puttin' it. I was out huntin' a Sasquatch."

"What's a Sasquatch?"

"Your generation calls him the Bigfoot, but that's just a nickname some dimwit yellow paper journalist called him. It'd be like callin' a raven a 'black feather,' just on account that the bird has black feathers. Not very inventive, if you ask me."

Freddy wrinkled his nose as if he smelled something that was beyond ripe. "A Bigfoot, Grandpa? There's no such thing as Bigfoot. That's just a fairy tale."

Grandpa abruptly sat back, visibly appalled at the heresy that fell across his ears. He looked at Freddy over the top rim of his thick reading glasses and laid the book onto one knee, tales of foreign adventure instantly forgotten. "A fairytale? Boy, fairy tales are for little girls where knights ride in on horseback and save some broad from an evil witch. Fairy tales ain't true, but the Sasquatch sure is. He's as real as the stink from a summer outhouse."

"Are you pulling my leg?"

"Your leg? Shoot, I was about to ask you the same question. Sweet mother of Abraham, what do they teach you in school these days?"

"Math and reading, I guess."

"Well, then, you need to get to readin' about Sasquatch. There's plenty written about him. Sasquatch is a wily beast. He ain't big on socializin', but there's enough folks all over the world that can attest to his livin' out there in the woods."

"How come I've never seen one?" Freddy asked.

"Have you ever looked for a Sasquatch?"

"Well, no, not specifically."

"Sasquatch ain't gonna come out to you and declare 'boy-howdy'! Besides, you don't ever want to see him anyways."

"So how did *you* see him?"

Grandpa let loose a long sigh and a fart. Fred the senior would be back in an hour to pick the kid up. He knew he shouldn't, but he figured it was time to tell his grandson about Sasquatch, to educate him a little on what lie out there lurking in the shadows of the world. He supposed if his own son and the school system had their way, Freddy would never hear otherwise. Grandpa peered out the dusty window. The sun was starting to go down and the night bugs were flying up. It was just about this time of dusk when the whole thing had first started.

"Well, Freddy, I must have been only about twenty-one or twenty-two years old back then and was courtin' your grandmother. I wanted some extra money to buy her pretty things, so I went out trappin' with some other fellers up in the mountains. Times sure were different back when I was a young man," he said, scratching the side of his whiskered cheek with the tip of the metal hook hand.

Freddy eagerly moved closer to him, turning sideways to sit cross-legged on the stained old cushion. He faced the chronicler of tale directly, eyes lighting up in anticipation.

Grandpa went on. "Like I was sayin', it was the early spring of '89 . . ."

◆　◆　◆

The sun was starting to go down and the night bugs were flying up. Mosquitoes, gnats and moths were hovering in the air fluttering toward the light of the campfire that Curtis had just kindled. The mesquite smoke wandered gently through the darkening air as the men sat down around the fire outside of the small log cabin. A tin of beans mixed with rabbit meat simmered over the fire and the men passed around a bota bag canteen half full of whiskey. The three white hunters sat on one side and their Indian guides, Joseph Redpaw and Tyee sat on the other.

"Well, boys, it's getting to be slim pickings out here. We've either killed everything off or scared it away. I'm saying it again. After tomorrow, I think it's time to pull in the traps and head on back."

The Indian guides looked at Curtis as he spoke, then at each other and shrugged their shoulders.

Willie spat into the fire. "I ain't ready to go back yet. We've hardly got anything. A few furs and some elk meat."

"Shoot, I'm agreeable with Curtis. I've got a little lady waitin' for me back in town that I'm fixin' on makin' an honest woman out of. The longer I'm up here, the more I get to thinkin' that some other feller's gonna make his move first," Fritz said.

"Now, Fritz, why'd you want to do something dumb like that? I can sell you an ass that'll kick just as hard, but at least you can put her out in the barn each night."

The men chuckled. Even with the marginal stores, they were in good spirits. The recent rain had let up and worries floated away like the mesquite smoke on the wind.

While they sat there, a sudden screaming roar thundered away nearby, up the mountain slope. Birds shot out of trees like arrows darting through the air. The men froze around the fire at the volume of the echoing vulgar sound. Joseph Redpaw and Tyee spoke Klickitat stealthily in swift hushed tones and started to creep away from the others.

Fritz grabbed his rifle and stood up in excitement. "Sounds like maybe we caught us a bear? I'll go check it out."

Willie stood with him. "I'll go with you. That don't sound like any bear I ever heard."

They loaded up their rifles, older model Winchesters from post-Civil War industry, and then commenced to jog quickly up a gentle dirt path brushing through branches of pacific silver fir and mountain hemlock. The sun had nearly descended from sight and the sky was now a murky swirl of indigo and maroon. Dark shadows crawled through the underbrush and twigs snapped. Ahead, a strained commotion was heard, that of loud grunting and thrashing.

Fritz reached the edge of the clearing first. He stopped abruptly under a conifer's thick cover. He knelt down slowly and motioned for Willie to do the same. Before them struggled an image that nightmares were born of.

They had caught a monster in their steel bear trap. A monster Fritz could never have imagined: twice the size of a grizzly bear, but black as a fresh-tar road. The bear trap's massive metal jaws were locked tight, slicing through the monster's lower leg, like a skewered summer kabob. The trap's metal jaws were almost as fearsome as the fanged jaws of the monster itself, cruel and stained from past prey. It sat on its haunches in the dirt, bulky hands each the size of a cooked chicken, trying to figure out how to pull the bear trap apart. The monster grunted and muttered, its mouth opening and closing, revealing glistening sabers of teeth, jutting out from behind syrupy lips like a twisted iron rake.

"Holy Hannah . . . what is that?"

"I don't know," Fritz whispered, "but I ain't aimin' on findin' out too closely." He raised his rifle and sighted it on the horrendous beast. The beast swiftly jerked its head when it noticed them in the underbrush. In a rush, it stood up, posturing like a man and bellowed a shrieking roar at them. Bushes flattened and Fritz, who was over thirty feet away, felt the roar strike his face like a balmy slap. He fired at the monster and a spiral of its blood and black ooze flung into the cascading night air.

The monster leapt at them. Willie screamed like a Yankee girl and dropped his rifle to the dirt. He spun a wild half-circle and fled back down the trail. Fritz tried to load his rifle and fire again, but he quickly started shaking as Willie's panic spread to him. The monster was halted by its first charge from the length of five-foot chain, bolting the trap into the ground. It grasped the chain with both hands and with another shrieking bellow, snapped it apart into flying fragmented shards.

Fritz turned around and followed Willie in a race back to the cabin.

"Get your guns! Get your guns!" he shouted down the trail to the others.

He felt the monster's presence behind him, a lurching, swinging of a mighty clawed hand. Then the monster stumbled in the brush, buckled by the skewered leg, sunk bear trap and broken chain trailing behind like a devil's tail. Another echoing roar followed, clinging after Fritz.

Fritz burst onto the campsite yelping and sweating.

Curtis was there holding a shotgun at him, rigid as an arrow shaft. "Is it behind you?"

"I didn't stop to look!" Fritz gasped for breath and regained his composure. He took up position next to Curtis, aiming his rifle at the direction he had run down from.

Willie slunk up behind them holding a six-shot revolver in each hand. "I'm sorry I ran, Fritzy. I'm gonna have to live with that, I reckon."

"'Yellow Willie's' your name now."

"That was a Sasquatch monster back there, Fritz."

"That's what the Injuns said, too," Curtis announced softly, still intently aiming his shotgun up the dirt path.

"Where's the Injuns at?" Fritz asked.

"After that second roar sounded, them two lit out of here like their rears was on fire. They called it the Sésquac and said it was angered."

"A Sasquatch, just like the Injuns told us. I thought they were trying to spook us with their ghost stories," Willie said.

Nothing came out of the bushes charging toward them. The three men stood by the cabin entrance with guns raised. The campfire was starting to dim, casting an ominous red glow upon the land around them. The pack mules were tied up nearby, quietly pushed up against each other in a huddle, sensing something lingering in the forest.

"We saw a Sasquatch," Willie started again, "and you shot it. It wasn't even hurt. It just got madder."

"I hit that thing dead center," Fritz spoke quietly.

"The Injuns said those monsters live further up the mountain. They said don't ever bother them and they'll just leave you alone."

"Well, you set the trap that it stepped in. I think it was bothered already by the time it saw us."

"You shot him, Fritzy. The Injuns say Sasquatch can't be killed. We gotta get outta here before that thing comes back looking to get even."

"Hells bells," Curtis said. "I only heard one gun shot between the two of you. If that thing's as fearsome and big as y'all say, then you just need to shoot it to Dutch. I mean, you don't shoot a grizzly just once, do you? You open up with everything you've got. Anything living can be killed."

"You didn't see it, Curtis, it wasn't natural. It was a demon incarnate."

"Listen you two," Curtis said calmly. "Have you ever heard about Sasquatch before?"

Fritz pondered and nodded his head. "Yeah, a couple times out in the saloons. Just from prospectors and lumberjacks, but no one believes the stories those old coots tell."

"How 'bout you, Willie?"

"I heard it before the Injuns from a couple railroad men, but their story just didn't seem truthful, like they was talking about dragons or something."

"Exactly. Nobody believes this thing is real, unless they see it with their own eyes. You boys say you saw the Sasquatch monster up there and I'm inclined to believe you. I'm saying that if we haul a Sasquatch carcass back into town, we're gonna be national known men, like Andrew Jackson or Carnegie."

Willie and Fritz looked at each other, muttering and shaking their heads. Willie's moody eyes were downcast in shame and Fritz was still shaking from his hasty retreat.

Curtis continued, "I even heard Barnum and Bailey Circus will pay ten thousand dollars for any creature never before seen. We wouldn't have to work another day in our lives!"

Willie's shaking head halted and he raised his eyes. "Nobody has that kind of money to toss around."

"Believe it. I heard that P.T. Barnum has more money than every man in Europe put together."

Fritz contemplated Curtis's words and kicked around the glowing edges of the campfire embers. "I don't care how much money Barnum's worth. You'd need an army to take that thing down, not just the three of us. Yellow Willie here was scared off with one look."

"I was just surprised, is all," Willie said defensively. "I wasn't expecting no Sasquatch to be sitting in our backyard. I tell you what, I'm with Curtis now. I'm gonna redeem myself. I ain't letting you call me 'Yellow Willie' no more."

"Fritzy, don't let us down, or your name's gonna be Yellow Fritz." Curtis glared at him as he spoke.

"Sister of mercy, I'll go, I'll go. But if Willie runs again, I'm hightailin' it back to town with or without y'all."

Curtis beamed and bounced up and down on the edge of his faded leather boots. Curtis was the oldest of the three young men, but Fritz thought he was also the most impetuous. His judgment didn't extend further than a silver coin on a stick. Fritz felt a portentous foreboding, the way the sky stills before a twister hurtles down.

Each man took stock of his weapons. Curtis gave Willie his shotgun and went into the cabin to load up his hunting rifle, a long Trapdoor Springfield. Fritz scanned the murky woodland surrounding them, then followed Curtis into the cabin to get his buck knife and extra shot for his gun. Willie holstered his revolvers and paused by the fire pit, cradling the shotgun and imagining himself standing under a waterfall of currency pouring down upon him, paper bills with the profile of P.T. Barnum on each face.

Willie struck up a little humming whistle, an army melody which he could not place a name to. He spat into the fire. An owl hooted nearby and then promptly halted in mid-call. The forest went silent but for a rustling through the boughs. Willie caught the downward draft scent of a pungent odor. He raised the shotgun and searched quickly in all directions, waving his head from right to left like a flag unfurling in the wind.

"Fritz, Curtis," he hissed faintly. "Something's out here."

The two other men anxiously popped their heads out from the shelter of the doorway.

A whistling windy sound grew from the ghostly darkness and a granite boulder the size of a Conestoga wagon wheel rocketed through the air, striking and decapitating poor old Willie. The boulder slammed into him so hard his head crumpled up like a rotten flapjack and popped clean off its scrawny unshaven neck. The shorn body flipped a cartwheel into the nighttime and fell in a limp pile of splayed limbs, half in the fire pit. Immediately, his flannel shirt and greasy skin started to smolder and burn.

Fritz and Curtis gasped in horrific duet. They fired their guns into the forest where the boulder had departed, but the black forest shadows were many and the shadows were all ominous and great.

◆　◆　◆

"Grandpa, I have to tinkle," Freddy said.

"Tinkle?"

"Yes."

"You gotta take a piss?"

"Yes, Grandpa."

"Well, why didn't you just say so?"

"I did."

Grandpa shook his head in puzzlement and the two expectantly looked at each other, each waiting for the other to say something else.

Grandpa gave in first. "Are you askin' for my permission?"

"No, I just didn't want to have to interrupt your story."

"Well go, boy. When a feller's got to relieve himself, there's no use in debatin' the issue."

Freddy hopped off of the sagging linen couch and trotted to the small paneled bathroom outside of the living room.

Grandpa sighed. Freddy was his only grandchild and he often despaired to think the boy didn't have the sense of two toddlers. He loved the kid, but just wished he wasn't coddled so much by his parents. He decided spontaneously that he was going to show Freddy the *box*. A warm excitement rolled across his chest at the thought. He stood up, old bones creaking, and walked over to an incense cedar hope chest, quietly slumbering in the corner under a quilted comforter.

Grandpa's wedding picture was on top, a sepia-toned portrait of him and Ruth. She had loved him despite the loss of his hand. Maybe she loved him more because of it. She was the kind of woman to love a bird with a broken wing because of its frailty. He got along fine one-handed; there was nothing Grandpa Fritz couldn't accomplish that two-handed folks could. But he felt his disability most when he had embraced his wife. He lamented that he could only wrap one good arm around her and caress the small of her back, while he tucked his hooked hand neatly and coldly against his own side.

Under albums of photographs and newspaper clippings lay a warped wooden box, the size of a Sears catalogue, with a split running through the grain on one side. It was musty and locked under tarnished brass fittings. He brought the box out and a small key on a chain.

Freddy was back on the couch waiting for him when he returned. "What's that, Grandpa?"

"It's something very special, and I reckon it's your birthright."

"What's a birthright?"

The old man felt his exasperation rise up, but took a moment to push it back into the dim recesses where it simply lingered. He didn't want to get cross with the boy at a time like this. "It's like your inheritance. It's the heart of a Sasquatch."

Freddy scrunched up his face in evident doubt, obviously not certain how to comprehend what his grandfather said or even how to respond.

Grandpa continued, "You said there's no such thing as Sasquatch and I said that there is. This here's the proof. Sasquatch may have taken my hand, but I got his heart. I cut it out myself. It was still beatin' two days later."

Quiet astonishment spread across Freddy's face, widening eyes rippling to slackening jaw. He appeared to imagine the still, strange content slumbering inside. "Can I see it?"

"Yes, but you can't tell your father. Him and I ain't friendly about this matter. Honor?"

"Honor." Freddy's eyes grew even wider. Grandpa could not determine if those eyes were shimmering with fright or with excitement.

"Okay, where was I? Right. So me and Curtis started shootin' into the forest, but it was dark and everything was a great shadow that looked like it could be a Sasquatch monster, and—"

"Grandpa, but what about Bigfoot's heart?"

"Eh, what about it?"

"Aren't you going to show me the box?"

"Yeah, yeah, Freddy, I said I would. I've got to finish my story first so you'll have an appreciation of it."

"Oh, sorry."

"It's all right. I reckon I'd be restless to see it, too. I'll hasten my words to get to the good part."

Freddy resumed his position, sitting cross-legged sideways, facing him. His eyes fluctuated between the old man's face and the wooden box reverently held in his hand.

"So me and Curtis started shootin' into the forest . . ."

◆　◆　◆

. . . but the black forest shadows were many and menacing and great. A monstrous bellow rose from the woods and another slab of granite was hurled through the air. It crashed against the wall of the log cabin accompanying a victorious wail, buckling the cross members inward with a splintering din.

One shadow rose above all the others and stepped closer to the cabin. The three mules brayed in screaming fear, bucking at their leather tethers and kicking each other. The fire from the pit and Willie's headless body lit up the image. Dancing waves of light spread across the Sasquatch's face and chest. The beast stood with a limp, favoring one leg over the other. One of the legs was bloody and swollen above the ankle where the bear trap had skewered it. Its eyes glowed an insidious yellow with large black pupils staring down on the two men in the doorway.

Curtis gasped and fired his Springfield rifle at the Sasquatch. A reprisal spiral of the creature's blood and black ooze flung once again into the night air. The beast grunted and grabbed its chest and lurched backwards. Fritz fired his Winchester, but could not tell if his shot was successful. They popped open the rifle breeches and loaded new shells, but the Sasquatch disappeared back into the shadows amongst cracking branches and fleeing rodents.

"I got that bastard good," Curtis triumphantly declared. "We gotta go finish it off!"

"I dunno. I'm hesitatin' to go out there. Willie's dead. I'm thinkin' we outta just sit here 'til the sun's up."

"Sit here? Fritzy, it's hurt. All we gotta do is pour some more buckshot into its hide and it's done for. We're gonna be the first ones that ever brought down a Sasquatch!"

"You saw how easy Willie was just killed. It's a fool's mission, chasin' a demon in his own backyard."

"We owe it to Willie to get vengeance for him. You know, you outta think of that gal you're pining for. You and Ruth'll be sitting pretty after this is done."

Fritz paused and considered, his heart pounding like a bullfrog in heat. "All right, but I ain't gonna venture out there too far."

Curtis hopped out the door with a cry of glee. He wore a bandolier of rifle cartridges slung loose across his chest. Next to Willie's corpse, he picked up a wood bough, burning at one end from the fire pit, and held it high in the air. "Let's go get us a Sasquatch!"

Fritz sheathed a large buck knife into his rawhide belt and followed Curtis out into the nighttime, carrying his rifle tightly like an amulet. He picked out a burning stick from the campfire as well, in order to light their path. The new moon was waxing crescent, a thin lemon rind in the sky. Little moonlight filtered down upon the murky ground below.

The two men dodged quickly into the trees. Even if they did not have the torch light from the burning logs, it would have been effortless to follow the destructive path of torn brushes and snapped tree limbs left by the retreating creature.

Fritz recognized the familiar upward slope of the mount.

"He's headin' back to where I first saw him in the clearing," he whispered.

"He's headin' home to Hell, and we're gonna hasten that journey," Curtis said.

They reached the clearing amongst conifers. The gentle dirt path Fritz had earlier travelled ran parallel to the trail they were following now through the undergrowth. Across the clearing where the trees and shrubs grew thick again, the men saw a branch swing back, a dark movement in the gloomy woods. A quick snuffling growl barked out, hoarse and laced with assurances of their mortal ruin.

"He's waitin' for us," Fritz said.

A flash of yellow eyes rustled through the leaves, a glowering glimpse, and then the branch moved back to its place. Curtis fired his rifle into those shadowy woods. The branch didn't move again nor was any further sound heard.

"Did I get him?" Curtis asked.

"I can't see a thing over there."

"All right, I'm going in. Cover me."

The gunpowder smoke hovered lightly in the air. Curtis hunched down beneath it and crept into the clearing. A metal snapping clatter shattered the silence and Curtis screamed in agony.

"Ahhh!" he wailed and fell to the earth in a spasm. "I stepped on a trap!"

Curtis's lower leg was crushed in a bloody pulp of shredded trouser and splintered bone. He bawled in pain and rolled on the muddy dirt, clawing at the shut bear trap. "Help me get this thing off!"

Fritz stepped forward holding the dim torch and saw the bear trap was connected to a length of chain. The chain was snapped apart after a few feet in length, the last metal link gnarled and crooked as it had been heaved asunder. He realized it was the same bear trap the Sasquatch had stepped into. The creature had pulled off the trap and figured out how to reset it. It must have laid the bear trap out in the middle of the clearing and lured Fritz and Curtis to it.

The Sasquatch rose from the dense woods, yellow eyes gleaming large and bright like two flaming cannon balls fast approaching.

Fritz dropped the burning bough. He fired his rifle at the monster and Curtis screamed anew. The Sasquatch took the bullet as he had taken the others. It reached down and grabbed the broken length of chain, violently pulling Curtis toward him.

Curtis's screams went two tones higher. His babbling shrieks turned incoherent so that Fritz couldn't tell if he was trying to say words in a meaningful language or just exuding cries of guttural terror in a final primordial defense.

Fritz loaded another cartridge into his Winchester rifle. Sasquatch and Curtis disappeared behind the wild trees.

The open clearing was about forty feet wide and Fritz bounded across it in several leaping strides. He passed through the first line of trees and almost collided directly into Curtis and the creature. The Sasquatch held him upside down by one leg. The beast shoveled its clawed hand into Curtis's chest and an explosion of wet innards poured out from between the cleaved ribs, like a bowl of beet stew. Curtis's moans dropped to a choked gurgle and then silenced. In an instinctual flash, Fritz fired his rifle nearly point-blank into Sasquatch's face. The monster yelled in pain and rage and one yellow eye rolled uncontrollably upwards, deadened from the shot. Still holding Curtis's body by one leg, the creature swung him at Fritz like a medieval mace. Curtis's head cracked into Fritz's own and Fritz bowled over backwards, nose snapped askew and ringing flashes circling his head. His consciousness waned.

Fritz's eyes blinked open, his head pounding. Sasquatch limped over to stand above him, straddling him with black-haired bowed legs each as thick as a stone chimney. It reached down and lifted him up into the air by the throat, massive clawed fist encircling and crushing Fritz's neck. Fritz stopped breathing and his body seized in the air. He looked the monster directly into its one good eye. They stared at each other as the world slowed around them.

Fritz wrapped his right arm around the Sasquatch's and tried to lift himself up to relieve the pressure on his suffocating, collapsing throat. He kicked at the monster; futile strikes into Sasquatch's side and legs. Sasquatch held him still and a sinister smirk of conquest arose upon its gory face. The bullet Fritz had shot from his rifle had gone in at an angle through the creature's lower cheek. It left a gaping bloody cavity, charcoaled and ragged. Fritz didn't know how the Sasquatch could be standing so resiliently. He lashed out with his left hand, trying to dig his fingers inside the spewing hole in the beast's face. Sasquatch dodged its head sideways and then with a mighty snap, bit off Fritz's hand just above the wrist.

Fritz would have screamed had he the breath to allow it. The only fortune he felt was the pain was not as severe had it occurred with all his senses in full capacity. He grew faint and the amputation of his hand struck him almost as a delayed afterthought. His vision dimming, he heard nothing but a sharp ringing in the middle of his skull. His legs stopped kicking at Sasquatch. He saw the monster chew, its jaws working up and down in quick succession, and then swallow heartily.

Fritz's life began to fade, but he fought. He let go of the creature's arm; his windpipe constricted more with the increased stress from the weight of his hanging, weakening body, like dangling from a hangman's noose. He reached onto his knife, which was holstered in the rawhide belt. With a desperate lurch, he swung out the knife and plunged it deep into Sasquatch's functioning eye. Sasquatch shrieked and dropped Fritz. The beast fell back onto its knees and brought both arms up to its sightless eyes. Fritz collapsed to the mud with a tremendous gasp of air and tears. He paused for but a moment, then leapt at the monster. He still held the large buck knife and thrust it between the beast's upraised arms into its exposed leathery throat.

The Sasquatch let loose a wheezing gargle and swung its arms outwards, the back of its hand catching Fritz and knocking him away. Fritz righted himself and leapt again and stabbed the monster in the chest, burying the blade up to its hilt. The Sasquatch feebly batted its arms out one last time as if brushing away the nuisance of a hovering gnat, then fell onto its back, mewling and spewing inky blood.

Fritz sat next to the creature, watching it convulse and then turn still. The pain and shock from his broken nose and severed arm grew and he felt dizzy as his own blood poured from his wounds. He took off his cotton shirt and wrapped it tightly around his arm, temporarily stemming the blood flow. He sat and stared at the creature's corpse for a long time. Things began to creep and rustle in the thick bushes and towering trees around him. Fritz retrieved his knife, pulling it from the Sasquatch's chest. He started to walk away then paused and turned again to the fallen monster on the forest floor. He thought he saw more glowing eyes appear in the distant woods, waiting, probing. His half-stunned mind dreamt feral images. He found it difficult to think rationally, but knew he must flee.

Before doing so, he returned back to the beast and with his buck knife, carved out the Sasquatch's heart.

◆ ◆ ◆

"Wow," Freddy said with a sigh.

"I then stumbled back to the cabin and took one of the mules and rode it down to town. The next morning I returned to that mountain with a posse of soldiers and ranchers, walkin' uphill in the rain, limpin' and freshly one-handed. I was told to bed rest, but I wouldn't hear of it. I swallowed the pain and did what needed doin'. Our Injun guides, Joseph Redpaw and Tyee, came with us back to the cabin and we followed the trail to where I had killed Sasquatch. They couldn't look me in the eyes, they was so shamed. I showed them the heart I had cut out and they fell to their knees. They knew what I had done and they were in awe. Folks call them 'braves,' but they weren't so brave that night." Grandpa chuckled and cleared his throat with a wheezy hack.

"What then? Did you find Bigfoot, er, I mean Sasquatch again? What'd you do with him?"

"Nothin'. Sasquatch's body was gone. Vanished like a banshee. Plenty of blood and mud where we struggled. We buried the bodies of my two friends up there. Nobody doubted me back then. They called me a conqueror; I was what a man was supposed to be. These days though . . ." Grandpa trailed off. "At least I still have this."

The cracked wooden box that Grandpa held as he spoke was shut under a tarnished brass lock. It rested evenly upon one hand of warm flesh and one of cold steel. The key lay on top of the box lid. Grandpa offered it to Freddy. "Would you like the honors?"

"Yes. Thank you." Freddy's hand quivered slightly. He grasped the small gold key as if it were a mystical talisman.

A gasp behind them.

"Dad! What are you doing?"

Fritz and Freddy both startled, jolted by the new voice.

"We didn't hear you pull up," Fritz said cautiously, like a guilty child with cookie crumbs smeared across his lips.

"I guess not. Put that box away."

"Dad, Grandpa has a Sasquatch heart!"

Fred glared at his father. "No, he doesn't, Freddy. It's a Grandpa story. There's no such thing as monsters in the woods."

Fritz locked glares with his son. "It's true and you sure well know it."

"There's nothing inside that old box. It's just a cruel joke," Fred senior said.

Freddy gulped involuntarily, a bystander in a wicked crossfire. "But he said Sasquatch is out there—"

"And I say he's not. Freddy, go wait outside in the car."

"But, Dad—"

"Now!"

Freddy sulked out, evidently heartbroken. He turned back and glumly waved. "Bye, Grandpa."

"See you around, kiddo."

"Not likely," Fred muttered to his father. "How many times have I told you to lay off the Bigfoot stories? It's getting really old."

"I've always told you the truth. Sasquatch lives in those mountains and I fought him and I survived. It changed my life in more ways than you'll ever know. I think that's something worth passin' down to my kin."

"Don't you remember how much you terrified me of Bigfoot as a kid? For years, I had horrible nightmares of monsters chasing after me. I was afraid to ever step foot outside, much less into the forest."

"Son, you don't need to live a life of fear in order to know what's around you. It's called appreciation and respect for your surroundings. Sasquatch don't bother folks unless they bother him. I know because I was the one that attacked him first."

Fred lowered his voice and looked pleadingly to his father. "Dad, I know you lost your hand and I know whatever occurred to you was unimaginably horrific. You survived a terrible ordeal. But Bigfoot doesn't exist. It was just a bear."

Rage bubbling within, Fritz said, "I know what I saw, boy. I have the proof right here." He held up the locked wooden box.

"What proof? There's nothing inside that old box. I've seen it. It's just a moldy stain."

"It was in here."

"How long ago was it when you fought your monster?"

"It was the early spring of 1889."

"So it happened over half a century ago. Things die, Dad, and they decay and rot away. If you had something that was remarkable, you should have taken it to the museum or to a scientist back then."

"The beast took my hand! Sasquatch's heart was mine. I earned it. I wasn't gonna hand it over to some stuffy antiquarian. It belonged to me."

Fred shook his head. "Dad, I've told you before and I mean it: no more Bigfoot stories, especially around my son. I forbid it. He gets teased enough at school as it is, without repeating your fables." Fred concluded his statement with an abrupt turn and, dismissing his father, walked away and out the door.

Fritz stood there quietly holding the box. He didn't move. He listened to the car outside turn over its engine and then accelerate with a haunting growl. The sound soon dimmed as the last of his family legacy gradually drove away into the distance. He felt an inward collapse, a fainting of his spirit, but he stood there still.

He remained there for a long time, then slowly walked to the hope chest in the corner. He placed the wooden box back beneath the photographs and newspaper clippings and wedding portrait, then closed the lid, the legend of Sasquatch buried under the sentimental trappings of an old man.

About the Editors

Eric S. Brown is the author of numerous books including the *Bigfoot War* series, *The War of the Worlds Plus Blood Guts and Zombies*, *Season of Rot*, and *World War of the Dead* to name only a few. His short fiction has been published hundreds of times in the small press and beyond. He lives in NC with his wife and son, where he continues to write as many tales of the hungry dead, blazing guns, and the things that lurk in the woods. Visit his Website at **ericsbrown.wordpress.com**

A.P. Fuchs is the author of many novels and short stories, most of which have been published. His most recent books are the first three installments in the *Blood of my World* vampire series, *Possession of the Dead* and *Zombie Fight Night: Battles of the Dead*, in which zombies fight such classic monsters as werewolves, vampires, Bigfoot, and even go up against awesome foes like pirates, ninjas, and . . . Bruce Lee. He is also known for his superhero series, *The Axiom-man Saga*, and the author of the shoot 'em up zombie trilogy, *Undead World*. Fuchs lives and writes in Winnipeg, Manitoba. Visit him on the Web at **www.canisterx.com**

About the Authors

Janice Gable Bashman is the author of *Wanted Undead or Alive* with *New York Times* bestseller Jonathan Maberry, nominated for a Bram Stoker Award. She is managing editor of *The Big Thrill*, the International Thriller Writers' newsletter and webzine. Her short fiction has appeared in a variety of anthologies, and she has written for *Novel & Short Story Writers' Market*, *The Writer*, *Wild River Review*, and many others. Find Janice's website at **www.janicegablebashman.com**

David Bernstein is a member of the HWA. His short stories have appeared in numerous anthologies and magazines. He has two novels: *Amongst the Dead* and *Tears of No Return*. He is currently working on a trilogy entitled, *Machines of the Dead*. He lives in NYC and really hates car horns. You can visit him at **davidbernsteinauthor.blogspot.com** and email him at **dbern77@hotmail.com**

Tonia Brown lives in North Carolina with her genius husband and an ever fluctuating number of cats. When not writing she raises unicorns and fights crime with her husband under the code names "Dr. Weird" and his sexy sidekick "Butternut." You can learn more about her and her pen name, Regina Riley, at **www.thebackseatwriter.com**

Frank Collia was born and raised in Staten Island, NY, but now lives in Tampa, FL. That's not exactly Bigfoot territory, but no one's made a Skunk Ape anthology yet.

Eric Dimbleby in Maine with his wife and three children. His third novel, *The Klinik*, will be released this winter. For more information, visit **www.ericdimbleby.com**

Bruce Durham lives in Mississauga, Ontario. He has appeared in publications such as *Paradox, Lovecraft eZine, Flashing Swords, Return of the Sword, Rage of the Behemoth* and *Lawyers in Hell*. In 2009 his short story *The Marsh God* was adapted into a graphic novel. *The Marsh God* and *Homecoming* won Preditors & Editors Readers polls for Best SF&F in 2005 and 2006, *Yaggoth-Voor* from *Rage of the Behemoth* received Harper's Pen and Prix Aurora nominations in 2010 and *The Crane Horror*, appearing in the *Lovecraft eZine,* won the Preditors & Editors Readers poll for Best Horror in 2011. Currently he writes for Janet Morris and her HUGO award winning *Heroes in Hell franchise*. You can visit his website at **www.brucedurham.ca**

Eric J. Guignard writes dark and speculative fiction from his office in southern California. His most recent credits include *Stupefying Stories Magazine, Horror Library Vol 5, The Horror Zine Magazine,* and *Indie Gypsy*. He's a member of the Horror Writer's Association and the Greater Los Angeles Writer's Society. Although his passion is for fiction, he's also a published essayist and editor, including this year's acclaimed collection, *Dark Tales of Lost Civilizations*. Look for the next anthology, *After Death . . .*, to be released in Spring 2013. Visit Eric at **www.ericjguignard.com** or at his blog, **www.ericjguignard.blogspot.com**

Jason Hughes grew up in Texas. He has been a lifelong fan of the Horror genre for thirty-five years and counting. He graduated *The Tom Savini's Special Effects Make-Up Program* in 2004 and still does Special

Effects today. Jason is the Editor of the anthology *Moral Horror*, available now in stores everywhere. He is a contributing Writer for *The Houston Examiner, Beyond the Dark Horizon* and Writer/Reviewer for *Horrornews.net.* His writings can be found in such anthologies as *Nocturnal Illumination, Thirsty are the Damned, Ladies and Gentlemen of Horror 2010, Bleed and They Will Come, Quakes & Storms* along with *Twisted Dreams Magazine* and *House of Horror Magazine* among others. He is also a multi-published (and transferred to audio) Poet. Jason was chosen as one of the top ten best Horror Authors of 2009-2011. He has written screenplays for Mudd Miller Films/Rebellious Cinema, Sick Flick Productions & American – International Pictures. He is also a Drummer, T-shirt Printer, Sky Diver and avid Supporter of *The West Memphis Three* (**www.wm3.org**)

Giovanna Lagana is a freelance editor and writer and three-time Eppie finalist

E.M. MacCallum is the author of the zombie/western novella, *Zombie-Killer Bill*, as well as several short stories in various horror anthologies. As an avid reader, writer, hiker, camper and video gamer, she rarely finds a dull moment unless she was looking for one.

Christine Morgan works the overnight shift in a residential psychiatric facility, a lonely job rough on the health and sleep schedule, but it provides considerable writing time, as well as the occasional moment of inspiration. Christine is a lifelong reader of horror, a roleplaying gamer, a cat person, and a general geek with interests including superheroes, pirates, zombies, Vikings, history, oddball crafts, and cheesy disaster movies.

Suzanne Robb is the author of *Z-Boat* and *Were-wolves, Apocalypses, and Genetic Mutation, Oh my!*. She is also a contributing editor at Hidden Thoughts Press, and co-edited *Read the End First* with Adrian Chamberlin. In her free time she reads, watches movies, plays with her dog, and enjoys chocolate and LEGOs.

R.J. Sevin is the bearded half of Creeping Hemlock Press/Print Is Dead, an acclaimed indie press specializing in all sorts of terrifying literary magic. His short fiction has appeared in *The Living Dead II, The Magazine of Bizarro Fiction, Bits of the Dead* and *Cemetary Dance*. His first novel, *Buster Voodoo*, is due in early 2012 from Ravenous Shadows, a new horror/crime/thriller imprint spear-headed by splatterpunk legend John Skipp. He lives in New Orleans with his brilliant wife, his son (also brilliant), and their deranged cat, Kitty Velcreaux, and has very small feet.

Rosalind Sevin, who raised her son R.J. on a steady diet of monster movies, wrote the first draft of "The Thing Under The House" in 1999. She asked him to polish it and find a market, but he never got around to doing it. The original handwritten pages were lost in Hurricane Katrina, but R.J. recreated the story from memory. Before losing her sight to glaucoma, Rosalind worked as a folk artist, selling hundreds of paintings to collectors across the world. She has a collection of inspirational poetry coming in 2012, and she still wonders when her son is going to grow up. Her feet are also very small.

The author of six novels and numerous shorter works of fiction and nonfiction, **Franklin E. Wales** prefers the title of Storyteller to Novelist or Journalist. Born and raised in Conway, NH, Frank now lives with his beautiful photographer wife, Jacki, in the South Florida home they share with their two dogs and a cat named Oz (as in Wizard of).

Thrillers, Suspense, Horror . . .

. . . this is what we do.